purpose:
capture the sound of voices speaking
of local flavor

NEW STORIES
FROM THE SOUTH

The Year's Best, 1991

edited by
Shannon Ravenel

NEW STORIES
FROM THE SOUTH

The Year's Best, 1991

Algonquin Books of Chapel Hill

published by
Algonquin Books of Chapel Hill
Post Office Box 2225, Chapel Hill, North Carolina 27515–2225
a division of Workman Publishing Company, Inc.
708 Broadway, New York, New York 10003

ISSN 0897-9073
ISBN 0-945575-82-3

CONTENTS

PREFACE

"Is it possible that publishers, not writers, have defined the new generation of Southern writing? Has the literary South been reduced to an easily packageable genre that is dotted with crossroads and hamlets and peopled with beauty operators and eccentric old coots?"

—MARC K. STENGEL
The Nashville Scene, 1990

Those are good questions.

They appeared in an article entitled "Why Is Nobody Writing about the South We Know?" first published last year in a Nashville, Tennessee, alternative weekly. The article caught the attention of editors in the South and was reprinted at least once (in *The Memphis Flyer*) and was the basis for the *North Carolina Independent*'s hard look at Algonquin Books in its September 26 issue. The *Independent*'s headline was "Grit Lit—More Than Dead Mules?"

Although I'd prefer to shrug off the implied criticism, all of us publishers—and especially Southern ones—ought to give these questions a second thought. If we are indeed guilty of pandering to an appetite for "Southren" caricature in fiction, if we really are rejecting any Southern fiction that ignores it, then a pox on us. No. Three poxes on us, for our guilt would be threefold.

First, we'd be guilty of a kind of literary bigotry, one that discriminates against images of the modern South in favor of those that memorialize an older South. My belief is that the American publishing trade is NOT guilty on this score and that the proof is in the pudding. If the work of writers like Richard Ford, Gail Godwin, and William Styron doesn't include images of today's South, then it's impossible to define those images fictionally.

Second, we in the trade would be guilty of choosing to publish the kind of broadly recognizable Dixie literature that sells simply to make money. I say we're not guilty of this either. We're not fools. Today's most commercially successful Southern writer is Pat Conroy. Nothing old magnolia or "Hee Haw" about *The Great Santini* or *The Prince of Tides*.

Third, we'd be guilty of misinforming the rest of the world about the true character of today's South. As Mr. Stengel put it, "For national readers . . . the South is still the land of Mayberry." Where, he wants to know, is the literature of the thriving contemporary Southern megalopolis? Where, he asks, is the literature of downtown and suburban—and the following are the cities cited by Mr. Stengel—Atlanta, Nashville, Memphis, Charlotte, Birmingham?

This is probably the most interesting of the accusations.

I am looking, with Mr. Stengel's question in mind, at the stories selected for this sixth annual collection of my favorite new stories from the South, chosen from among short stories published in the 1990 editions of about 100 American magazines and literary journals. Score one for Mr. Stengel! Not a single one of these sixteen stories is set in one of the metropolitan centers he listed in his article. There are stories set in Richmond (Elizabeth Hunnewell's "A Life and Death Matter"), in Tallahassee (Nanci Kincaid's "This Is Not the Picture Show"), in New Orleans (Robert Olen Butler's "Relic"), and in Mobile (Thomas Phillips Brewer's "Black Cat Bone"). None of the stories, however, has to do with business opportunities, boardrooms, bank accounts, brokers' fees—the stuff so many people who live in the contemporary South deal with daily. Not one of them concerns itself with carpooling, country clubs, catering companies, Call-Waiting, cash machines.

And where, Mr. Stengel wants to know, is the literature of Southern politics in a South "where scandal-prone, small-time politicians are trying to come to terms with the metropolises their sleepy little hamlets have become?" Another good question. And again he scores a point. Not one of these sixteen stories focuses on the sweep of contemporary American politics. There are stories about drug dealing ("Black Cat Bone") and Vietnamese immigrants ("Relic") and highway construction (Robert Morgan's "Poinsett's Bridge") and even about a politician's funeral (Peter Taylor's "Cousin Aubrey"). But the focus in all these stories springs off the political issue in its eagerness to dive into the characters' motivations.

And in the stories with the settings Mr. Stengel so deplores, those hamlets and crossroads, the challenges faced by the bumpkins involved—death (Lee Smith's "Intensive Care," Reynolds Price's "His Final Mother," and Jill McCorkle's "Waiting for Hard Times to End"), illness (Barbara Hudson's "The Arabesque" and Mark Richard's "The Birds"), treachery and betrayal (Larry Brown's "Big Bad Love" and Susan Starr Richards's "The Screened Porch"), love as opposed to romance (Bobbie Ann Mason's "With Jazz," Hilding Johnson's "South of Kittatinny," and Rick Bass's "In the Loyal Mountains")—are universal concerns which have dominated literature from earliest time. What's more, they still do. Nobody complains about *Hamlet* taking place in a remote Danish castle instead of Elizabethan London. Shakespeare cared about how his character responded to a given challenge more than he cared about where or when. The same seems true of the sixteen writers whose stories are gathered here.

So I find myself guilty of the last accusation. Mr. Stengel is right. In selecting the short stories for this collection, I am not much interested in informing readers of the socioeconomic or political climate of the contemporary South. But more to the point, neither are the writers. I don't believe they understand that as their mission. I believe they see it, rather, as informing us of other kinds of conditions—the temperature under the skins and inside the hearts of their characters. And since my strong belief is that those temperatures are very likely to match the ones found under commuters' skins and in country clubbers' hearts, North, West, and East of here, I am letting myself off all three prongs of Mr. Stengel's hook.

Shannon Ravenel
Chapel Hill, North Carolina
1991

PUBLISHER'S NOTE

The stories reprinted in *New Stories from the South, The Year's Best, 1991* were selected from American short stories published in magazines issued between January and December 1990. Shannon Ravenel annually consults a list of more than 175 nationally distributed American periodicals and makes her choices for this anthology based on criteria that include original publication first-serially in magazine form and publication as short stories. Direct submissions are not considered.

NEW STORIES
FROM THE SOUTH

The Year's Best, 1991

Peter Taylor

COUSIN AUBREY

(from *The Kenyon Review*)

In the Tennessee country of my forebears it was not uncom-
mon for a man of good character suddenly to disappear. He
might be a young man or a middle-aged man or even sometimes
a very old man. Few questions were ever asked. Only rarely was it
even speculated that perhaps he had an "ugly situation at home."
It was always assumed, moreover, that such a man had gone away
of his own volition and that he had good and sufficient reason
for resettling himself elsewhere. Such disappearances were especially common in our earliest history, before Tennessee achieved
statehood even, but they continued all through the nineteenth
century and even into the twentieth. We were brought up on
stories of such disappearances. I very early came to think of them
as a significant part of our history: the men who had disappeared
without leaving behind any explanation of their going.

When in recent years I found myself strangely preoccupied
with the possible present whereabouts of one of my mother's
aged cousins, one Aubrey Tucker Bradbury, I could not but be
mindful of those old stories I had heard about other men who
had vanished. By this time I was already a middle-aged man with
grown-up children of my own, and my mother herself had been
dead for some while. This middle-aged preoccupation of mine
would soon develop into what amounted to an obsession. What
seemed particularly impressive to me was that this Cousin Aubrey

had managed to vanish three times from our midst before his disappearance was complete and permanent, so to speak. Anyhow, I came to find myself wishing above all things, almost, to know what had finally happened to my old cousin and where he might be living out his days. It did not occur to me either that he had had some great good fortune in life or that he had come to an ignominious or perhaps violent end. But somehow I could not rest until I knew what had become of the man. I realized that even as a child I had a good many times wondered what had happened to him. I suppose I had reason enough to wonder, since on every occasion of our meeting before his final departure he had taken particular pains to show a special dislike for the small boy—and later, the adolescent—who was brought forward to meet him, a dislike which seemed totally unwarranted since our meetings were so few and so brief. But all that aside, my sudden and otherwise unaccountable preoccupation with finding Cousin Aubrey Bradbury was like some old passion of my youth that had been suppressed and was now in late middle age manifesting itself in a more virulent form.

All the while that I was making the first, few, tentative inquiries and investigations concerning this missing cousin and even later when we had found him—as a result of mine and my younger son's efforts—I continued to think of those other vanished men who had captured my imagination when I was a boy. I felt that they might offer an explanation of Aubrey's disappearance. I knew how little similarity there could have been between those men and himself—as little as there could also have been between himself and any one of our great achievers, such as my maternal grandfather, for instance, who scaled the great heights of Tennessee politics to end his days in a no less exalted role than that of United States Senator and an entrenched power in the capitol at Washington. But nonetheless, the names and stories of those other men's disappearances would keep returning to my inflamed and strangely excited mind. My constant reference to them in conversation during this time very nearly drove my wife Eliza as

well as my son Braxton to distraction. They spoke of this habit I
had fallen into as my "mania." But they listened sympathetically,
too—they and the rest of the family—as again and again I cata-
loged the names of vanished Tennesseans. Apparently I spoke of
them always in tones of such a particular veneration that Braxton
especially found it wonderfully amusing. He compared it to the
listing of Homeric heroes! At any rate, by all means the most
famous name in my said catalog was that of our old warrior-
hero, Governor Sam Houston. Everyone, especially Braxton and
his mother, knew the story: On the morning following the night
of Governor Sam Houston's marriage to a Nashville belle, he
abandoned his bride and abandoned as well his newly won guber-
natorial chair. It is well known that Houston went then for a time
to live among the Indians. And afterward, of course, he went
on to found the independent Republic of Texas. But, for us, the
point is that he never returned to Tennessee. . . . Only somewhat
less famous in the annals of the state was a man who had been
one of our two Confederate senators and who, after the War,
without seeing his family or his constituents again, went off to
live in Brazil. From there he sent back photographs of himself
posed in opulent surroundings and attired in romantic Portu-
guese costume. But when some relative, later on, made a point
of looking him up, he was found in pathetic rags living in dread-
ful squalor and quite alone in the slums of Rio de Janeiro. . . .
Not all of our vanished men, however, were public men. They
were, some of them, simple, landless men who seemed unable
to put down roots anywhere. Sometimes they took their wives
right along with them when they went away, as well as whatever children they had and perhaps an old grandmother or some
other dependent relative or, in the earliest time, perhaps a little
clutch of black slaves and even an indentured servant or two.
But even these rootless men, when they departed, frequently left
under the cover of night, as if the act of moving in itself were a
disgrace. I am told that in the first quarter of the last century it
was indeed quite common in Tennessee to see a crudely lettered

sign nailed to a tree trunk in the front yard of an abandoned farmhouse, reading simply "Gone to Texas." And that was only a manner of speaking, of course. It was merely a statement that another disenchanted man had put forever behind him the long, green hinterland that is Tennessee, and that he never intended returning to her salubrious clime.

Certainly among my earliest memories is my experience aboard the special funeral train bearing the body of my late grandfather, who was in the United States Senate and who died in Washington in 1916. I was the only grandchild taken along on this journey since the others were of school age and would have been too long absent from classes. Aboard that funeral train the Senator's widow occupied the drawing room in the first of the two Pullman cars. I remember such details not merely because I was present but because I would afterward hear accounts of that train ride repeated endlessly by other members of the family, for whom without exception it was the most important journey of their entire lives. I particularly remember that in the drawing room of the second Pullman car were the late Senator's three daughters by an earlier marriage, one of them being my mother—young matrons they must be called in the language of that day, though despite each being married and the mother of one or more children they were scarcely more than girls, really. And in lower berths nearest to their private compartment would sleep their young husbands, each taking his turn during the long journey to Tennessee at sitting with the dead Senator's corpse up in the baggage car. Among these, also taking his turn at sitting with the corpse, was of course my father. A certain nephew of the Senator, the aforementioned Aubrey Tucker Bradbury, would from time to time offer to relieve one or another of three sons-in-law at his watch. But the sons-in-law regarded their vigil by the Senator's coffin as their exclusive privilege. And the fact was that the very presence on the train of this odd-looking and eccentric kinsman of the Senator's—this Aubrey Tucker Bradbury—was resented by all members of the immediate family. The three sons-in-law agreed among themselves that even the wide black armband on the sleeve of Aubrey's dark suit was a presumption and an affront. More than anyone else perhaps, they bore in mind a certain ir-regularity in Aubrey's very kinship to the family—that is, that he had been born out of wedlock, being the child of the Sena-tor's deceased elder brother and a "mountain woman" of obscure background. In the eyes of the family there was something infi-nitely lugubrious, if not sinister, in the young man's very bearing. The eldest of the three sisters was moved to remark (while I, her little nephew, was sitting on her lap in the drawing room) that only by the black mourning band on his sleeve could their cousin Aubrey be distinguished from the long-faced undertakers who had abounded on the scene at the railway platform as they were setting out.

That special train would leave the Union Station in Washing-ton at 2:40 in the afternoon on September 18. The year of course was 1916. Although the funeral procession from the Willard Hotel to the station had been led by a horse-drawn hearse bedecked with a mountain of floral wreaths, the rest of the official proces-sion consisted of four elegant black limousines and eleven other black motor cars. In the uncovered driver's seat of each of the high-set limousines rode not only a chauffeur uniformed in black but a black-uniformed footman as well. I remember my father's commenting that these funeral vehicles and their funeral atten-dants were supplied not by the federal government, as one might have supposed, but by the Washington undertaker who would be in charge of all procedure and all protocol until that moment when the Senator's coffin would be lifted onto the baggage car.

It must be mentioned that alongside the highly polished limou-sines rode a number of government-provided plainclothesmen—outriders on horseback, as it were. And it cannot go without mention that these men were present because inside the lim-ousines, among other notables, rode two very great personages indeed. Though the American manners of the day forbade that the bereaved family openly acknowledge the presence of any such personage at this solemn occasion, I think it all right, so long afterward and in this latter day, so to speak, for me to make known the rank of those great personages. They were none other than a former president of the United States and the present incumbent himself! Their presence is, however, scarcely a significant part of my story. The important point is that the mounted presidential guards with automatic pistols showing on their belts underneath their jackets seemed impressive to me, at the age of four, and actually frightening to my mother and her two sisters. It gave those young-lady daughters of the dead Senator the uneasy and altogether absurd feeling that the funeral procession might be attacked as it moved along Pennsylvania Avenue.

One of these three sisters who had this irrational response to the armed guards was of course my mother. This youngest daughter of the Senator was of an apprehensive and nervous temperament. Already, at earlier events of the funeral, she had kept glancing almost suspiciously in the direction of her eccentric cousin, Aubrey Tucker Bradbury, as if to see if he were experiencing an anxiety similar to her own. (I do think I observed this for myself at the time and was not merely told of it by Mother long afterward.) It was always at Aubrey she glanced during the funeral service and not at her handsome and youthful husband. The sight of Aubrey Bradbury was somehow reassuring to her during the early period of the funeral, as his presence had oftentimes been to her as a child and particularly just after the death of her own mother. Aubrey had actually been her confidant in those earlier times, as he had been also for her sisters during certain times of insecurity in *their* girlhood, and there had even been a period when this cousin had lived in the house with them and served briefly as their Papa's private secretary. And at one time or another this same Aubrey had made declarations of undying love to each of the three sisters. (All three of the sisters would in later life give me hints of these outbursts of Aubrey's.) Anyhow, my mother knew of Aubrey's sensitive, serious nature, and though she had since her marriage—and probably through the influence of her husband—come to think of Aubrey as a ridiculous, unmanly sort of creature, she wondered if he were not today imagining, like herself, that outrageous and terrifying things were going to happen to the funeral party. As a matter of fact, I think that probably without being conscious of it my mother sensed that this occasion marked the end of an era in the life they all had known.

The two other sisters, my two aunts, who were destined to help bring me up after my father's early death, were persons of a far less apprehensive nature than was my mother, and so they were able to speak more openly of the absurd anxiety they felt that day. Even as they rode along the Avenue between the Willard Hotel and the Union Station and observed total strangers standing at the curb, with hats removed in the old-fashioned way in the presence of death, my Aunt Bertie and Aunt Felicia spoke to each other openly of their anxiety. But my mother, whose name was Gertrude, was of a more introspective and questioning temperament and was unable to speak out about her fear. Her hesitation was due, in part at least, to the peculiar nature of her anxieties. The fantasy she entertained was not merely that those men on horseback would suddenly turn on the procession and perhaps upset the coffin and the precious corpse inside. (*That* was the "crazy feeling" openly confessed to by my aunts and which, as a matter of fact, they would long afterward laughingly tell me about.) But Trudie, as my mother was always called by her older sisters, imagined those armed men as actually forcing open the coffin and revealing to her that her worst fantasy-fear was come true: that it was not Senator Nathan Tucker's body locked in the casket but that of someone known to her but whom she could not quite recognize, someone whose identity somehow eluded her or, rather, whose identity she could not quite bring herself to acknowledge.

My mother knew in reason, of course, that her father's body *was* present, but during the short funeral service in the hotel ballroom it had occurred to her several times that her father was not really dead at all and locked away in the elaborate, brass-trimmed coffin. She would learn in later years that during the very moments when the three sons-in-law, along with her cousin Aubrey Bradbury and two other young kinsmen, were bearing the coffin down a center aisle that was arranged between hotel ballroom chairs—she would learn, that is to say, that other mourners besides herself had had that same fantasy.

Perhaps it seemed to nearly everyone present that day that whatever else might be inside that coffin it could not be the body of Senator Nathan Tucker of Tennessee. The Senator had always seemed to nearly everybody the liveliest and most alive of men. To all present, moreover, the tragedy of the Senator's death seemed almost beyond belief, if only because of the unlikeliness of the circumstance. They could not accept that this noble, gifted, vigorous, healthy man of sixty who had been more of a gentleman–folk hero than a mere politician, had been brought down by something as ignoble and trivial-sounding as a gallstone operation.

Of far greater and more lasting significance, though, was the shock to the mourners that this ambitious and talented man would be destroyed at the very peak of his illustrious career in public life. (He had served three terms as governor and was at the beginning of his second term in the Senate.) No doubt the most difficult fact to be faced—or perhaps *not* to be faced—was that this distinguished son of an old country family, a family that had been distinguishing itself to an ever-greater degree during every generation for more than a hundred years, should now be stricken at the very peak of his family's supreme elevation. Perhaps all the kin and connections assembled at the funeral were in fact saying to themselves: "We have invested so much confidence and hope in this man as chief of our tribe! In him who helped lead us back into the Union and resolved so many other conflicts within us! If he be dead now, to whom shall we turn to bolster our collective ego, and *where* shall we turn?" These Ten-

nessee people were, in 1916, a people who still identified themselves most often in terms of family ties. To them the Senator's
achievement represented generations of hanging together in all
things. Perhaps everyone present at the funeral service understood this. Perhaps the notables present as well as the fashionable
Washington friends of the three daughters were more observ-
ing of the antediluvian family feelings than were members of the
family themselves. There was something altogether archaic about
this family, something that made it seem to step out of an earlier,
simpler, nobler age.

Even while riding in the procession to the Union Station and
even when the coffin was being hoisted clumsily into the baggage car of the waiting train, Gertrude Tucker Longford, my
mother, continued now and again to entertain her ugly fantasy.
Her papa's body *could not* lie inside that coffin! It was not her
gentle, witty, silver-maned, silver-tongued, her almost beautiful
papa who was dead but some other senator, somebody else's head
of family and chief of tribe, or just some other, ordinary man
of lower degree and less beloved than her papa. Probably this
seemed so to a lesser extent for her two sisters also. Because once
the three of them were closeted in their drawing room, there
in the second Pullman car of the funeral train, with me sitting
on the lap of first one of them and then another, then each young
woman positioned herself in the remotest-seeming corner of the
green-upholstered seats, fondling or vaguely trying to entertain
me from time to time but totally disregarding her sisters and
staring disconsolately into space as if the end of the world had
come and she were entirely alone with her grief.

As Trudie Longford, my mother, quietly closed the drawing-
room door that afternoon the last face she saw out in the aisle of
the Pullman car was that of her cousin Aubrey Bradbury. I was
standing close by Mother's side, and Aubrey must have observed
the both of us there. I don't recall what my own impression was.
But Trudie observed, as she would tell me many times afterward,
that Aubrey wore a wounded expression on his heavy but weak-

chinned face, and as she closed the door he lowered his eyelids submissively as if acknowledging Trudie's right to shut the door in his face. My own impression was, and remained so ever afterward, that his seemingly lowering his eyes actually represented his glancing down at me with a mixture of ire and resentment. My mother, at any rate, would be confronted by her cousin a good many other times before that journey was over, but she retained her impression always that that was the last time they ever looked directly into each other's eyes, that there was never again the exchange of communicative glances there once had been. After the Senator's lying-in-state in Nashville and after the subsequent burial at the cemetery in Knoxville, Trudie would never in effect look upon his countenance again. When he did return rather mysteriously to attend my two aunts' funerals, not too many years later, he was unrecognizable to most people, and Mother had no substantive exchanges with him. His reappearances on those occasions seemed afterward more like apparitions, in most respects. And nobody learned anything of the whereabouts of his present residence or of his present mode of life— not that anybody knew how he learned about the funerals he attended, either. For more than forty years his real whereabouts would remain unknown to any member of the Tucker clan or to anyone in the entire connection. It was, as my mother and her sisters said, as though that day in the Knoxville cemetery the earth of East Tennessee had simply opened up and swallowed Aubrey Bradbury whole. From that moment he was no more among them, no more among us. From that time he became another of those men of good character who disappeared without leaving any explanation of their going.

My points of reference regarding Cousin Aubrey's severance from the world he knew best would not be complete without mention of some other examples that come to mind. My father had a cousin in West Tennessee who set fire to his house and went off with a woman from a neighboring farm. His house was long since heavily insured, perhaps by design, and so he supposed he was not behaving dishonorably or even inconsiderately with his family. He had no concern about the welfare of his wife and children. At a later time word would come that this man wished to return home. But his wife's brothers went to him, wherever he had revealed himself to be, and forbade his coming back or even manifesting his present whereabouts to his wife and children. Most of us never knew where it was he had resettled or whether or not he and the woman from the neighboring farm had stayed together.

And then there was a banker in Nashville that I would hear about during my childhood who left his office in the middle of one afternoon, without so much as taking his derby hat or his gold-headed cane with his monogram on the crown. They say he went out through the revolving door, like one of the ordinary clerks, with a pencil stuck behind his ear and just as though he were only stepping across the street for a few moments. His whereabouts were not known to us for more than twenty-five years. And he did not abscond with any bank funds when he left, and his affairs were in perfect order. His greatest problem was said to be with demon rum. One sad part of the story was that when at last he was found he had altogether rid his life of that difficulty and was regarded as a model citizen in his new location. Sad, though, was not the word for what happened after he was discovered. When he was at last hunted down by a Nashville newspaper reporter ("Just for the story in it," so it was said), the two oldest children of the new family he had started locked themselves in their rooms and put bullets through their heads. It turned out that the banker and his former secretary, whom he had run off with, had opened a small hardware store somewhere in the Northeast and were operating a moderately successful business there. . . . I can assure you there were other instances, all the details of which I once knew as well as I know these. As for my wife and my son Braxton, they have always shown more interest in these stories with unhappy endings than in those that end merely in tantalizing mystery, which are more to my liking. My son Brax used to predict perversely that to find my cousin Aubrey Bradbury might do him irreparable harm. From the outset I felt that it was likely that the old man's rediscovery by a long-lost cousin, scarcely more than half his own age, might just as easily turn out to be a great boon for the old fellow—and would somehow certainly turn out so for me. Yet in my nightly dreams about him throughout the entire period of my search it would sometimes turn out one way and sometimes another. I cannot even now say for sure what our eventual reunion meant either to Aubrey or to me.

If when I was growing up I asked one of my fragile and ever-ailing aunts or my fragile but long-enduring mother whatever became of Aubrey, she was apt to stare off into space, genuinely bewildered—so it seemed to me—and murmur something like: "We don't know what ever happened to poor Aubrey. I am afraid none of us has kept track of him. Finally he just seemed to have vanished into thin air." They did not want to think about what may have become of him. They only wanted to talk of the trying times they had had with him on the funeral train. If at some other time and in quite another mood I asked whether Aubrey had been like my manly father or like my equally manly uncles as a young man, I would likely be answered with a hoot of laughter. They thought my question utterly ridiculous. If all three of these ladies were present when I asked this question, there would come a chorus of "Oh, heavens, no! Not a bit! Not in the least! Not at all like any one of *them*! They were real men, your father and your uncles!" If at still another time I persisted, trying to arrive at some notion of the man, and suggested that perhaps after all he had been rather like those other men who had disappeared, I was apt to be given a very straight look. Then there came an emphatic answer: "No *indeed*! Aubrey Tucker Bradbury was most certainly not like one of them! For Aubrey there was no ugly situation at home that *he* had to run away from!"

The phrase "ugly situation at home" was one often used in

connection with the hero Sam Houston and with our relative in West Tennessee who burned his own house, as well as with a good many others. Once during recent years I happened to use that very phrase in discussing Cousin Aubrey with my son Brax, and when I quoted my mother to him on this subject I was at first shocked by Brax's burst of laughter. The fact was, Braxton was quite a young man at the time I speak of, and it only recently had been revealed to him that Aubrey Bradbury was actually an "outside cousin" of the Tucker family. I think this had not consciously been concealed from him, but it was rather that Aubrey's irregular kinship was seldom referred to by anyone. I don't recall at what age I myself stumbled upon the information that Aubrey was the illegitimate son of one of my maternal great-uncles and that Bradbury was actually his mother's surname. Upon my use of the all-too-familiar phrase, Brax, laughing out at me and slapping his thigh in the coarse manner he sometimes exhibits, exclaimed to me: "And you, Daddy—you and your mother and your aunts—you didn't call *that* 'an ugly situation at home?' Poor Cousin Aubrey! I hope you will never find him again!"

What I then felt I must explain to this son of mine was that in my mother's day—if not quite in my own—an illegitimate child like Aubrey was not put out for adoption and was not left to be brought up in disgrace by his unwed mother. Rather, he was drawn into the extended family, which was a reality in those quaint and distant days in Tennessee, and he was given the family's special protection both at home and abroad in the world. I said this was so, at any rate—or that I had been told so by my forebears—in the really best, the "most long-settled and best regulated families" in our little up-country corner of the world. As soon as I had insisted upon this to Brax, however, I found myself recalling how my mother and aunts had come at last to regard Aubrey with the condescension and even contempt that their husbands had taught them to feel for him, and that the husbands, in their particular, masculine pride of that period, had always felt. My father and my uncles were all three of them sons of Confederate veterans and were themselves so thoroughly versed in Civil

War history that aboard the funeral train they delighted in pointing out the sites of great battles and even small skirmishes. More than once I heard them laughing at Aubrey's ignorance of military history. At Culpeper, my father (whose name, incidentally, was Braxton Bragg Longford) went through the Pullman cars announcing to all that nearby was the spot where "the Gallant Pelham fell," and it had to be explained to Aubrey who that hero had been. Aboard the train there were many whispered conversations about the eccentric cousin's behavior. One night he was discovered in the area between the two Pullman cars, with his face in the crook of his arm, weeping aloud—ostensibly out of grief for his dead benefactor, the Senator. My two uncles discovered him there and led him into the men's smoking room where they administered large doses of whiskey out of their own flasks. And it was at some time on that long journey that I heard Uncle Hobart repeating what allegedly was my grandfather's own account of how he had gone to the simple mountain cabin where Aubrey was being reared until he was about school age and had "rescued" him from the rough people there, had placed him in Mr. Webb's school at Bell Buckle, where he was rather harshly disciplined and received a severely supervised classical education. But I think these incidents and stories did not impress me so strongly as did Cousin Aubrey's own contumelious glances at myself. Very early, though, I began to understand the resentment inspired in him by the mere sight of a boy who enjoyed every protection such a life as mine provided and the affection and even adoration of those three particular women who presided over my every activity. And by the time I was an adolescent I believe I could already conceive that an experience so totally different from mine could have a hardening and corrupting effect upon a being as sensitive to the affection and consideration of others as I believed myself to be.

I must tell you now that when Aubrey Tucker Bradbury resurfaced in my life at last—nearly forty years after his first disappearance—he would resurface little by little, so to speak, inch by inch. That is, I began first of all merely to hear rumors of the existence of a man with a name much like his own, though not exactly like. The surname and the middle name had been reversed. And on the second occasion of my hearing of him it was indicated that the two names had been hyphenated—a most unusual practice for someone hailing from Tennessee. The old Cousin Aubrey in all representations of him had been so modest-sounding and unpretentious that I tended to dismiss the possibility of the two being one and the same. But once I had heard of the existence of this other man it registered indelibly on my mind. After the first report of him I was ever-conscious of the remote possibility that this obviously different sort of man might still somehow be Aubrey.

Though it was always some place other than Tennessee that I heard his name spoken, it was inevitably added that his origins were there. It was this that made me first suspect that my mother and my two aunts might have been wrong in their assumption that Aubrey had merely disappeared into the East Tennessee countryside and had there resumed the role of a Tennessee bumpkin. It so happened that the first mention of his name reached my ears not in this country even but while I was traveling in Europe. Since I was not over there on a pleasure trip and was not paying my own expenses, I was put up at a rather better hotel than I normally would have been booked into. (My expenses were being paid by the very generous university where I taught art history in those days and partly by the Italian government, for whom I was helping to direct restoration of artworks after the disastrous flood in Florence.) There in the dining room of the great hotel by the Arno I heard someone at the next table pronounce the name Aubrey Bradbury-Tucker. The people at that table were alternately speaking English, German, and Italian. I listened carefully but was unable to grasp precisely the subject of conversation. But I heard once again the articulation of that name. The party left the dining room without my ever making out their identity, though I assumed, correctly I think, that they too were involved somehow in the restoration at the Uffizi.

The next time I heard the man's name spoken was on a shuttle flight between New York City and Washington. A garrulous old lady sitting beside me on that short flight insisted on knowing where I was "from." When I told her I was from Charlottesville, she said knowingly that my accent didn't sound like "old Charlottesville" and that I must teach at the university there. (She of course "knew people" there and had often been a visitor.) I confirmed that all she said was so and confessed that I was originally from Tennessee. "Ah, Tennessee!" she exclaimed. "Nashville I'll bet it is!" Then she proceeded to tell me about a wonderfully attractive man from Nashville—"so he claimed." She had made his acquaintance aboard a South American cruise ship and he had flirted with her "most scandalously." His name was Mr. Bradbury-Tucker—"Hyphenated no less!" she said. And then she laughed her merry laugh again. Suddenly I could see just how attractive she herself had once been, and I could understand how delightful it would have been then to have found oneself on the South American cruise with her. She said that Mr. Bradbury-Tucker had had the most beautiful Vandyke beard she had ever seen on any man. And she said that when she told him so, he replied, with a twinkle in his bewitching brown eyes, that he only wore the beard in order to conceal "a very weak chin." Then she went on to say that Mr. Bradbury-Tucker had deceived her wickedly and that *she* had clearly meant nothing to *him*. Only on the last day of the cruise did she discover that Mr. Bradbury-Tucker was traveling in the company of another woman, a rich woman older than herself who during the voyage had kept mostly to their stateroom. I tried to reassure her—facetiously I suppose—that all Tennesseans were not such rascals, and I told her that my mother's maiden name had been Tucker and she had had a cousin named Bradbury. At this, that lady blushed to the roots of her snow white hair. She made no further effort at conversation and managed not to hear further questions that it now struck me to ask. I felt she was berating herself for having once again talked too much to a stranger. When she got off the plane she hurried away with the crowd without my learning so much as her name. But it was then that the fantasy first occurred to me that the country bumpkin, the outside cousin, had not disappeared into the countryside of East Tennessee but had been interred with his erstwhile protector, the late Senator Tucker, and that a new Aubrey had been released to make his own way, to take on a new persona and perhaps in that persona take revenge upon the world.

At a party in Charlottesville some two years after that ride on the shuttle, I obtained a really conclusive piece of evidence that Mr. Bradbury-Tucker and our Cousin Aubrey Bradbury were indeed one and the same. It was at a men's "smoker"—so-called in old-fashioned academic circles—given one afternoon in honor of a visiting lecturer, a man who was being considered for an appointment at the university. Though I was on the selections committee, I felt reasonably certain that he would not accept such an appointment as we would be able to offer. He was too celebrated, too "international" an expert in his field, to be willing to settle down in Charlottesville, Virginia. But he was our guest lecturer of the day and we wished to please him. We happened on the subject of the old days of railways and what a delight traveling had been then. It turned out that our lecturer was a veritable collector of stories about trains. And of course, wishing to please him, we all brought forward our stories on the subject. Perhaps I, more than the others, insisted on being heard and was soon running through my own repertoire. Yet I think everyone present would have acknowledged that our guest more or less urged me on.

When at length I proceeded to tell our lecturer about Grand-father's funeral train, I was careful to speak only of the comic aspects of the journey. In fact, I told him only about how my two uncles ended by getting very drunk and so altogether out of control that they had finally, first one and a while later the other, to be turned over to the constabulary in the first two county seats where the train stopped after passing over the Tennessee state border.

Indeed, I had hardly sketched in my account of those two incidents when our guest lecturer burst out at me, exclaiming, "What a strange coincidence this is!" He bent forward and placed his well-manicured hand on my arm. But he was not even looking at me as he spoke. "This is a true story that I have heard before!" he said, bending toward me as he spoke. "How very strange! How I do love such stories and most of all how I love to have them turn up in such dissimilar circumstances. I first heard of that train journey from a man by the name of Colonel A. N. Bradbury-Tucker and who himself was present on that funeral train and who was, moreover, a relative of this dead senator who you referred to up in the baggage car." (Obviously our guest lecturer had not bothered to catch my own name and my connection with the Senator, though I had already spent a day and a half in his company, squiring him about the university, introducing him to senior professors, deans, and one vice-president. Clearly he did not recall that I had identified the dead senator as my grandfather.) Presently he continued: "He was a very odd sort of person, this Colonel Bradbury-Tucker, who told me his version of this same story. He was a very urbane and distinguished-seeming person. He was more like someone you might meet in Europe. One could not have guessed that his clothes even were American. He had a handsome beard, very beautifully trimmed. Altogether he was wonderfully well-groomed in the old-fashioned way. He and I met in the house of a very wealthy lady in Bristol, Rhode Island. I never knew exactly what *that* relationship was—his and the Rhode Island lady's—but I gathered from little things he let drop that he saw himself as a great ladies' man. Anyway, he loved to talk about women—ever so confidingly. Perhaps he had a lot of money. He wished one, at any rate, to think so. Or perhaps he was the sort of man who lives off women. But the thing that interested me most about that funeral train he had been aboard was the presence there of the dead Senator's three young married daughters. I remember his holding up his forefinger and thumb like this and saying, 'They were absolutely delicious.' He was like some very cultivated gourmet describing a variety of his favorite dishes! He made great distinctions and differentiations with regard to the young ladies' three kinds of beauty. He referred to them as innocent young matrons all properly married and perfectly protected of course but knowing nothing of the world. 'Genuine provincials!' he said. 'And absolutely delicious!'"

Suddenly I felt deeply offended and wished to hear no more from our lecturer and no more of Colonel Bradbury-Tucker's view of my mother and my aunts. It was undoubtedly my Cousin Aubrey that the lecturer had known, but the picture that this latter-day Colonel Bradbury had painted was so far from what I had received from my mother and my aunts that I felt a kind of electric shock pass through me. When presently our talk was interrupted, I moved away from our guest lecturer and soon took my leave from the smoker. I was afraid that some faculty colleague present might mention to him that my mother's maiden name had been Tucker and that like the Colonel, I too originally hailed from Tennessee. . . . I hardly need add that the lecturer did not receive the nomination of the selection committee, and that though I continued to read his distinguished scholarly works I never saw him in person again.

From that day forward I was sure of course that the man I had kept hearing about was my mother's cousin. For a certain period after that I was less sure than formerly that I still wished to come face to face with Cousin Aubrey. Yet curiosity about his incredible transformation caused my interest in his whereabouts and his ultimate fate to persist. If the long-ago journey on the Senator's funeral train changed all our lives in some degree and if the significance of those changes was what I longed to understand, then a meeting with Colonel Bradbury-Tucker—surely the most altered of us all—might facilitate my understanding. Only to look upon the man's countenance might solve mysteries about myself.

Very soon Aubrey's resurfacing in my life was destined to

come one inch closer. In Charlottesville, Virginia, there are many people, especially among the university faculty, who subscribe to the *Washington Post* as their morning newspaper. But since my wife is a native of a small town in Southside Virginia, we have always read the *Richmond Times-Dispatch* for our morning paper and purchased the *New York Times* at the newsstand on the corner. And that is how I happened to miss—or very nearly miss— seeing the newspaper picture of Colonel Bradbury-Tucker. I first beheld his visage not in a paper that was delivered to my doorstep, and not in one for sale at a newsstand, but in a fragment of newsprint wrapped around a vegetable that my wife Eliza brought from the curb market. It was from an issue of the *Washington Post* that was at least three weeks old. Even as the paper crossed my vision on its way to the trash can I received an impression of the erect figure and the slightly out-of-focus face that was in the background of the photograph reproduced thereon. I quickly fished it out and spread it on the enamel-topped kitchen table. It purported to be a picture of one of those Washington hostesses whose entertainments one generally avoids unless one is seeking office or has some other self-interested purpose requiring one's presence there. The caption under the picture gave the famously rich hostess's name, of course, describing her as one of Washington's most celebrated socialites. She was apparently so rich and so celebrated that it seemed worthwhile to mention even her slightly out-of-focus escort in the background, one Colonel A. N. Bradbury-Tucker. At last I had a blurred but indubitable image of the man Aubrey Tucker Bradbury had become. Though his beard was white, it seemed to me an absolute facsimile of the streaked gray beard my grandfather had worn in pictures taken not long before his death. And even though the image of his face was blurred, the dark eyes looked out piercingly toward the camera, just as the Senator's had always done in his campaign pictures, those which Mother kept locked away in her leather-bound scrapbook and produced periodically for my admiration and edification. And I had the eerie feeling that indeed it had been the old Cousin Aubrey whose death had come that September day in 1916 and that it was his body that had been substituted for the dead Senator's in the elaborately brass-trimmed coffin that was handed so clumsily onto the special funeral train.

Barbara Hudson

THE ARABESQUE

(from *Apalachee Quarterly*)

[handwritten annotation: Kate - older sis / arden - younger sis]

Sometimes Arden's mother would get them up in the middle of the night to clean the house. The first time Arden was four. The room was dark and her mother stood in the light from the hall.

"It's time to get up," she said and turned on the overhead light, and Arden saw the crack that began above the door and ran across the ceiling. Her sister Kate rose from the other bed. The ceiling was blue and their beds were white. Her mother wore an old print dress and tennis shoes. "We're going to clean. Before your father gets home." She turned and moved away, her feet soft on the carpet, heavy against the stairs. Soon *The Firebird* by Stravinsky filled the house.

"Come on," said Kate, pulling at her arm. "Get out of bed. Get out."

"What is Mommy doing?" Arden asked.

"Hell," said Kate, who was nine. "I don't know."

Arden had never heard her say that word, and she was scared.

Later, when the beds were made and the baseboards dusted, they sat at the kitchen table eating cornflakes; their mother was talking. "I'm going to paint the living room today. Kate, when you get home from school, Arden and I will have painted the entire living room. What color shall we paint it?" She turned to Arden. "My little angel, what color shall we paint it?"

Arden was worried. She had no idea how to paint. "I don't know," she whispered.

"Think," her mother said and rose from the table.

Arden heard the car door slam and she slipped out of her chair.

"Sit down," her mother said. "I'll greet your father."

"This is terrible." Kate twisted a piece of her long blond hair tighter and tighter. "Maybe you should go with me. Maybe I should take you to school."

Their father, who was a doctor and who had been up all night working in the emergency room, walked into the kitchen. His fine light hair fell across his forehead, his shoulders sagged, his eyes slipped past theirs and dropped to their shoes. He touched them on their heads. "How are my girls?"

"Fine, Daddy," Arden said.

"Yeh," said Kate. "Just fine. We've been listening to *The Firebird.*"

"Oh?" He raised his head and looked at their mother.

She smiled, her face radiant, one hand pushing her dark hair from her oval face. "Go upstairs and get in bed and I'll bring your breakfast. Whatever you want. Just tell me. Whatever. Waffles, strawberries, whipped cream."

He reached out his arm and drew her to him and she laughed. "Your mother is crazy," he said and kissed her nose.

They painted the living room that day, while her father slept upstairs. First they stood in the cold gray outside the paint store until the man with the key came. "Colors!" her mother said. "Show me all your colors!" Arden chose white for the walls— Silver Butterflies, or something like that—and a very light pink for the molding. Fairy Pink, she called it. And later when they were almost finished and her father was at the top of the stairs, asking if he could come down, her mother shouted, "Wait," and said, "Here, Arden, right here. Paint a fairy." And Arden painted a little pink fairy on the wall where the edge of the desk would cover it.

It was a strange and wonderful day. And a horrible night. When her father left again for the hospital, her mother wouldn't let them go to sleep. Arden was so tired, but her mother kept shaking her or slapping her face. Kate was supposed to be dancing to *Swan Lake*—she wore pink tights and a black leotard and her black ballet shoes.

"Wake up," her mother said. "You're being rude. Kate is dancing for us." And Kate would lift her arms into a big circle one more time. Arden couldn't help it. She had never been so tired.

Finally the phone rang and their mother went away, long enough for them to climb the stairs and crawl into their beds, still clothed. Kate locked the door.

It wasn't the first day her mother had been like that, Arden was sure—people don't go mad overnight—but it was the first day she could remember. A whole day. From beginning to end.

Later she would ask Kate when it started, and Kate would say, "I don't want to talk about her."

One day Arden tried to tell her father. She was six and had walked out of her first-grade class, where Mrs. Engelhardt spoke softly and looked at her with steady eyes. Arden was going to clench her teeth and catch the bus and ride home with children who yelled. But there he was, all by himself, waiting in the old Chevrolet, and she didn't even ask why.

"Bright Arden," he said and touched her hair. "How are you?"

"I'm fine, Daddy," she answered.

"Are you always fine?" he asked. "Are you always bright and fine?"

"Yes," she said and rolled down the window to feel the warm air. "Did you save anyone last night?"

"Yes," he said. "We saved a mommy who took too many pills."

"What kind of pills?" she asked and watched the trees go by. They were covered with pale green buds.

"Sleeping pills," he said. "She thought she wanted to sleep a long time, but maybe she really didn't. Maybe she wanted something else." He put on his sunglasses. "To be happy. Happy people don't take too many pills."

Arden didn't say anything for a while. They passed the yard with the willows and the creek bank covered with late daffodils. "I don't think I would have saved her," she finally said, thinking of her own mother.

"What do you mean?" he asked, raising his sunglasses.

"Then I could sleep at night."

"What's the problem, Arden?"

"I have nightmares," she said. It was always one hand. Always going for her face. Sometimes with talons. Sometimes changing at the last into something else: a bird that would light on her shoulder, a butterfly that would brush her nose. On the bad nights she would crawl into Kate's bed and Kate would let her stay.

"Have you told your mother?" her father asked.

She shuddered. He didn't understand.

He said it again. "Have you told your mother?"

"No." She looked down at her dress. They had picked it out last week and it was wonderful, finding the dark blue with pink flowers. But now she had to wear it every day and she didn't like it anymore. Every morning her mother sent her back upstairs to put it on. She wanted to tear it into pieces.

"Maybe I should tell her," he said.

"No," she said. "I think I made it up. I sleep fine at night."

He put out his arm and she moved across the seat and let him hold her until they got home. Then she kept her distance. It was safer.

Some days their mother didn't even get up, and they would tiptoe down the stairs and into the kitchen. No chaos. Order and peace. Heaven. They would eat their cereal and smile. Once Kate leaned over and kissed Arden's cheek for no reason. Arden started to cry. Then she began to laugh, then they were both laughing, loud and hard, and Kate took the cereal box and dumped the cornflakes on the table, and they began to throw cornflakes in the air, all over everything. They smashed them on the floor. Arden climbed on the table and let them fall through her hands like rain, and Kate pretended she was taking a shower. Then they got out the brooms and swept them around the kitchen and finally out the back door, where Brothers Grimm, the dog, began to eat them.

On those days their mother might still be in bed when they came home from school, the house just as it was when they'd left—curtains drawn, her door still closed, no music, none of her smells. Suddenly Arden would miss her and want to sneak into her room, but Kate would say no, not when Daddy's in there. He would come out later, his hair rumpled, and take a shower. They didn't bother him. He would speak when he wanted to. And later they would eat potpies together, and he would tell them about his patients. Very sick people, sometimes children, who would probably die unless he was there, and sometimes even that didn't work. He would leave for the hospital, and they would do their homework and go to bed, and still their mother wouldn't get up.

When Arden was eleven and Kate was sixteen they moved into a new house with all new furniture. Arden's bedroom was white with blue trim, no cracks in the ceiling, and Kate's was pale green like an aquarium. Their mother hired a housekeeper who came twice a week, and they thought that maybe she wouldn't get them up anymore. Besides, if Kate locked her door, then Arden couldn't get in when she had a nightmare. In the old house, locking the door had sometimes worked. Arden would hear her mother's hand on the knob, then the pull on the door that wouldn't open. Sometimes she went away and never said anything. Other times she banged until Arden opened the door. "Get your sister up," she'd say. "We have work to do."

One night in the new house Arden woke up because Kate was yelling.

"I'm not going to get up anymore," she shouted. "You can't make me. Something's wrong with you."

"What's wrong with me?" her mother yelled, her voice growing until it swallowed all sound.

"Nobody's mother does this," Kate shouted but her voice quivered.

"How do you know?" her mother yelled. "How do *you* know?" Arden could imagine her reaching for Kate's shoulders, and she began to tremble.

"Don't touch me," Kate yelled. Then Arden heard the slap, and Kate was silent.

Someone moved down the hall and stood in the doorway, but Arden didn't move. She tried to breathe as though she were asleep. One breath in. I can change this into a dream. Hold it. Slowly let it out. I can make this person disappear. Hold it. Slowly let it out. But maybe it was Kate. Maybe she had slapped their mother. Suddenly Arden wanted to open her eyes, to whisper, Kate come here. But no. It wouldn't be this quiet. Slowly let it out.

After a while, her mother turned on the light. She moved into the room and sat on the edge of Arden's bed and ran one hand over her eyes, again and again. "I'm sorry," she whispered. "I'm sorry." She sat for a long time looking down, that hand passing over her eyes. "I'm so sorry." Finally she stood and straightened her dress. Her eyes brightened and she lifted her long fingers to touch her brow, as though to remember something. "We have work to do. Before your father gets home. I'll put on the music." She moved down the hall. Stopped. Came back. "Maybe you could tell Kate." She was gone again, her feet on the stairs.

Arden could hardly get out of bed, but she crept down the hall and found Kate on the carpet, face down, crying.

She knelt and whispered in her ear, "She says she's sorry."

"I don't care," mumbled Kate.

The music was coming up from downstairs. Arden whispered louder, "I think she really means it."

"Go away," said Kate. "Go away forever."

Arden got up and left the room. She didn't know what to say. Even now it was hard. Pushed out into the cold where it was dark with no moon. No one left. A door slammed shut and a note shoved beneath it. Don't come back. You've taken the other side. Find your friends among the traitors.

She went downstairs and their mother left Kate alone and Arden polished the silver.

Later that morning Kate talked to their father, and after a few days, he put their mother into the hospital for a while. Arden missed her in the afternoons when she came home from school. At night she had the same dreams. In the morning she wasn't sure how she felt. Their father's mother came and cooked runny scrambled eggs and talked to herself as she moved about the house. Arden worried that she might suddenly discover she wasn't talking to anyone. Kate loved her and broke into her murmurings to chatter on and on as she followed her from room to room. Their father kept to himself; he went to the hospital and he went to visit their mother. Never again would he laugh and say that she was crazy.

When their mother left it was fall. When she came home it was winter, and they were all waiting for her—Kate, Grandmother, Arden. They sat on the sofa and watched the late afternoon snow fall, the squirrels at the birdfeeder. Kate was talking to their grandmother, using a name she'd heard. "Mema, I saw this boy again yesterday."

Arden was trying to decide what she would do when her mother walked through the door. Would she stand and say, "I'm so sorry, Mother. What have they done to you?"

"He walked me to my locker, you know, kind of slow, like he wanted to ask me something."

Maybe she would yell from the sofa, "Why have you come back? I don't want you here."

"Finally I just said, 'Do you want to ask me something?' He

looked me straight in the eye and said no. I was so embarrassed."
Their grandmother coughed.

She could run up the stairs, into her room, lock the door, crawl
under the bed.

"But later he came back and said, 'Yeh, do you want to go
out?'"

Or she could stay on the couch and not move and not say
anything.

Their grandmother lifted a wrinkled hand and picked a piece
of lint from the sofa. "Ask your mother about it, Kate. Give her
a day and then ask her. I think she'd want to know."

Kate took her grandmother's hand and squeezed it. "You tell
me. *You* tell me what I should do. Should I go out with him?
Should I call him up on the phone and tell him to pick me up
across the street? At the Stanways across the street?"

Their grandmother lifted her other hand and touched Kate's
hair. "Ask your mother, dear. You don't need to send him across
the street."

"Hell I don't. She doesn't give a damn." Kate stood up, and
Arden moved over and put her head on their grandmother's
lap. She didn't know her grandmother that well, but when she
saw her touch Kate's hair, that was what she wanted to do. Her
grandmother began to stroke her head, and Arden began to cry.
She couldn't help it. Then Kate began to cry. She sat down
and put her head on Arden's back and Arden could see their
grandmother's arm come around to touch Kate while she stroked
Arden's head, and their grandmother began to hum softly, nothing Arden knew, but it was a wonderful song.

Then the car was in the driveway and they all straightened up
and sniffed and smoothed their dresses, and it was almost like
nothing had happened, nothing with their grandmother, that is;
too much of the other had happened to forget now.

Two car doors opened and closed. The trunk slammed. Boots
crunched through the snow on the stone path. Then onto the
porch. The door opened and Arden's father stepped in with a

suitcase. He looked taller than he had that morning, his shoulders more broad. Her mother followed, dressed in new clothes: a long red coat, a brilliant scarf, strands of her dark hair electric in the dry air. She paused for a moment, her eyes uncertain, her hands at the scarf. Then she laughed and threw her arms wide. "I almost went crazy," she said. Arden ran to her—she couldn't help it—and her mother pulled her close and whispered, "Do you still love me, little angel?" And she smelled as she always had.

"Yes," Arden whispered back. She did in that moment. It was a true answer but not complete.

"And Kate, what about you?" She extended an arm. Their father was beaming. Their grandmother rose from the sofa. Kate didn't move.

"Do you want me to lie?" Nobody said anything. "I think you are the most wonderful mother in the entire world. You are such a wonderful mother I think you should teach classes, and I will personally invite all my friends who have never been here—all my friends who ask, 'Why don't we go to your house?' and I say, 'It smells bad. A cat died underneath it.' Do you know how many cats have died underneath our house?"

Arden began to scream. That's all she could remember. Screaming as her father took her outside where the snow was falling. He picked her up and began to swing her slowly around and around, like he'd done when she was five, when she would laugh and ask for more. She was small and thin for eleven, and he swung her until she was quiet. Then he stopped and held her for a while. Finally he said, "It's time to go in now," and they went in together, and nothing more was said about it.

Life together was too much for them. Arden could see that now. Too intense. People cannot live like that for long.

When their mother came home from the hospital, she was different. She had fooled Arden that first afternoon, but gradually Arden began to see that her mother's mountains and valleys had been stretched by some hand, maybe her own, into one long thin line. She rose in the morning at 7:00; she went to bed at 10:00. The housekeeper came three days a week and did all the cleaning. She attended the Medical Auxiliary luncheons and ran a few errands. She and Arden went to Kate's ballet recitals, where she sat quietly and clapped with no sound. Sometimes she would say, "Arden, why don't you have a friend over to spend the night," and she asked nice questions of Kate's boyfriends—what they liked to do instead of what their parents did. She and their father went to the symphony once a month, and Arden watched them leave, her father's arm wrapped around her mother.

Arden was happy; she slept well at night. Sometimes she would sit on Kate's bed and they would talk about those bad days when their mother was mean, the good days now that she was nice, and oh yes tell me and smile big, isn't it easier, especially for our father, who has to work so hard anyway. And for us, too, because we're young and have to navigate such a complicated world. And for our grandmother, who won't have to worry so much anymore. Yes and giggle, our heads together, murmuring, muttering, trying to make her sounds of wandering through the house. And for our mother, too. It must be easier. Of course we can't ask her; how do you ask someone, "Are you happy now that you're not crazy? Do you know what a bitch you were?" But surely she was happy, or she wouldn't be so nice. Yes, Mother, we want so much for you to be happy.

Finally one night after Kate had gone away to college, to a small school in North Carolina where she could study dance, their mother sat down at the kitchen table and lowered her head into her hands. "I have a terrible headache," she whispered. "Please call your father." Arden ran to the phone, her whole body shaking, and she dialed as fast as she could, but when she came back her mother had lost consciousness, her head on the table, her hands limp. The ambulance came, and she was gone.

Later her father called. "Arden," he said, "your mother died on the way to the hospital."

"I see."

"We think she burst an aneurysm."

"Thank you for calling, Dad." She put down the phone, walked into her bedroom, crawled under the bed, and went to sleep.

During the service, her father leaned over and whispered, "I always knew she would die before me." Then he leaned the other way and said something to Kate, who smiled, a grim sort of smile, their grandmother beside her, but Arden could only see her black hat. She was overwhelmed with relief; they had escaped, all of them. The past would die with their mother, and Arden would live on as somebody else, not trapped on a wall behind the edge of a desk. She could be anyone. Her mother could be anyone. They were all free.

And for a while it worked—that vigorous suppression of history. But eventually she wore out—what with all the energy it took just to live—and her mother came rumbling back. In women who laughed too hard, who were too kind, who had long fingers and dark hair. In the middle of the night when she couldn't sleep and finally rose to put on *The Firebird*, sitting with her ear to the speaker so as not to wake her father, who worked during the day now. In the department store that sold her mother's perfume, buying some, standing too long, forgetting why she was there and how to get out, until her friend Abby found her. In a boy who held her hand, whose mouth was thin like her mother's, and she wouldn't let him kiss her. In her father, who took her to the symphony, his arm on the back of her chair, not touching her shoulder.

Then it was summer and Kate was home. She was nineteen and Arden was fourteen, and one day Arden was sitting in the bathtub, clothed and dry, trying to remember the song her grandmother hummed. She looked up, and Kate stood in the doorway, dressed in her leotard and tights.

"It's gone," Arden said. "I can't remember."

Kate walked into the room, bent low, and peered into her eyes. "How long have you been in the bathtub?" she asked.

"I don't know." She looked down at her clothes and couldn't remember when she'd put them on.

"Don't let her do this to you," Kate said and grabbed her shoulders.

"What?"

"She's making you crazy. Do you hear me?" Kate shook her. "Do you hear what I'm saying?"

Arden pushed her hands away and stood up. "She's dead."

Kate rolled her eyes. "Can't you see?" She lifted her long fingers and touched Arden's forehead. "You can't get rid of her without destroying your mind."

Arden sat down again in the bathtub and put her head on her knees. "Sometimes I want her back."

"You miss somebody else," Kate said. "Somebody else's mother," and Arden began to cry.

"Maybe you miss me." Kate climbed into the bathtub and sat facing Arden, her knees pulled to her chest. "We had the same mother." Kate took one of her hands. "She was a strange woman."

"Not always," Arden said.

"But we didn't know her long enough," Kate answered.

"I was alone with her when she died."

"She died in the ambulance."

"But I thought I'd killed her, that I'd done it without realizing, and Dad was calling to ask why."

Kate pressed her hand.

The words kept coming. "Then he told me and I was so happy. She was dead and I hadn't killed her. I could love her always and things would be better, but they're not. They're worse."

She looked at Kate, who was quiet for a moment, before she released Arden's hand and rose from the bathtub. "This is what you do," she said, and Arden followed her into the living room, where Kate stood in the middle of the Oriental rug, in first position, her shoulders back, her chin lifted, her heels, calves, and fingertips meeting. "This is what you do. You take your mother," and she pushed onto her toes and turned, stepping with the leg that would become her base, one arm moving forward, lifting her upper body, the other leg and the other arm rising slowly behind her. "You take your mother and you turn her into something else."

It was the most beautiful arabesque Arden had ever seen: one long smooth arc stretching from Kate's fingertips to her pointed toe, and the leg on the carpet so straight and sure. "Do you see?" Kate asked.

"Yes," Arden whispered. "I think I do."

Lee Smith

INTENSIVE CARE

(from *Special Report*)

Cherry Oxendine is dying now, and everybody knows it. Everybody in town except maybe her new husband, Harold Stikes, although Lord knows he ought to, it's as plain as the nose on your face. And it's not like he hasn't been *told* either, by both Dr. Thacker and Dr. Pinckney and also that hotshot young Jew doctor from Memphis, Dr. Shapiro, who comes down here once a week. "Harold just can't take it in," is what the head nurse in Intensive Care, Lois Hickey, said in the Beauty Nook last week. Lois ought to know. She's been right there during the past six weeks while Cherry Oxendine has been in Intensive Care, writing down Cherry's blood pressure every hour on the hour, changing bags on the IV, checking the stomach tube, moving the bed up and down to prevent bedsores, monitoring the respirator—and calling in Rodney Broadbent, the respiratory therapist, more and more frequently. "Her blood gases is not but twenty-eight," Lois said in the Beauty Nook. "If we was to unhook that respirator, she'd die in a day."

"I would go on and do it then, if I was Harold," said Mrs. Hooker, the Presbyterian minister's wife, who was getting a permanent. "It is the Christian thing."

"You wouldn't either," Lois said, "because she *still knows him*. That's the awful part. She still knows him. In fact she peps right

35

up ever time he comes in, like they are going on a date or something. It's the saddest thing. And ever time we open the doors,
here comes Harold, regular as clockwork. Eight o'clock, one
o'clock, six o'clock, eight o'clock, why shoot, he'd stay in there
all day and all night if we'd let him. Well, she opens her mouth
and says *Hi honey,* you can tell what she's saying even if she can't
make a sound. And her eyes get real bright and her face looks
pretty good too, that's because of the Lasix, only Harold don't
know that. He just can't take it all in," Lois said.

"Oh, I feel so sorry for him," said Mrs. Hooker. Her face is as
round and flat as a dime.

"Well, I don't." Dot Mains, owner of the Beauty Nook, started
cutting Lois Hickey's hair. Lois wears it too short, in Dot's opinion. "I certainly don't feel sorry for Harold Stikes, after what
he did." Dot snipped decisively at Lois Hickey's frosted hair.
Mrs. Hooker made a sad little sound, half sigh, half words, as
Janice stuck her under the dryer, while Miss Berry, the old-
maid home-demonstration agent waiting for her appointment,
snapped the pages of *Cosmopolitan* magazine one by one, blindly,
filled with somewhat gratuitous rage against the behavior of
Harold Stikes. Miss Berry is Harold Stikes's ex-wife's cousin. So
she does not pity him, not one bit. He got what's coming to
him, that's all, in Miss Berry's opinion. Most people don't. It's a
pleasure to see it, but Miss Berry would never say this out loud
since Cherry Oxendine is of course dying. Cherry Oxendine!
Like it was yesterday, Miss Berry remembers how Cherry Oxendine acted in high school, wearing her skirts too tight, popping
her gum.

"The doctors can't do a thing," said Lois Hickey.

Silence settled like fog then on the Beauty Nook, on Miss
Berry and her magazine, on Dot Mains cutting Lois Hickey's
hair, on little Janice thinking about her boyfriend Bruce, and
on Mrs. Hooker crying gently under the dryer. Suddenly, Dot
remembered something her old granny used to say about such
moments of sudden absolute quiet: "An angel is passing over."

After a while, Mrs. Hooker said, "It's all in the hands of God, then." She spread out her fingers one by one on the tray, for Janice to give her a manicure.

And as for Harold Stikes, he's not even considering God. Oh, he doesn't interfere when Mr. Hooker comes by the hospital once a day to check on him—Harold was a Presbyterian in his former life—or even when the Baptist preacher from Cherry's mama's church shows up and insists that everybody in the whole waiting room join hands and bow heads in prayer while he raises his big red face and curly gray head straight up to heaven and prays in a loud voice that God will heal these loved ones who walk through the Valley of Death, and comfort these others who watch, through their hour of need. This includes Mrs. Eunice Sprayberry, whose mother has had a stroke, John and Paula Ripman, whose infant son is dying of encephalitis, and different others who drift in and out of Intensive Care following surgery or wrecks. Harold is losing track. He closes his eyes and bows his head, figuring it can't hurt, like taking out insurance. But deep down inside, he knows that if God is worth His salt, He is not impressed by the prayer of Harold Stikes, who knowingly gave up all hope of peace on earth and heaven hereafter for the love of Cherry Oxendine.

Not to mention his family.

He gave them up too.

But this morning when he leaves the hospital after his eight-o'clock visit to Cherry, Harold finds himself turning left out of the lot instead of right toward Food Lion, his store. Harold finds himself taking 15-501 just south of town and then driving through those ornate marble gates that mark the entrance to Camelot Hills, his old neighborhood. Some lucky instinct makes him pull into the little park and stop there, beside the pond. Here comes his ex-wife, Joan, driving the Honda Accord he paid for last year. Joan looks straight ahead. She's still wearing her shiny blond hair in the pageboy she's worn ever since Harold met her at Mercer

College so many years ago. Harold is sure she's wearing low heels and a shirtwaist dress. He knows her briefcase is in the backseat, containing lesson plans for today, yogurt, and a banana. Potassium is important. Harold has heard this a million times. Behind her, the beds are all made, the breakfast dishes stacked in the sink. As a home ec teacher, Joan believes that breakfast is the most important meal of the day. The two younger children, Brenda and Harold Jr., are already on the bus to the Academy. James rides to the high school with his mother, hair wet, face blank, staring straight ahead. They don't see Harold. Joan brakes at the stop sign before entering 15-501. She always comes to a complete stop, even if nothing's coming. Always. She looks both ways. Then she's gone.

Harold drives past well-kept lawn after well-kept lawn and lovely house after lovely house, many of them houses where Harold has attended Cub Scout meetings, eaten barbecue, watched bowl games. Now these houses have a blank, closed look to them, like mean faces. Harold turns left on Oxford, then right on Shrewsbury. He comes to a stop beside the curb at 1105 Cambridge and just sits there with the motor running, looking at the house. His house. The Queen Anne house he and Joan planned so carefully, down to the last detail, the fish-scale siding. The house he is still paying for and will be until his dying day, if Joan has her way about it.

Which she will, of course. Everybody is on her side: *desertion*. Harold Stikes deserted his lovely wife and three children for a redheaded waitress. For a fallen woman with a checkered past. Harold can hear her now. "I fail to see why I and the children should lower our standards of living, Harold, and go to the dogs just because you have chosen to become insane in mid-life." Joan's voice is slow and amiable. It has a down-to-earth quality which used to appeal to Harold but now drives him wild. Harold sits at the curb with the motor running and looks at his house good. It looks fine. It looks just like it did when they picked it out of the pages of *Southern Living* and wrote off for the plans. The only difference is, that house was in Stone Mountain, Georgia, and this house is in Greenwood, Mississippi. Big deal.

Joan's response to Harold's desertion has been a surprise to him. He expected tears, recriminations, fireworks. He did not expect her calm, reasonable manner, treating Harold the way she treats the Mormon missionaries who come to the door in their black suits, for instance, that very calm sweet careful voice. Joan acts like Harold's desertion is nothing much. And nothing much appears to have changed for her except the loss of Harold's actual presence, and this cannot be a very big deal since everything else has remained exactly the same.

What the hell. After a while Harold turns off the motor and walks up the flagstone walk to the front door. His key still fits. All the furniture is arranged exactly the way it was arranged four years ago. The only thing that ever changes here is the display of magazines on the glass coffee table before the fireplace, Joan keeps them up to date. *Newsweek, National Geographic, Good Housekeeping, Gourmet.* It's a mostly educational grouping, unlike what Cherry reads—*Parade, Coronet, National Enquirer.* Now these magazines litter the floor at the side of the bed like little souvenirs of Cherry. Harold can't stand to pick them up.

He sits down heavily on the white sofa and stares at the coffee table. He remembers the quiz and the day he found it, four years ago now, although it feels like only yesterday, funny thing though that he can't remember which magazine it was in. Maybe *Reader's Digest.* The quiz was titled "How Good Is Your Marriage?" and Harold noticed that Joan had filled it in carefully. This did not surprise him. Joan was so law-abiding, such a *good girl,* that she always filled in such quizzes when she came across them, as if she *had to,* before she could go ahead and finish the magazine. Usually Harold didn't pay much attention.

This time, he picked the magazine up and started reading. One of the questions said: "What is your idea of the perfect vacation? (a) a romantic getaway for you and your spouse alone; (b) a family trip to the beach; (c) a business convention; (d) an organized tour of a foreign land." Joan had wavered on this one. She had marked and then erased "an organized tour of a foreign land." Finally she had settled on "a family trip to the beach." Harold skimmed along. The final question was: "When you think of the love between yourself and your spouse, do you think of (a) a great passion; (b) a warm, meaningful companionship; (c) an average love; (d) an unsatisfying habit." Joan had marked "(c) an average love." Harold stared at these words, knowing they were true. An average love, nothing great, an average marriage between an average man and woman. Suddenly, strangely, Harold was filled with rage.

"It is not enough!" He thought he actually said these words out loud. Perhaps he *did* say them out loud, into the clean hushed air-conditioned air of his average home. Harold's rage was followed by a brief period, maybe five minutes, of unbearable longing, after which he simply closed the magazine and put it back on the table and got up and poured himself a stiff shot of bourbon. He stood for a while before the picture window in the living room, looking out at his even green grass, his clipped hedge, and the impatiens blooming in their bed, the clematis climbing the mailbox. The colors of the world fairly leaped at him—the sky so blue, the grass so green. A passing jogger's shorts glowed unbearably red. He felt that he had never seen any of these things before. Yet in another way it all seemed so familiar as to be an actual part of his body—his throat, his heart, his breath. Harold took another drink. Then he went out and played nine holes of golf at the country club with Bubba Fields, something he did every Wednesday afternoon. He shot 82.

By the time he came home for dinner he was okay again. He was very tired and a little lightheaded, all his muscles tingling. His face was hot. Yet Harold felt vaguely pleased with himself, as if he had been through something and come out the other side of it, as if he had done a creditable job on a difficult assignment. But right then, during dinner, Harold could not have told you exactly what had happened to him that day, or why he felt this way. Because the mind will forget what it can't stand to remember, and anyway the Stikeses had beef Stroganoff that night, a new recipe that Joan was testing for the Junior League cookbook, and Harold Jr. had written them a funny letter from camp, and for once Brenda did not whine. James, who was twelve that year, actually condescended to talk to his father, with some degree of interest, about baseball, and after supper was over he and Harold went out and pitched to each other until it grew dark and lightning bugs emerged. This is how it's supposed to be, Harold thought, father and son playing catch in the twilight.

Then he went upstairs and joined Joan in bed to watch TV, after which they turned out the light and made love. But Joan had greased herself all over with Oil of Olay, earlier, and right in the middle of doing it, Harold got a crazy terrified feeling that he was losing her, that Joan was slipping, slipping away.

But time passed, as it does, and Harold forgot that whole weird day, forgot it until *right now,* in fact, as he sits on the white sofa in his old house again and stares at the magazines on the coffee table, those magazines so familiar except for the date, which is four years later. Now Harold wonders: If he hadn't picked up that quiz and read it, would he have even *noticed* when Cherry Oxendine spooned out that potato salad for him six months later, in his own Food Lion deli? Would the sight of redheaded Cherry Oxendine, the Food Lion smock mostly obscuring her dynamite figure, have hit him like a bolt out of the blue the way it did?

Cherry herself does not believe there is any such thing as coincidence. Cherry thinks there is a master plan for the universe, and what is *meant* to happen will. She thinks it's all set in the stars. For the first time, Harold thinks maybe she's right. He sees part of a pattern in the works, but dimly, as if he is looking at a constellation hidden by clouds. Mainly, he sees her face.

Harold gets up from the sofa and goes into the kitchen, suddenly aware that he isn't supposed to be here. He could be arrested, probably! He looks back at the living room but there's not a trace of him left, not even an imprint on the soft white cushions of the sofa. Absentmindedly, Harold opens and shuts the refrigerator door. There's no beer, he notices. He can't have a Coke. On the kitchen calendar, he reads:

Harold Jr. to dentist, 3:30 P.M. Tues
Change furnace filter 2/18/88 (James)

So James is changing the furnace filters now, James is the man of the house. Why not? It's good for him. He's been given too much, kids these days grow up so fast, no responsibilities, they get on drugs, you read about it all the time. But deep down inside, Harold knows that James is not on drugs and he feels something awful, feels the way he felt growing up, that sick little flutter in his stomach that took years to go away.

Harold's dad died of walking pneumonia when he was only three, so his mother raised him alone. She called him her "little man." This made Harold feel proud but also wild, like a boy growing up in a cage. Does James feel this way now? Harold suddenly decides to get James a car for his birthday, and take him hunting.

Hunting is something Harold never did as a boy, but it means a lot to him now. In fact Harold never owned a gun until he was thirty-one, when he bought a shotgun in order to accept the invitation of his regional manager, "Little Jimmy" Fletcher, to go quail hunting in Georgia. He had a great time. Now he's invited back every year, and Little Jimmy is in charge of the company's whole eastern division. Harold has a great future with Food Lion too. He owns three stores, one in downtown Greenwood, one out at the mall, and one over in Indianola. He owned two of them when his mother died, and he's pleased to think that she died proud—proud of the good little boy he'd always been, and the good man he'd become.

Of course she'd wanted him to make a preacher, but Harold never got the call, and she gave that up finally when he was twenty. Harold was not going to pretend to get the call if he never got it, and he held strong to this principle. He *wanted* to see a burning bush, but if this was not vouchsafed to him, he wasn't going to lie about it. He would just major in math instead, which he was good at anyway. Majoring in math at Mercer College, the small Baptist school his mother had chosen for him, Harold came upon Joan Berry, a home ec major from his own hometown who set out single-mindedly to marry him, which wasn't hard. After graduation, Harold got a job as management trainee in the Food Lion store where he had started as a bagboy at fourteen. Joan produced their three children, spaced three years apart, and got her tubes tied. Harold got one promotion, then another. Joan and Harold prospered. They built this house.

Harold looks around and now this house, his house, strikes him as creepy, a wax museum. He lets himself out the back door and walks quickly, almost runs, to his car. It's real cold out, a gray day in February, but Harold's sweating. He starts his car and roars off toward the hospital, driving—as Cherry would say— like a bat out of hell.

They're letting Harold stay with her longer now. He knows it, they know it, but nobody says a word. Lois Hickey just looks the other way when the announcement "Visiting hours are over" crackles across the PA. Is this a good sign or a bad sign? Harold can't tell. He feels slow and confused, like a man underwater. "I think she looks better, don't you?" he said last night to Cherry's son Stan, the TV weatherman, who had driven down from Memphis for the day. Eyes slick and bright with tears, Stan went over to Harold and hugged him tight. This scared Harold to death, he has practically never touched his own sons, and he doesn't even *know* Stan, who's been grown and gone for years. Harold is not used to hugging anybody, especially men. Harold breathed in Stan's strong go-get-'em cologne, he buried his face in Stan's long curly hair. He thinks it is possible that Stan has a permanent. They'll do anything up in Memphis. Then Stan stepped back and put one hand on each of Harold's shoulders, holding him out at arm's length. Stan has his mother's wide, mobile mouth. The bright white light of Intensive Care glinted off the gold chain and the crystal that he wore around his neck. "I'm afraid we're going to lose her, Pop," he said.

But Harold doesn't think so. Today he thinks Cherry looks the best she's looked in weeks, with a bright spot of color in each cheek to match her flaming hair. She's moving around a lot too, she keeps kicking the sheet off.

"She's getting back some of that old energy now," he tells Cherry's daughter, Tammy Lynn Palladino, when she comes by after school. Tammy Lynn and Harold's son James are both members of the senior class, but they aren't friends. Tammy Lynn says James is a "stuck-up jock," a "preppie," and a "country-clubber." Harold can't say a word to defend his own son against these charges, he doesn't even *know* James anymore. It might be true, anyway. Tammy Lynn is real smart, a teenage egghead. She's got a full scholarship to Millsaps College for next year. She applied for it all by herself. As Cherry used to say, Tammy Lynn came into this world with a full deck of cards and an ace or two up her sleeve. Also she looks out for Number One.

In this regard Tammy Lynn is as different from her mama as night from day, because Cherry would give you the shirt off her back and frequently has. That's gotten her into lots of trouble. With Ed Palladino, for instance, her second husband and Tammy Lynn's dad. Just about everybody in this town got took by Ed Palladino, who came in here wearing a seersucker suit and talking big about putting in an outlet mall across the river. A lot of people got burned on that outlet mall deal. But Ed Palladino had a way about him that made you want to cast your lot with his, it is true. You wanted to give Ed Palladino your savings, your time-sharing condo, your cousin, your ticket to the Super Bowl. Cherry gave it all.

She married him and turned over what little inheritance she had from her daddy's death—and that's the only time in her life she ever had *any* money, mind you—and then she just shrugged and smiled her big crooked smile when he left town under cover of night. *"C'est la vie,"* Cherry said. She donated the rest of his clothes to the Salvation Army. *"Que será, será,"* Cherry said, quoting a song that was popular when she was in junior high.

Tammy Lynn sits by her mama's bed and holds Cherry's thin dry hand. "I brought you a Chick-Fil-A," she says to Harold. "It's over there in that bag." She points to the shelf by the door. Harold nods. Tammy Lynn works at Chick-Fil-A. Cherry's eyes are wide and blue and full of meaning as she stares at her daughter. Her mouth moves, both Harold and Tammy Lynn lean forward, but then her mouth falls slack and her eyelids flutter shut. Tammy sits back.

"I think she looks some better today, don't you?" Harold asks.

"No," Tammy Lynn says. She has a flat little redneck voice. She sounds just the way she did last summer when she told Cherry that what she saw in the field was a cotton picker working at night, and not a UFO after all. "I wish I did but I don't, Harold. I'm going to go on home now and heat up some Beanee Weenee for Mamaw. You come on as soon as you can."

"Well," Harold says. He feels like things have gotten all turned around here some way, he feels like he's the kid and Tammy Lynn has turned into a freaky little grown-up. He says, "I'll be along directly."

But they both know he won't leave until Lois Hickey throws him out. And speaking of Lois, as soon as Tammy Lynn takes off, here she comes again, checking something on the respirator, making a little clucking sound with her mouth, then whirling to leave. When Lois walks, her panty girdle goes *swish, swish, swish* at the top of her legs. She comes right back with the young black man named Rodney Broadbent, Respiratory Therapist. It says so on his badge. Rodney wheels a complicated-looking cart ahead of himself. He's all built up, like a weightlifter.

"How you doing tonight, Mr. Stipe?" Rodney says.

"I think she's some better," Harold says.

Lois Hickey and Rodney look at him.

"Well, lessee here," Rodney says. He unhooks the respirator

tube at Cherry's throat, sticks the tube from his own machine down the opening, and switches on the machine. It makes a whirring sound. It looks like an electric ice-cream mixer. Rodney Broadbent looks at Lois Hickey in a significant way as she turns to leave the room.

They don't have to tell him, Harold knows. Cherry is worse, not better. Harold gets the Chick-Fil-A, unwraps it, eats it, and then goes over to stand by the window. It's already getting dark. The big mercury arc light glows in the hospital parking lot. A little wind blows some trash around on the concrete. He has had Cherry for three years, that's all. One trip to Disney World, two vacations at Gulf Shores, Alabama, hundreds of nights in the old metal bed out at the farm with Cherry sleeping naked beside him, her arm thrown over his stomach. They had a million laughs.

"Alrightee," Rodney Broadbent nearly sings, unhooking his machine. Harold turns to look at him. Rodney Broadbent certainly looks more like a middle linebacker than a respiratory therapist. But Harold likes him.

"Well, Rodney?" Harold says.

Rodney starts shadow-boxing in the middle of the room. "Tough times," he says finally. "These is tough times, Mr. Stipe." Harold stares at him. Rodney is light on his feet as can be.

Harold sits down in the chair by the respirator. "What do you mean?" he asks.

"I mean she is drowning, Mr. Stipe," Rodney says. He throws a punch which lands real close to Harold's left ear. "What I'm doing here, see, is suctioning. I'm pulling all the fluid up out of her lungs. But now looka here, Mr. Stipe, they is just too damn much of it. See this little doohickey here I'm measuring it with? This here is the danger zone, man. Now Mrs. Stipe, she has been in the danger zone for some time. They is just too much damn fluid in there. What she got, anyway? Cancer and pneumonia both, am I right? What can I tell you, man? She is *drowning*." Rodney gives Harold a short affectionate punch in the ribs, then wheels his cart away. From the door, apparently struck by some misgivings, he says, "Well, man, if it was me, I'd want to know what the story is, you follow me, man? If it was me, what I'm saying." Harold can't see Rodney anymore, only hear his voice from the open door.

"Thank you, Rodney," Harold says. He sits in the chair. In a way he has known this already, for quite some time. In a way, Rodney's news is no news, to Harold. He just hopes he will be man enough to bear it, to do what will have to be done. Harold has always been scared that he is not man enough for Cherry Oxendine, anyway. This is his worst secret fear. He looks around the little Intensive Care room, searching for a sign, some sign, anything, that he will be man enough. Nothing happens. Cherry lies strapped to the bed, flanked by so many machines that it looks like she's in the cockpit of a jet. Her eyes are closed, eyelids fluttering, red spots on her freckled cheeks. Her chest rises and falls as the respirator pushes air in and out through the tube in her neck. He doesn't see how she can sleep in the bright white light of Intensive Care, where it is always noon. And does she dream? Cherry used to tell him her dreams, which were wild, long Technicolor dreams, like movies. Cherry played different parts in them. If you dream in color, it means you're intelligent, Cherry said. She used to tease him all the time. She thought Harold's own dreams were a stitch, dreams more boring than his life, dreams in which he'd drive to Jackson, say, or be washing his car.

"Harold?" It's Ray Muncey, manager of the Food Lion at the mall.

"Why, what are you doing over here, Ray?" Harold asks, and then in a flash he *knows*, Lois Hickey must have called him, to make Harold go on home.

"I was just driving by and I thought, Hey, maybe Harold and me might run by the Holiday Inn, get a bite to eat." Ray shifts from foot to foot in the doorway. He doesn't come inside, he's not supposed to, nobody but immediate family is allowed in Intensive Care, and Harold's glad—Cherry would just die if people she barely knows, like Ray Muncey, got to see her looking so bad.

"No, Ray, you go on and eat," Harold says. "I already ate. I'm leaving right now, anyway."

"Well, how's the missus doing?" Ray is a big man, afflicted with big, heavy manners.

"She's drowning," Harold says abruptly. Suddenly he remembers Cherry in a water ballet at the town pool, it must have been the summer of junior year, Fourth of July, Cherry and the other girls floating in a circle on their backs to form a giant flower—legs high, toes pointed. Harold doesn't know it when Ray Muncey leaves. Out the window, the parking lot light glows like a big full moon. Lois Hickey comes in. "You've got to go home now, Harold," she says. "I'll call if there's any change." He remembers Cherry at Glass Lake, on the senior class picnic. Cherry's getting real agitated now, she tosses her head back and forth, moves her arms. She'd pull out the tubes if she could. She kicks off the sheet. Her legs are still good, great legs in fact, the legs of a beautiful young woman.

Harold at seventeen was tall and skinny, brown hair in a soft flat crew cut, glasses with heavy black frames. His jeans were too short. He carried a pen-and-pencil set in a clear plastic case in his breast pocket. Harold and his best friend, Ben Hill, looked so much alike that people had trouble telling them apart. They did everything together. They built model rockets, they read every science-fiction book they could get their hands on, they collected Lionel train parts and Marvel comics. They loved superheroes with special powers, enormous beings who leaped across rivers and oceans. Harold's friendship with Ben Hill kept the awful loneliness of the only child at bay, and it also kept him from having to talk to girls. You couldn't talk to those two, not seriously. They were giggling and bumping into each other all the time. They were immature.

So it was in Ben's company that Harold experienced the most private, the most *personal* memory he has of Cherry Oxendine in high school. Oh, he also has those other memories you'd expect, the big public memories of Cherry being crowned Miss Greenwood High (for her talent, she surprised everybody by reciting "Abou Ben Adhem" in such a stirring way that there wasn't a dry eye in the whole auditorium when she got through), or running out onto the field ahead of the team with the other cheerleaders, red curls flying, green-and-white skirt whirling out around her hips like a beach umbrella when she turned a cartwheel. Harold noticed her then, of course. He noticed her when she moved through the crowded halls of the high school with her walk that was almost a prance, she put a little something extra into it, all right. Harold noticed Cherry Oxendine then in the way that he noticed Sandra Dee on the cover of a magazine, or Annette Funicello on "American Bandstand."

But such girls were not for the likes of Harold, and Harold knew it. Girls like Cherry always had boyfriends like Lamar Peebles, who was hers—a doctor's son with a baby-blue convertible and plenty of money. They used to drive around town in his car, smoking cigarettes. Harold saw them, as he carried out grocery bags. He did not envy Lamar Peebles, or wish he had a girl like Cherry Oxendine. Only something about them made him stand where he was in the Food Lion lot, watching, until they had passed from sight.

So Harold's close-up encounter with Cherry was unexpected. It took place at the senior class picnic, where Harold and Ben had been drinking beer all afternoon. No alcohol was allowed at the senior class picnic, but some of the more enterprising boys had brought out kegs the night before and hidden them in the woods. Anybody could go back there and pay some money and get some beer. The chaperones didn't know, or appeared not to know. In any case, the chaperones all left at six o'clock, when the picnic was officially over. Some of the class members left then too. Then some of them came back with more beer, more blankets.

It was a free lake. Nobody could *make* you go home. Normally, Harold and Ben would have been among the first to leave, but because they had had four beers apiece, and because this was the first time they had ever had *any* beer ever, at all, they were still down by the water, skipping rocks and waiting to sober up so that they would not wreck Harold's mother's green Gremlin on the way home. All the cool kids were on the other side of the lake, listening to transistor radios. The sun went down. Bullfrogs started up. A mist came out all around the sides of the lake. It was a cloudy, humid day anyway, not a great day for a picnic.

"If God is really God, how come He let Himself get crucified, is what I want to know," Ben said. Ben's daddy was a Holiness preacher, out in the county.

But Harold heard something. "Hush, Ben," he said.

"If I was God I would go around and really kick some ass," Ben said.

Harold heard it again. It was almost too dark to see.

"Damn." It was a girl's voice, followed by a splash.

All of a sudden, Harold felt sober. "Who's there?" he asked. He stepped forward, right up to the water's edge. Somebody was in the water. Harold was wearing his swim trunks under his jeans, but he had not gone in the water himself. He couldn't stand to show himself in front of people. He thought he was too skinny.

"Well, *do something*." It was the voice of Cherry Oxendine, almost wailing. She stumbled up the bank. Harold reached out and grabbed her arm. Close up, she was a mess, wet and muddy, with her hair all over her head. But the thing that got Harold, of course, was that she didn't have any top on. She didn't even try to cover them up either, just stomped her little foot on the bank and said, "I am going to *kill* Lamar Peebles when I get ahold of him." Harold had never even imagined so much skin.

"What's going on?" asked Ben, from up the bank.

Harold took off his own shirt as fast as he could and handed it over to Cherry Oxendine. "Cover yourself," he said.

"Why, thank you." Cherry didn't bat an eye. She took his shirt and put it on, tying it stylishly at the waist. Harold couldn't believe it. Close up, Cherry was a lot smaller than she looked on the stage or the football field. She looked up at Harold through her dripping hair and gave him her crooked grin.

"Thanks, hey?" she said.

And then she was gone, vanished into the mist and trees before Harold could say another word. He opened his mouth and closed it. Mist obscured his view. From the other side of the lake he could hear "Ramblin' Rose" playing on somebody's radio. He heard a girl's high-pitched giggle, a boy's whooping laugh.

"What's going on?" asked Ben.

"Nothing," Harold said. It was the first time he had ever lied to Ben. Harold never told anybody what had happened that night, not ever. He felt that it was up to him to protect Cherry Oxendine's honor. Later, much later, when he and Cherry were lovers, he was astonished to learn that she couldn't remember any of this, not who she was with or what had happened or what she was doing in the lake like that with her top off, or Harold giving her his shirt. "I think that was sweet, though," Cherry told him.

When Harold and Ben finally got home that night at nine or ten o'clock, Harold's mother was frantic. "You've been drinking," she shrilled at him under the hanging porch light. "And where's your shirt?" It was a new madras shirt which Harold had gotten for graduation. Now Harold's mother is out at Hillandale Cemetery. Ben died in Vietnam, and Cherry is drowning. This time, and Harold knows it now, he can't help her.

Oh, Cherry! Would she have been so wild if she hadn't been so cute? And what if her parents had been younger when she was born—normal-age parents—couldn't they have controlled her better? As it was, the Oxendines were sober, solid people living in a farmhouse out near the county line, and Cherry lit up their lives like a rocket. Her dad, Martin "Buddy" Oxendine, went to sleep in his chair every night right after supper, woke back up for the eleven-o'clock news, and then went to bed for good. Buddy was an elder in the Baptist church. Cherry's mom, Gladys Oxendine, made drapes for people. She assumed she would never have children at all because of her spastic colitis. Gladys and Buddy had started raising cockapoos when they gave up on children. Imagine Gladys's surprise, then, to find herself pregnant at thirty-eight, when she was already old! They say she didn't even know it when she went to the doctor. She thought she had a tumor.

But then she got so excited, that old farm woman, when Dr. Grimwood told her what was what, and she wouldn't even consider an abortion when he mentioned the chances of a mongoloid. People didn't use to have babies so old then as they do now, so Gladys Oxendine's pregnancy was the talk of the county. Neighbors crocheted little jackets and made receiving blankets. Buddy built a baby room onto the house and made a cradle by hand. During the last two months of the pregnancy, when Gladys had to stay in bed because of toxemia, people brought over casseroles and boiled custard, everything good. Gladys's pregnancy was the only time in her whole life that she was ever pretty, and she loved it, and she loved the attention, neighbors in and out of the house. When the baby was finally born on November 1, 1944, no parents were ever more ready than Gladys and Buddy Oxendine. And the baby was everything they hoped for too, which is not usually the case—the prettiest baby in the world, a baby like a little flower.

They named her Doris Christine, which is who she was until eighth grade, when she made junior varsity cheerleader and announced that she was changing her name to Cherry. Cherry! Even her parents had to admit it suited her better than Doris Christine. As a little girl, Doris Christine was redheaded, bouncy, and busy—she was always into something, usually something you'd never thought to tell her not to do. She started talking early and never shut up. Her old dad, old Buddy Oxendine, was so crazy about Doris Christine that he took her everywhere with him in his red pickup truck. You got used to seeing the two of them, Buddy and his curly headed little daughter, riding the country roads together, going to the seed-and-feed together, sharing a shake at the Dairy Queen. Gladys made all of Doris Christine's clothes, the most beautiful little dresses in the world, with hand-smocking and French seams. They gave Doris Christine everything they could think of—what she asked for, what she didn't. "That child is going to get spoiled," people started to say. And of course she did get spoiled, she couldn't have helped *that*, but she was never spoiled rotten as so many are. She stayed sweet in spite of it all.

Then along about ninth grade, soon after she changed her name to Cherry and got interested in boys, things changed between Cherry and the old Oxendines. Stuff happened. Instead of being the light of their lives, Cherry became the bane of their existence, the curse of their old age. She wanted to wear makeup, she wanted to have car dates. You can't blame her—she was old enough, sixteen. Everybody else did it. But you can't blame Gladys and Buddy either—they were old people by then, all worn-out. They were not up to such a daughter. Cherry sneaked out. She wrecked a car. She ran away to Pensacola with a soldier. Finally, Gladys and Buddy just gave up. When Cherry eloped with the disc jockey, Don Westall, right after graduation, they threw up their hands. They did not do a thing about it. They had done the best they could, and everybody knew it. They went back to raising cockapoos.

Cherry, living up in Nashville, Tennessee, had a baby, Stan, the one that's in his twenties now. Cherry sent baby pictures back to Gladys and Buddy, and wrote that she was going to be a singer. Six years later, she came home. She said nothing against Don Westall, who was still a disc jockey on WKIX, Nashville. You could hear him on the radio every night after 10:00 P.M. Cherry said the breakup was all her fault. She said she had made some mistakes, but she didn't say what they were. She was thin and noble. Her kid was cute. She did not go back out to the farm then. She rented an apartment over the hardware store, down by the river, and got a job downtown working in Ginger's Boutique. After a year or so, she started acting more like herself again, although not *quite* like herself, she had grown up somehow in Nashville, and quit being spoiled. She put Stan, her kid, first. And if she did run around a little bit, or if she was the life of the party sometimes out at the country club, so what? Stan didn't want for a thing. By then the Oxendines were failing and she had to take care of them too, she had to drive her daddy up to Grenada for dialysis twice a week. It was not an easy life for Cherry, but if it ever got her down, you couldn't tell it. She was still cute. When her daddy finally died and left her a little money, everybody was real glad. Oh *now,* they said, Cherry Oxendine can quit working so hard and put her mama in a home or something and have a decent life. She can go on a cruise. But then along came Ed Palladino, and the rest is history.

Cherry Oxendine was left with no husband, no money, a little girl, and a mean old mama to take care of. At least by this time Stan was in the Navy. Cherry never complained, though. She moved back out to the farm. When Ginger retired from business and closed her boutique, Cherry got another job, as a receptionist at Wallace, Wallace, and Peebles. This was her undoing. Because Lamar Peebles had just moved back to town with his family, to join his father's firm. Lamar had two little girls. He had been married to a tobacco heiress since college. All this time he had run around on her. He was not on the up-and-up. And when he encountered redheaded Cherry Oxendine again after the passage of so many years, all those old fireworks went off again. They got to be a scandal, then a disgrace. Lamar said he was going to marry her, and Cherry believed him. After six months of it, Mrs. Lamar Peebles checked herself into a mental hospital in Silver Hill, Connecticut. First, she called her lawyers.

And then it was all over, not even a year after it began. Mr. and Mrs. Lamar Peebles were reconciled and moved to Winston-Salem, North Carolina, her hometown. Cherry Oxendine lost her job at Wallace, Wallace, and Peebles, and was reduced to working in the deli at Food Lion. Why did she do it? Why did she lose all the goodwill she'd built up in this community over so many years? It is because she doesn't know how to look out for Number One. Her own daughter, Tammy Lynn Palladino, is aware of this.

"You have got a fatal flaw, Mama," Tammy said after learning about fatal flaws in English class. "You believe everything everybody tells you."

Still, Tammy loves her mother. Sometimes she writes her mother's whole name, Cherry Oxendine Westall Palladino Stikes, over and over in her Blue Horse notebook. Tammy Lynn will never be half the woman her mother is, and she's so smart she knows it. She gets a kick out of her mother's wild ideas.

"When you get too old to be cute, honey, you get to be eccentric," Cherry told Tammy one time. It's the truest thing she ever said.

It seems to Tammy that the main thing about her mother is, Cherry always has to have *something* going on. If it isn't a man it's something else, such as having her palm read by that woman over in French Camp, or astrology, or the grapefruit diet. Cherry believes in the Bermuda Triangle, Bigfoot, Atlantis, and ghosts. It kills her that she's not psychic. The UFO Club was just the latest in a long string of interests, although it has lasted the longest, starting back before Cherry's marriage to Harold Stikes. And then Cherry got cancer, and she kind of forgot about it. But Tammy still remembers the night her mama first got so turned-on to UFOs.

Rhonda Ramey, Cherry's best friend, joined the UFO Club first. Rhonda and Cherry are a lot alike, although it's hard to see this at first. While Cherry is short and peppy, Rhonda is tall, thin, and listless. She looks like Cher. Rhonda doesn't have any children. She's crazy about her husband, Bill, but he's a workaholic who runs a string of video rental stores all over northern Mississippi, so he's gone a lot, and Rhonda gets bored. She works out at the spa, but it isn't enough. Maybe this is why she got so interested when the UFO landed at a farm outside her mother's home-town of Como. It was first spotted by sixteen-year-old Donnie Johnson just at sunset, as he was finishing his chores on his parents' farm. He heard a loud rumbling sound "in the direction of the hog house," it said in the paper. Looking up, he suddenly saw a "brilliantly lit mushroom-shaped object" hovering about two feet above the ground, with a shaft of white light below and glowing all over with an intensely bright multicolored light, "like the light of a welder's arc."

Donnie said it sounded like a jet. He was temporarily blinded and paralyzed. He fell down on the ground. When he came back to his senses again, it was gone. Donnie staggered into the kitchen where his parents, Durel, fifty-four, and Erma, forty-nine, were eating supper, and told them what had happened. They all ran back outside to the field, where they found four large imprints and four small imprints in the muddy ground, and a nearby clump of sage grass on fire. The hogs were acting funny, bunching up, looking dazed. Immediately, Durel jumped in his truck and went to get the sheriff, who came right back with two deputies. All in all, six people viewed the site while the bush continued to burn, and who knows how many people—half of Como—saw the imprints the next day. Rhonda saw them too. She drove out to the Johnson farm with her mother, as soon as she heard about it.

It was a close encounter of the second kind, according to Civil Air Patrol head Glenn Raines, who appeared on TV to discuss it, because the UFO "interacted with its surroundings in a significant way." A close encounter of the first kind is simply a close-range sighting, while a close encounter of the third kind is something like the most famous example, of Betty and Barney Hill of Exeter, New Hampshire, who were actually kidnapped by a UFO while they were driving along on a trip. Betty and Barney Hill were taken aboard the alien ship and given physical exams by intelligent humanoid beings. Two hours and thirty-five minutes were missing from their trip, and afterward, Betty had to be treated for acute anxiety. Glenn Raines, wearing his brown Civil Air Patrol uniform, said all this on TV.

His appearance, plus what had happened at the Johnson farm, sparked a rash of sightings all across Mississippi, Louisiana, and Texas for the next two years. Metal disk-like objects were seen, and luminous objects appearing as lights at night. In Levelland, Texas, fifteen people called the police to report an egg-shaped UFO appearing over State Road 1173. Overall, the UFOs seemed to show a preference for soybean fields and teenage girl viewers. But a pretty good photograph of a UFO flying over the Gulf was taken by a retired man from Pascagoula, so you can't generalize. Clubs sprang up all over the place. The one that Rhonda and Cherry went to had seventeen members and met once a month at the junior high school.

Tammy recalls exactly how her mama and Rhonda acted the night they came home from Cherry's first meeting. Cherry's eyes sparkled in her face like Brenda Starr's eyes in the comics. She started right in telling Tammy all about it, beginning with the Johnsons from Como and Betty and Barney Hill.

Tammy was not impressed. "I don't believe it," she said. She was president of the Science Club at the junior high school.

"You are the most irritating child!" Cherry said. "*What* don't you believe?"

"Well, any of it," Tammy said then. "All of it." And this has remained her attitude ever since.

"Listen, honey, *Jimmy Carter* saw one," Cherry said triumphantly. "In nineteen seventy-one, at the Executive Mansion in Georgia. He turned in an official report on it."

"How come nobody knows about it, then?" Tammy asked. She was a tough customer.

"Because the government covered it up!" said Rhonda, just dying to tell this part. "People see UFOs all the time, it's common knowledge, they are trying to make contact with us right now, honey, but the government doesn't want the average citizen to know about it. There's a big cover-up going on."

"It's just like Watergate." Cherry opened a beer and handed it over to Rhonda.

"That's right," Rhonda said, "and every time there's a major incident, you know what happens? These men from the government show up at your front door dressed all in black. After they get through with you, you'll wish you never heard the word 'saucer.' You turn pale and get real sick. You can't get anything to stay on your stomach."

Tammy cracked up. But Rhonda and Cherry went on and on. They had official-looking gray notebooks to log their sightings in. At their meetings, they reported these sightings to each other, and studied up on the subject in general. Somebody in the club was responsible for the educational part of each meeting, and somebody else brought the refreshments.

Tammy Lynn learned to keep her mouth shut. It was less embarrassing than belly dancing; she had a friend whose mother took belly dancing at the YMCA. Tammy did not tell her mama about all the rational explanations for UFOs that she found in the school library. They included: (1) hoaxes; (2) natural phenomena, such as fungus causing the so-called fairy rings sometimes found after a landing; (3) real airplanes flying off course; and Tammy's favorite, (4) the Fata Morgana, described as a "rare and beautiful type of mirage, constantly changing, the result of unstable layers of warm and cold air. The Fata Morgana takes its name from fairy lore and is said to evoke in the viewer a profound sense of longing," the book went on to say. Tammy's biology teacher, Mr. Owens, said he thought that the weather patterns in Mississippi might be especially conducive to this phenomenon. But Tammy kept her mouth shut. And after a while, when nobody in the UFO Club saw anything, its membership declined sharply. Then her mama met Harold Stikes, then Harold Stikes left his wife and children and moved out to the farm with them, and sometimes Cherry forgot to attend the meetings, she was so happy with Harold Stikes.

Tammy couldn't see *why*, initially. In her opinion, Harold Stikes was about as interesting as a telephone pole. "But he's so *nice!*" Cherry tried to explain it to Tammy Lynn. Finally Tammy decided that there is nothing in the world that makes somebody as attractive as if they really love you. And Harold Stikes really did love her mama, there was no question. That old man—what a crazy old Romeo! Why, he proposed to Cherry when she was still in the hospital after she had her breast removed (this was back when they thought that was *it,* that the doctors had gotten it all).

"Listen, Cherry," he said solemnly, gripping a dozen red roses. "I want you to marry me."

"What?" Cherry said. She was still groggy.

"I want you to marry me," Harold said. He knelt down heavily beside her bed.

"Harold! Get up from there!" Cherry said. "Somebody will see you."

"Say yes," said Harold.

"I just had my breast removed."

"Say yes," he said again.

"*Yes, yes, yes!*" Cherry said.

And as soon as she got out of the hospital, they were married out in the orchard, on a beautiful April day, by Lew Uggams, a JP from out of town. They couldn't find a local preacher to do it. The sky was bright blue, not a cloud in sight. Nobody was invited except Stan, Tammy, Rhonda and Bill, and Cherry's mother, who wore her dress inside out. Cherry wore a new pink lace dress, the color of cherry blossoms. Tough little Tammy cried and cried. It's the most beautiful wedding she's ever seen, and now she's completely devoted to Harold Stikes.

So Tammy leaves the lights on for Harold when she finally goes to bed that night. She tried to wait up for him, but she has to go to school in the morning, she's got a chemistry test. Her mamaw is sound asleep in the little added-on baby room that Buddy Oxendine built for Cherry. Gladys acts like a baby now, a spoiled baby at that. The only thing she'll drink is Sprite out of a can. She talks mean. She doesn't like anything in the world except George and Tammy, the two remaining cockapoos.

They bark up a storm when Harold finally gets back out to the farm, at one-thirty. The cockapoos are barking, Cherry's mom is snoring like a chain saw. Harold doesn't see how Tammy Lynn can sleep through all of this, but she always does. Teenagers can sleep through anything. Harold himself has started waking up several times a night, his heart pounding. He wonders if he's going to have a heart attack. He almost mentioned his symptoms to Lois Hickey last week, in fact, but then thought, What the hell. His heart is broken. Of course it's going to act up some. And everything, not only his heart, is out of whack. Sometimes he'll break into a sweat for no reason. Often he forgets really crucial things, such as filing his estimated income tax on January 15. Harold is not the kind to forget something this important. He has strange aches that float from joint to joint. He has headaches. He's lost twelve pounds. Sometimes he has no appetite at all. Other times, like right now, he's just starving.

Harold goes in the kitchen and finds a flat rectangular casserole, carefully wrapped in tinfoil, on the counter, along with a Tupperware cake carrier. He lifts off the top of the cake carrier and finds a piña colada cake, his favorite. Then he pulls back the tinfoil on the casserole. Lasagna! Plenty is left over. Harold sticks it in the microwave. He knows that the cake and the lasagna were left here by his ex-wife. Ever since Cherry has been in Intensive Care, Joan has been bringing food out to the farm. She comes when Harold's at work or at the hospital, and leaves it with Gladys or Tammy. She probably figures that Harold would refuse it, if she caught him at home, which he would. She's a great cook, though. Harold takes the lasagna out of the microwave, opens a beer, and sits down at the kitchen table. He loves Joan's lasagna. Cherry's idea of a terrific meal is one she doesn't have to cook. Harold remembers eating in bed with Cherry, tacos from Taco Bell, sour-cream-and-onion chips, beer. He gets some more lasagna and a big wedge of piña colada cake.

Now it's two-thirty, but for some reason Harold is not a bit sleepy. His mind whirls with thoughts of Cherry. He snaps off all the lights and stands in the darkened house. His heart is racing. Moonlight comes in the windows, it falls on the old patterned rug. Outside, it's as bright as day. He puts his coat on goes out, with the cockapoos scampering along beside him. They are not even surprised. They think it's a fine time for a walk. Harold goes past the mailbox, down the dirt road between the fields. Out here in the country, the sky is both bigger and closer than it is in town. Harold feels like he's in a huge bowl turned upside down, with tiny little pinpoints of light shining through. And everything is silvered by the moonlight—the old fenceposts, the corn stubble in the flat long fields, a distant barn, the highway at the end of the dirt road, his own strange hand when he holds it out to look at it.

He remembers when she waited on him in the Food Lion deli, three years ago. He had asked for a roast beef sandwich, which come prepackaged. Cherry put it on his plate. Then she paused, and cocked her hip, and looked at him. "Can I give you some potato salad to go with that?" she asked. "Some slaw?"

Harold looked at her. Some red curls had escaped the required net. "Nothing else," he said.

But Cherry spooned a generous helping of potato salad onto his plate. "Thank you so much," he said. They looked at each other.

"I know I know you," Cherry said.

It came to him then. "Cherry Oxendine," said Harold. "I remember you from high school."

"Lord, you've got a great memory, then!" Cherry had an easy laugh. "That was a hundred years ago."

"Doesn't seem like it." Harold knew he was holding up the line.

"Depends on who you're talking to," Cherry said.

Later that day, Harold found an excuse to go back over to the deli for coffee and apple pie, then he found an excuse to look through the personnel files. He started eating lunch at the deli every day, without making any conscious decision to do so. In the afternoons, when he went back for coffee, Cherry would take her break and sit at a table with him.

Harold and Cherry talked and talked. They talked about their families, their kids, high school. Cherry told him everything that had happened to her. She was tough and funny, not bitter or self-pitying. They talked and talked. In his whole life, Harold had never had so much to say. During this period, which lasted for several weeks, his whole life took on a heightened aspect. Everything that happened to him seemed significant, a little incident to tell Cherry about. Every song he liked on the radio he remembered, so he could ask Cherry if she liked it too. Then there came the day when they were having coffee and she mentioned she'd left her car at Al's Garage that morning to get a new clutch.

"I'll give you a ride over there to pick it up," said Harold instantly. In his mind he immediately canceled the sales meeting he had scheduled for four o'clock.

"Oh, that's too much trouble," Cherry said.

"But I insist." In his conversations with Cherry, Harold had developed a brand-new gallant manner he had never had before.

"Well, if you're sure it's not any trouble . . ." Cherry grinned at him like she knew he really wanted to do it, and that afternoon when he grabbed her hand suddenly before letting her out at Al's Garage, she did not pull it away.

The next weekend Harold took her up to Memphis and they stayed at the Peabody Hotel, where Cherry got the biggest kick out of the ducks in the lobby, and ordering from room service.

"You're a fool," Harold's friends told him later, when the shit hit the fan.

But Harold didn't think so. He doesn't think so now, walking the old dirt road on the Oxendine farm in the moonlight. He loves his wife. He feels that he has been ennobled and enlarged, by knowing Cherry Oxendine. He feels like he has been specially selected among men, to receive a precious gift. He stepped out of his average life for her, he gave up being a good man, but the rewards have been extraordinary. He's glad he did it. He'd do it all over again.

Still walking, Harold suddenly knows that something is going to happen. But he doesn't stop walking. Only, the whole world around him seems to waver a bit, and intensify. The moonlight shines whiter than ever. A little wind whips up out of nowhere. The stars are twinkling so brightly that they seem to dance, actually dance, in the sky. And then, while Harold watches, one of them detaches itself from the rest of the sky and grows larger, moves closer, until it's clear that it is actually moving across the sky, at an angle to the earth. A falling star, perhaps? A comet?

Harold stops walking. The star moves faster and faster, with an erratic pattern. It's getting real close now. It's no star. Harold hears a high whining noise, like a blender. The cockapoos huddle against his ankles. They don't bark. Now he can see the blinking red lights on the top of it, and the beam of white light shooting out the bottom. His coat is blown straight out behind him by the wind. He feels like he's going blind. He shields his eyes. At first it's as big as a barn, then a tobacco warehouse. It covers the field. Although Harold can't say exactly how it communicates to him or even if it does, suddenly his soul is filled to bursting. The ineffable occurs. And then, more quickly than it came, it's gone, off toward Carrollton, rising into the night, leaving the field, the farm, the road. Harold turns back.

It will take Cherry Oxendine two more weeks to die. She's tough. And even when there's nothing left of her but heart, she will fight all the way. She will go out furious, squeezing Harold's hand at the very moment of death, clinging fast to every minute of this bright, hard life. And although at first he won't want to, Harold will go on living. He will buy another store. Gladys will die. Tammy Lynn will make Phi Beta Kappa. Harold will start attending the Presbyterian church again. Eventually Harold may even go back to his family, but he will love Cherry Oxendine until the day he dies, and he will never, ever, tell anybody what he saw.

Susan Starr Richards

THE SCREENED PORCH

(from *The Southern Review*)

The porch was the temple of the gods, where vines crawled up the screens like snakes and outdoors was a wonderful green blur. It was being inside the world. The bricks of the porch floor were powdered with the spores of the giant tree fern, the oldest sort of tree on earth; its brown living dust sifted over them, straight from the forest primeval.

And the second-oldest sister had seen a woman on the porch one night, through the glass doors, as she was locking up. Locking up the glass doors at night was frightening. They fought about who would do it. The lock turned over like your tongue in your cheek when you make it click, and then the glass doors were staring at you, and as you walked away you felt something walking away behind you, into the dark, and you tried not to scream or run. It was hard not to scream, and harder not to run; these seemed to be their two main impulses—necessities—delights. The clutches in the small of the back, then the shrieks and giggles. The old house shook with their running, bare feet thudding on the Turkish carpets, and all the Peruvian pottery jumped up and down on the shelves above the library.

There were big wicker chairs on the porch, wing chairs with magazine racks woven into the arms, but everyone—everyone—sat on the long couch, all together, lined up, as if they were the audience at their own play. The cushions were old and soft and people tended to fall into each other—all distinctions blurred on the porch—looking out at the green blurred world. The lake was a blue glimpse in the daytime, and an erasure at night, the open dark behind the closure of the trees, and from there the great sounds of the frogs grew, honking and honking louder and louder as the night went on. In the garden thick vines roped from tree to tree, and the trees were full of epiphytes. The sisters called plants by names like epiphyte, as they had heard them called. Epiphyte, they said to each other, podocarpus, cocus plumosis, monstera deliciosa.

Here they were lined up now as they ever had been.

"Remember," the two younger sisters were asking the second-oldest, "remember how you used to make us sit on the gold couch and watch Uncle Joel till he took a drag on his cigarette?" A portrait of the uncle they meant hung over the fireplace in the living room. Its most noticeable feature was the cigarette that dangled from the long thin fingers of its subject. The second-oldest had always maintained that this portrait smoked, furtively, from time to time.

"And every time he got ready to do it," the second-oldest said, "every time—just at that moment—you'd both scream and throw yourselves face down on the brocade. So you never got to see him."

"Never. Never," they said.

"But he did do it," she went on. "And there would be just the faintest haze afterward, blue-gray, forming in front of his nostrils. You had to look hard, but it was there."

They were showing off, their silliness, their sisterliness, the peculiarity of their upbringing, like modest little savages, the virgins of this porch. After a certain point they had all rather raised themselves and each other, with small interference from the busy adults in their lives, who seemed anyway to think that worldly knowledge was mostly a matter of botanical names. Guided by the eclectic offerings of the family library, the sisters had learned etiquette from a book called *Perfect Behavior*, which included such matters as "A Correct Letter from a Young Lady to a Taxidermist Thanking Him for Having Stuffed Her Pet Alice." Recent history they learned from *Low on the War* (his cartoons of Germany as a storm trooper dragging off the young woman with "Czechoslovakia" written across her chest like a beauty queen), and anatomy from their grandfather's childhood encyclopedia, which showed little elves skipping through the digestive system. They all knew *What Your Handwriting Reveals*, and their view of sex came from *Peter Pauper's Limerick Book*. All more or less grown now, they were quaint girls, they were lively girls, and they were, above all, silly girls, inventively hysterical.

Each could do a good graceful swoon, blacking out slowly before her very own eyes. The oldest was best at this, having taken the title one day when, frustrated by their laughter at some minor sorrow, she had pitched headfirst down the stairway, the white bathrobe she was wearing billowing around her, and a wire coat hanger, which she had flung down, sliding in front of her, jingling like a cymbal on every step. Her sisters admired her high style, but they kept on laughing.

This oldest sister had periodically, when they were both very small, sent a playmate to report her death by rattlesnake to the second-oldest. A number of times the second-oldest had been led, in some anxiety, to the top of the hill above the house to view the corpse of her sister lying in the middle of the road. At last she had learned that a good vicious tickle in the ribs was the best cure for snakebite, and ever after she had a hard time believing in anyone's troubles.

The second-youngest sister was honorable and fainted only on the rare occasions when they went to church, and then she did it out of guilt, with complete conviction. The others couldn't help but feel the authenticity of the rifle-crack her head made when it hit the uncarpeted outside aisle on Easter morning.

The youngest sister was the pet of them all and the most hysterical, and it was hard to say if that was because she was four-teen years old or if she would always be that way. She had been laughed at by the others when she was little for saying from time to time that she had a pain in her heart. They all felt rather badly later when it appeared that she did have a little heart murmur, but said to each other, "Surely that wouldn't make your heart hurt? Just a murmur, after all." They had been fully relieved on that score when the second-oldest discovered that she had a heart murmur, too, and, she reported, it didn't hurt a bit.

And now here was the second-oldest, come home with a man. A young man with a dark tan and a white grin, thin-faced and hungry-looking, sitting on the porch amongst all the fair, soft, round-faced girls, with their foolish, exclusive talk and memory and self-conscious reflectiveness. They all sat right next to him, taking him into the sisterhood, surrounding him with blond, soft, girlish flesh, pressing against him.

The very first time the young man had come home with the second-oldest, the youngest sister (who was, of course, even younger then) had come and plumped herself right down on his lap. Later she confessed, solemnly and in confidence, that she had "dreamed" her sister had died in an automobile accident, so she could marry the young man herself. "But it didn't hurt you," she said, grinning anxiously, pleadingly. "It didn't hurt you at all."

"That's a comfort," the second-oldest said, grinning back.

That was the thing about being sisters. You told each other everything, even the awful things. They would have been awful indeed if you hadn't told them. The second-oldest didn't mind the "dream." Hadn't she simply erased the wife of her Classics professor often enough in her own imagination, without even considering euthanasia? But then, of course, she'd never met the woman; with a sister, you had some reason for tenderness.

But here was this peculiar circumstance. This young man had come back now as the second-oldest sister's husband. A young man in the family, on the porch, and on the couch, and one who would do—not a fool, as they all allowed the oldest sister's husband to be, but a clever one—one as silly, on occasion, as they were.

They had all, when they were growing up, tried walking on water; it had seemed something they were always on the verge of learning how to do, just as they had all at last learned how to drop off into the lake, yodeling like Tarzan, from the highest arc of the bag swing. The youngest, one day this summer, had continued their old experiment, stepping off the dock flat-footed, with her sneakers on—it was, she had announced, simply a matter of maintaining surface tension—and had been called by him, ever after, Squashy Foot.

"Old Squashy Foot," he would say, nodding at her.

"Old Squashy Foot," her sisters would say, nodding at him.

"Cow!" Old Squashy Foot would say. But she said this on every occasion.

"Cow!" he would say. "The cry of the wild Squashy Foot!"

"Squash, squash, squash, squash," Old Squashy Foot would say, doing a jaunty, squashy little dance.

"Pardonnez-moi," he would sing, dancing back at her, "is that the Squashanooga Shoe-Shoe?" Then murmur at them sideways, one eyebrow up, "You don't mind if I speak in my native tongue?"

How could they mind? It was *their* native tongue. It was, in fact, as if a stranger had appeared in some isolated tribe and had, from the beginning, spoken the language.

And for all that he was marvelously strange. The younger sisters fingered his clothing, patted his hair, stared at him in wonder. It made him theirs, his being the husband of the second-oldest. Not more seriously than before, but permanently; they could keep him. It was hard to take the marriage seriously as a marriage—it seemed mostly an arrangement for their delight and convenience, the better to be silly with him. It seemed that way to the sister who had married him, too—that seemed to be the very best thing about it, to have this attractive strange man here in the scene of her dreamy childhood, all her old, lazy, longing days of ecstasy on the porch, quiet and alone, or giggling with her sisters.

She looked out into the dark and remembered the way they used to stand under the streetlight on pleasant evenings, puzzled by what they were looking for. There was something about that, standing under the streetlight. The dark all around, the lake behind them, beyond the trees, they stood in the yellow pool of light on the brick road that was still warm from the day's sun, waiting for a car to go by and see them standing there waiting. Restless, unsatisfying, very satisfactory as an activity for young summer evenings, doing nothing at all in the full view of whoever might come by. Few people did. It was not a traveled road. The palmetto bugs bombed down at them so they screamed occasionally when one got caught in their hair and sometimes were altogether silent in the solemnity of their waiting.

She was still not sure that he was what she had been waiting for. It had seemed something vaster, more mysterious than any particular man. Still, here he was, and he was something in himself. And what a lovely time they were all having together. They had felt quite thinned out when the oldest sister had married and left, but now they were back in force, foursquare again, as they always had been, and closer, in a way, than before, with her two sisters turning always to him—the youngest, in fact, clinging to him as if magnetized.

One night they went to the drive-in movie. The car was too small for them all to sit in the front seat, but the youngest sister couldn't bear the exile of the back for long and crawled up on the top of the front seat, as she often did on the couch at home, and lay there with her arms around the young man's neck. But the car seat was narrower than the couch and, at some exciting point in the first movie, she lost her balance and literally fell all over the young man, sliding off her perch and landing heavily, her hips hanging off one of his shoulders, her breasts over the other, legs and arms everywhere. "For God's sake!" the second-oldest said, not laughing for once. "Quit *bothering* him." That was enough to make the youngest subside into the backseat, in tears. The second-oldest had been surprised by her own outburst and was prepared not to be angry after that, but as the weeping went on, expansive, accusing, right through the double feature, she grew stony and silent. He cheered them all up on the way home by joking around with them, and everyone seemed to have forgotten about it by the time they reached the house. But once the young man and his bride were in bed, he reprimanded her, gently but seriously, for hurting her sister's feelings for no reason.

"I thought *you'd* mind," the second-oldest said, as her first defense.

"I can take care of myself," he said pointedly. "If I mind, I'll say so."

She thought about this. "Well, I'm sorry I was mean to her," she said then, truthfully. "But I wasn't all *that* mean," she added. She grinned a little in the dark, wondering what he would have thought of her the time she had, in a fit of pique, slung a ukulele at the second-youngest.

He was silent a moment, as if he were considering. "We ought to try to be nice to her," he said then, thoughtfully.

She turned her head slowly to stare at him in the dark. "As opposed to trying *not* to be?"

"I don't mean you," he said, hugging her persuasively. "I mean both of us. We ought to let her know we like her. Be *nice* to her," he said again. "I think she needs it," he added, in the little quizzical voice he used for making pronouncements.

She acquiesced, puzzled, but respectful of his sensibilities. She had never been deliberately cruel to her younger sisters; she had even, when she could, protected them from the depredations of the oldest, remembering herself what it was like to be younger. And she would, of course, have flung herself into any stormy sea to save them, if she had to. She had studied Advanced Lifesaving in school, in case someday she should have to, and in her dreams her sisters were always the ones she saved. But it had never occurred to her to be nice to them.

After that night, there was still a lot of silliness and giggling in the daytime, but they began to talk seriously about life, in the darkening porch, as the nights came on. Or the young man began to talk. He said that everyone was alone in the world, and you had to accept that. "But that's awful," the two younger sisters said indignantly. No, he said, it wasn't an awful thing to know; it was an exciting thing to know, and once you knew it you could live in the world alone and like it. And you were ready to love someone if someone came along and was worth loving, and if no one did, you were all right too. The two girls listened obediently, asking questions in hopeless little voices, with tears in their eyes, as if it were a lesson they despaired to learn. And he responded to their tears; he told them these things over and over, tenderness quickening his voice.

The second-oldest watched and wondered. You might be alone in the world, she said to herself, but you certainly weren't alone on the couch. Here they all were, squashed up together as usual. So why had her sisters gotten so sad? They had always been so jolly, alone together. How they had danced at night in the tall white living room, making their long shadows leap up together toward the high ceiling, like the Masai warriors they had seen in *King Solomon's Mines*. How they had played, banging on the dishpan and the rosewood spinet alike, making "modern music" for themselves. How they had sung, in what they called Chinese harmony, fifths sliding up and down parallel, turning "You Are My Sunshine" into some threatening Oriental shrillness. If you were sad in those days, you got laughed at, or left alone. Or tickled, as if you were faking snakebite. How had her sprightly sisters turned into these sad ladies who sat around crying in the dark? Her husband went on talking, in his deep voice with its rich timbre, that in its lowest register actually vibrated the springs of the couch they sat on. And the youngest sister wept steadily, slowly, as he talked, tears sliding down her face, silver and visible in the dark.

What was she crying for? He knew a lot, but he didn't know

that. He knew a lot about life. But he didn't know a thing about sisters.

The second-oldest recalled how, when she was even younger than her youngest sister was now, she had provoked her older sister's boyfriend to kiss her under a bed in a game of hide-and-seek, and then had skulked away silently into the dark. And she remembered how, when she was several years older than her youngest sister was now, she had danced a pure, pelvic rhumba with her older sister's date one night in a dark bar—all hips, no feet, as if she were dancing on a cake of ice, as her dancing teacher used to say. But the movements she was making they had never learned in dancing school. And when, back in the booth, alone with her for a moment, he had kissed her—his lips seeming to come out and touch hers without any of the rest of him moving, like the tongue of a snake—she had looked him right in the eye and said, "You got the wrong sister."

What had she wanted on those occasions? Not to seduce anyone, certainly—beyond the rhumba, seduction had been a mystery to her. No, she had wanted Safe Contact—to be kissed, to have the world put its mouth out and touch hers. That had been quite enough, a perfect little taste of the world, so safe and so dangerous—to be kissed by a man who was presumed to belong to your older sister. She hadn't even much liked those men. Of course, her older sister hadn't been married to them either, but what was marriage to a fourteen-year-old? Rather like a long date.

And it was clear that her youngest sister did like her husband very much; indeed, she liked him so much herself, this seemed only natural to her. She loved him, in fact; but she didn't need him. How much did you allow for need, among your sisters?

Because she had at last to understand, watching her sister weeping in the dark, that her husband might be right—that those tears might be coming from some real need. Perhaps, when the youngest was little and said that her heart hurt, it really did hurt. Perhaps her heart hurt now. Certainly she had some new seriousness in her tears—she cried quietly now, knowingly, as if suffused with all the sorrows of the world. And if she were indeed sinking into some sea of world sorrow, being snatched away by its rip-tides—why, the second-oldest couldn't leap in herself, she was no good at this sadness business. But here was her young husband, who seemed to have an unexpected knack for it, to be drawn to it, in fact—even to have the promise of salvation in him. An Advanced Lifesaver, indeed. His talent all wasted on her.

"But what if you don't find anybody ever?" the youngest would say to him falteringly. "What if there really *isn't* anybody?"

"Then you're all right anyway," he would say again. "It's more fun with someone, of course. But it's fun anyway."

"But you *have* someone," the youngest said back to that one night. She got up from the couch and moved across to one of the chairs, looking from him to the second-oldest, her eyes flashing with tears.

"We don't know we'll *always* have each other," he said. "No-body can know that."

"But how can you say *we'll* be all right?" the youngest went on. "How can you be all right if you're all alone?"

"You're not 'all alone,'" he said, imitating her sorrowful tone. "You're just"—he shrugged, smiled—"alone. It's not so bad."

"It's not worth it," the youngest said, shaking her head.

"What's not?"

"It's not worth it. If I'm all there is, for the rest of my life . . ." She couldn't finish the sentence.

"You've got to be worth it," he said sharply. "You *are* all there is."

"It's not worth it," she said again. "I'll never be enough. How can I be enough if I'm not? I won't do it," she said, starting to cry again.

"Oh," he said, leaning forward suddenly, speaking to her softly, crooningly. "Oh. Wait. Listen. It's not true. I lied. You won't be alone."

She raised her head, hopeful, doubtful.

"Someone will always be with you."

She pulled her chin in, looking at him severely.

"The friend you always needed," he went on in that crooning voice. "The one you always wanted. The one you've been waiting for, all these years."

She looked at her sisters. They looked back, blankly.

"You know who it is, of course," he said.

"Not God?" she said hopelessly.

"God?" he said. "God I don't know about. But—Squashy Foot is always with you."

Her head dropped. The tears started to slide out from under her lashes again.

"You know," he crooned tenderly, "Squashy Foot? The one that walks on water?"

She said nothing, looking up at him pitifully with her tear-stained face.

"Hey, Squashy Foot," he called, behind his hand. "How's your surface tension?"

She gave a little hiccup, halfway between a sob and a giggle. She widened her eyes, stared down at her lap. Very softly she said, "Cow."

"Uh huh," he said. "That's right. Cow. Cow is with you, too. Both of them. Call on them, anytime. They'll come running. Here they come now." He started stamping his feet softly. "Squash, squash, squash, squash, isn't that how they go? Squash, squash, squash, squash," he sang, on his feet now, stamping toward her, arms swinging, grin flashing. "Squash, squash, squash—"

But she had leapt up from the chair and flung herself on him, headlong, giggling. Saved. For the moment, saved. They embraced, turning together to the second-oldest, who was angled back in the corner of the couch, watching.

It is just possible, she said to herself, looking from one shining, triumphant face to the other, that he has got the wrong sister.

But his dark, gleaming gaze drew her in, beyond all ordinary lights, and she saw her sister's pleading, anxious grin. And she grinned back. Her sister was, after all, her sister. And he was, she told herself, loving enough, wise enough, man enough for all three of them.

Came the night when she wandered out to the porch a little late and found herself at the end of the line, with her two sisters already pressed close against him, one on each side. His arm was long enough to reach around her, too, but that didn't feel right. The second-youngest had become a wall of flesh, through which she must imagine her husband's warmth. But then that sister, being honorable, got up and said she was going to bed, nobly giving up her place.

The two of them beside her then, their familiar shapes growing strange, growing together in the dark. They sat for a long time in what she expected was soulful silence. The frogs screamed louder and louder outside, the screens fell away into the living tangle of the night, the porch stood all open to the larger dark. And at last she recognized, in the stillness that had filled the air, the waiting her out, the willing her to be gone. What she was not sure of, here at the last minute, was just where it was coming from. From her sister? From him? He sat rather sunk down between them, an arm looped around each of them, his eyes half-closed.

She was not quite ready to submit to euthanasia yet; still, it seemed to her that the least she could do was go up to bed herself. Which she did, briefly, with no fuss, no "You coming?" The second-oldest had a sporting instinct. What she felt, as she walked away, was release, and a certain quickening of the blood.

But an hour went by, and the house stayed quiet, and sticky sheets settled slowly around her. The bright emptiness of the upstairs hall faced her. Outside, the facade of leaves, white and unearthly in the outside light. Some part of her stood out there in the dark, glimpsing smooth white limbs and strange dark twinings—in the cage of the porch below, her little sister and the dark stranger, enmeshed. She herself lay cold and sweating, all alone in the stuffy bedroom. Had she really thought she could save her sister by offering to share her husband? Over and over again she struggled to rise up, thinking to rescue—her sister? Or her husband? And what if neither of them wanted to be rescued? The thought of what she might find, down in the porch, went through her like a knife through her middle, pinning her back to the bed.

Then the footsteps thudding through the house—all the things they had locked out in the dark, running back into it. No screaming this time; they were past the possibilities of screaming now. Just the noisy running, that heavy-footed adolescent gallop, back through the living room, rounding the stairs. She leapt a little in the bed, feeling the clutch at her own back, as if those were her own footsteps, pounding up the stairs, running down the hall. A pale, familiar figure ducked past her door, so bent on its escape as to look almost headless.

So, she said to herself. It was as she had first expected. Just Safe Contact, after all. An embrace—perhaps a kiss—and that had been quite enough. The noisy publicity of her sister's retreat made that obvious.

But when, sometime later, she heard her husband's footsteps coming up the stairs, she was not nearly as relieved as she had expected to be. And when he came in the room and slipped into bed beside her—in the perfect silence that followed—she wished herself back in her old bed at the other end of the hall, with her sisters giggling and whispering in the next room.

Still, there was, perhaps, no giggling on this occasion. "Is she all right?" she finally had to ask. For she knew it was possible to be really frightened, even if all you had seen was yourself.

There was another silence. "If you want to know . . ." he began—but in such an unfamiliar, muffled, boyish voice. She had been so ready to believe in his male magic—as if he were her smoking uncle hanging on the wall downstairs—she had given all of them over to his supposed powers. Now she did want to know that her sister was all right—it was, she found to her surprise, the one thing in the world she really wanted to know. And she understood, from the sound of his voice, that he couldn't tell her.

"*I'm* the one that's not . . ." he began again. Not all right, that was what he meant; she could hear it in his faltering voice. She glanced over at him, softening. He lay flattened to his side of the big bed, reciting upward to the dark. She turned to him, feeling the expanse of sheet like a vast white distance between them.

Then he gave a sharp, startled laugh, looking over at her with a sudden flash of certainty. His voice shot up high, cracking with amazement and rage: "*She knew what she was doing,*" he said. "*All along.*"

But the truth was, of course, they had none of them known what they were doing. And she herself—who was, after all, the second-oldest—had known least of all. She shut her eyes and saw a pale, familiar, almost-headless figure—someone who might have been her sister—running away from her forever, into the foliate dark. It wasn't his fault, she said to herself. She had agreed to marry him, and she did love him. Still, he had ruined everything.

Robert Olen Butler

RELIC

(from *The Gettysburg Review*)

You may be surprised to learn that a man from Vietnam owns one of John Lennon's shoes. Not only one of John Lennon's shoes. One shoe that he was wearing when he was shot to death in front of the Dakota apartment building. That man is me, and I have money, of course, to buy this thing. I was a very wealthy man in my former country, before the spineless poor threw down their guns and let the communists take over. Something comes into your head as I speak: this is a hard man, a man of no caring, how can he speak of the "spineless poor." I do not mean to say that these people are poor because they are cowards. I am saying that being poor can take away a man's courage. For those who are poor, being beaten down, robbed of rights, repressed under the worst possible form of tyranny is not enough worse than just being poor. Why should they risk the pain and the maiming and the death for so little benefit? If I was a poor man, I too would be spineless.

But I had wealth in Vietnam and that gave me courage enough even to sail away on the South China Sea, sail away from all those things I owned and come to a foreign country and start again with nothing. That is what I did. I came at last to New Orleans, Louisiana, and because I was once from North Vietnam and was Catholic, I ended up among my own people far east in Orleans

Parish, in a community called Versailles, named after an apartment complex they put us in as refugees. I lived in such a place
for a time. The ceilings were hardly eight feet high and there was
no veranda, nowhere even to hang a wind chime. The emptiness
of the rooms threatened to cast me down, take my courage. In
Saigon, I owned many wonderful things: furniture of teak, inlaid
with scenes made of tiles of ivory and pearl, showing how the
Trung sisters threw out the Chinese from our country in the year
40 A.D.; a part of an oracle bone from the earliest times of my
country, the bone of some animal killed by ritual and carved with
the future in Chinese characters; a dagger with a stag's antler
handle in bronze. You might think that things like this should
have protected me from what happened. There is much power in
objects. My church teaches that clearly. A fragment of bone from
a saint's body, a bit of skin, a lock of hair, all of these things have
great power to do miracles, to cure, to heal.

But you see, though the Trung sisters threw the Chinese out,
just one year later the Chinese returned and the Trung sisters
had to retreat, and finally, in the year 43, they threw themselves
into a river and drowned. And the oracle stone, though I did not
know exactly what it said, probably dealt with events long past
or maybe even foresaw this very world where I have ended up.
And the dagger looked ceremonial and I'm sure was never drawn
in anger. It would have been better if I had owned the tiniest
fragment of some saint's body, but the church does not sell such
things.

And here I sit, at the desk in the study in my house. I am growing rich once more and in the center of my desk sits this shoe. It is
more like a little boot, coming up to the ankle and having no laces
but a loop of leather at the back where John Lennon's forefinger
went through to pull the shoe onto his foot, even that morning
which was his last morning on this earth. Something comes into
your head when I tell you this. It is my talent in making wealth to
know what others are thinking. You wonder how I should come
to have this shoe, how I know it is really what I say it is. I cannot

give away the names of those who I dealt with, but I can tell you this much. I am a special collector of things. A man in New York who sells to me asked if I was interested in something unusual. When he told me about this shoe, I had the same response— how can I know for sure? Well, I met the man who provided the shoe, and I have photographs and even a newspaper article that identifies him as a very close associate of John Lennon. He says that certain items were very painful for the family, so they were disposed of and he was in possession of them and he knew that some people would appreciate them very much. He too is a Catholic. The other shoe was already gone, which is unfortunate, but this shoe was still available, and I paid much money for it.

Of course, I have made much money in my new country. It is a gift I have, and America is the land of opportunity. I started in paper lanterns and firecrackers and *cay neu*, the New Year poles. I sold these at the time of Tet, our Vietnam New Year celebration, when the refugees wanted to think about home. I also sold them sandwiches and drinks and later I opened a restaurant and then a parlor with many video games. Versailles already has a pool hall, run by another good businessman, but I have video games in my place and the young men love these games, fighting alien space-ships and wizards and kung-fu villains with much greater skill than their fathers fought the communists. And I am now doing other things, bigger things, mostly in the shrimp industry. In ten years people from Vietnam will be the only shrimp fishermen in the Gulf of Mexico. I do not need an oracle bone to tell you this for sure. And when this is so, I will be making even more money.

I may even be able to break free of Versailles. I sit at my desk and I look beyond John Lennon's shoe, through the window, and what do I see? My house, unlike the others on this street, has two stories. I am on the second story at the back, and outside is my carefully trimmed yard, the lush St. Augustine grass faintly tinted with blue, and there is my brick barbecue pit and my set-ting of cypress lawn furniture. But beyond is the bayou that runs through Versailles and my house is built at an angle on an acre and a half and I can see all the other backyards set side by side for the quarter mile to the place where the lagoon opens up and the Versailles apartments stand. All the backyards of these houses— all of them—are plowed and planted as if this was some provincial village in Vietnam. Such things are not done in America. In America a vegetable garden is a hobby. Here in Versailles the people of Vietnam are cultivating their backyards as a way of life. And behind the yards is a path and beyond the path is the border of city land along the bayou, and on this land the people of Vietnam have planted a community garden stretching down to the lagoon and even now I can see a scattering of conical straw hats there, the women crouched flat-footed and working the garden, and I expect any moment to see a boy riding a water buffalo down the path or perhaps a sampan gliding along the bayou, heading for the South China Sea. Do you understand me? I am living in the past.

I have enough money to leave Versailles and become the American that I must be. But I have found that it isn't so simple. Something is missing. I know I am wrong when I say that still more money, from shrimp or from whatever else, will finally free me from the past. Perhaps the problem is that my businesses are all connected to the Vietnam community here. There was no way around that when I started. And perhaps it's true that I should find some American business to invest in. But there is nothing to keep me in this place even if my money is made here. I do not work the cash registers in my businesses.

Perhaps it is the absence of my family. But this is something they chose for themselves. My wife was a simple woman and she would not leave her parents and she feared America greatly. The children came from her body. They belong with her, and she felt she belonged in Vietnam. My only regret is that I have nothing of hers to touch, not a lock of hair or a ring or even a scarf—she had so many beautiful scarves, some of which she wore around her waist. But if my family had come with me, would they not in fact be a further difficulty in my becoming American? As it is,

I have only myself to consider in this problem and that should make things simpler.

But there are certain matters in life that a man is not able to control on his own. My religion teaches this clearly. For a rich man, for a man with the gift to become rich even a second time, this is a truth that is sometimes difficult to see. But he should realize that he is human and dependent on forces beyond himself and he should look to the opportunity that his wealth can give him.

I do not even know John Lennon's music very well. I have heard it and it is very nice, but in Vietnam I always preferred the popular singers in my own language, and in America I like the music they call easy-listening, though sometimes a favorite tune I will hear from the Living Strings or Mantovani turns out to be a song of John Lennon. It is of no matter to a man like John Lennon that I did not know his music well before I possessed his shoe. The significance of this object is the same. He is a very important figure. This is common knowledge. He wrote many songs that affected the lives of people in America and he sang about love and peace and then he died on the streets of New York as a martyr.

I touch his shoe. The leather is smooth and is the color of teakwood and my forefinger glides along the instep to the toe, where there is a jagged scrape. I lift my finger and put it on the spot where the scrape begins, at the point of the toe, and I trace the gash, follow the fuzzy track of the exposed underside of the leather. All along it I feel a faint grinding inside me, as if this is a wound in flesh that I touch. John Lennon's wound. I understand this scrape on the shoe. John Lennon fell and his leg pushed out on the pavement as he died. This is the stigmata of the shoe, the sign of his martyrdom.

With one hand I cup the shoe at its back and slide my other hand under the toe and I lift and the shoe always surprises me at its lightness, just as one who has moments before died a martyr's death might be surprised at the lightness of his own soul. I angle the shoe toward the light from my window and I look inside. I see the words Saville Row on the lining, but that is all. There is no size recorded here and I imagine that this shoe was made special for John Lennon, that they carefully measured his foot and this is its purest image in the softest leather. I am very quiet inside but there is this great pressure in my chest, coming from something I cannot identify as myself. This is because of what I will now do.

I wait until I can draw an adequate breath. Then I turn in my chair and gently lower the shoe to the floor and I place it before my bare right foot. I make the sign of the cross and slip my foot into John Lennon's shoe, sliding my forefinger into the loop at the back and pulling gently, just as John Lennon did on the day he joined the angels. The lining is made of something as soft as silk and there is a chill from it. I stand up before my desk and the shoe is large for me, but that's as it should be. I take one step and then another and I am in the center of my room and I stand there and my heart is very full and I wait for what I pray will one day be mine, a feeling about what has happened to me that I cannot even imagine until I actually feel it. I have asked the man in New York to look for another of John Lennon's shoes, a left shoe. Even if it is from some other pair, I want to own just one more shoe. Then I will put both of John Lennon's shoes on my feet and I will go out into the street and I will walk as far as I need to go to find the place where I belong.

WITH JAZZ

(from *The New Yorker*)

Jim Ed – 1st husband
george is the 2nd husband

I never paid much attention to current events, all the trouble in the world you hear about. I was too busy raising a family. But my children have all gone now and I've started to think about things that go on. Why would my daughter live with a man and get ready to raise a baby and refuse to marry the guy? Why would my son live in a cabin by the river and not see a soul for months on end? But that's just personal. I'm thinking of the bigger picture, too. It seems a person barely lives long enough to begin to see where his little piece fits in the universal puzzle. I'm not old but I imagine that old people start to figure out how to live just when it's too late.

These thoughts come up at my weekly neighborhood group. It started out as a weight-reducing club, but we kept meeting even after we all got skinny. Now on Fridays after work a bunch of us get together at somebody's house and talk about life, in a sort of talk-show format. Although we laugh a lot, for us it's survival. And it helps me think.

It's so hard to be nice to people. It's something you have to learn. I try to be nice, but it's complicated. You start feeling guilty for your own failures of generosity at just about the same point in life when you start feeling angry, even less willing to give. The two feelings collide—feeling gracious and feeling mean. When you get really old, they say, you go right back to being a child, spiteful and selfish, and you don't give a damn what people think. In between childhood and old age, you have this bubble of consciousness—and conscience. It's enough to drive you crazy.

After our group session last Friday, I went up to Paducah, across the county line, hoping to see this guy I know. He calls himself Jazz, but his real name is Peter. He always hated that name. Kids in school would tease him. "Where's your peter?," "Oh, you don't look like a peter," etc. Some kids from my distant past used the word "goober," the first name I ever heard for the secret male anatomy. I thought they were saying "cooper." That didn't make any sense to me. Then I learned that the correct word was "goober." I learned that in the fourth grade from Donna Lee Washam, the day she led me on an expedition to a black-walnut tree on the far edge of the playground. She came back to the classroom with two black walnuts in her panties and giggled all afternoon as she squirmed in her seat. Across the aisle and a couple of seats up, Jerry Ray Baxter sometimes took his goober out and played with it. He couldn't talk plain, and after that year he stopped coming to school.

Jazz was at the Top Line, where I thought he'd be. He was lounging at the bar, with a draught beer, shooting the breeze. When he saw me he grinned slowly and pulled a new brassiere out of his pocket, dangling it right there between the jug of beet-pickled eggs and the jug of pickled pigs' feet. Ed, the bartender, swung his head like he'd seen it all. "There you go again, Jazz, pulling off women's clothes."

Jazz said, "No, this is my magic trick."

I stuffed the bra in my purse. "Thanks, Jazz, I guess you knew my boobs were falling down."

He came from down in Obion, Tennessee, and grew up duck hunting around Reelfoot Lake. Now he goes to France and brings back suitcases full of French underwear. He sells it to a boutique and occasionally to friends. It's designer stuff and the sizes are different from here. His ex-wife gets it at cost from a supplier in Paris where she works. He goes over there once a year or so to see his kids. Jazz works construction and saves his money, and then quits and lights out for France. I've got a drawerful of expensive bras he's given me—snap-fronts, plunges, crisscrosses, strapless—all in lace and satin.

"That's a special number," he said, moving close to me. "Scalloped lace and satin stretch. Molded cup, underwire. I'll want to check the fitting later."

I grinned. "We'll see about that, Jazz. Tonight I feel like getting drunk."

"You're gonna be a granny again in a few months, Chrissy. Is that how an old granny's supposed to act?" he teased.

"But I'm happy, damn it! I feel like I'm in love."

"One of these days I'll make you fall in love with me, Chrissy."

I ordered a bourbon. What Jazz needed, I thought, was a woman who felt romantic about him. But he'd never make a claim on a woman who cared about him. He'd always step aside and let the woman go fall in love with some clod who jerked her around.

Glancing up at a TV newsbreak—a local update on water pollution—I said, "All the mussels in the lake are dying. It's all those pesticides."

"I heard it was last year's drought," said Jazz. "That's natural."

"Here I am celebrating a new baby coming into the world— for what? To see a dead lake? And air not fit to breathe?"

Jazz touched my shoulder, to steady me. "World's always had trouble. No baby ever set foot in the Garden of Eden."

I laughed. "That's just like you to say that, Jazz."

"You think you know me, don't you?" he said.

"I know you well enough to feel sorry I always treat you so bad."

Ed set my drink before me and I took it eagerly. I said to Jazz, "Why don't you ever get mad at me, tell me off?"

He punched my arm, buddy style. "You should never go away mad at a person, because one of you might get killed on the way home."

The regular crowd was there at the Top Line—good old boys who worked at the plants, guys wandering around loose on a Friday night while their wives took the kids to the mall. A tall man entering the bar caught my eye. He walked like he had money. He had on an iridescent-green shirt, with a subtle paisley design that made my eyes tingle. His pants had cowboy-style piping on the pocket plackets. Over the shirt he wore a suède vest with fuschia embroidery and zippered pockets.

"That's Buck Joiner, the radio guy," Jazz said, reading my mind.

Buck Joiner was the d.j. I listened to while I was getting ready for work. His "Morning Mania" show was a roaring streak of pranks and risqué jokes and call-in giveaways. Once, he actually telephoned Colonel Qaddafi in Libya. He got through to the palace and talked to some official who spoke precise English with a Middle Eastern accent.

As soon as I felt I'd had enough bourbon, I marched over to Buck Joiner's table, wielding my glass.

"I listen to you," I said. "I've got your number on my dial."

He seemed bored. It was like meeting Bob Dylan or some big shot you know won't be friendly.

"I called you up once," I went on recklessly. "You were giving away tickets to the Ray Stevens show. I was trying to be the twenty-fifth caller. But my timing wasn't right."

"Too bad," he said, deadpan. He was with a couple of guys in suits. Blanks.

"I've got to work on my timing." I paused, scrambling for contact. "You should interview my Friday-afternoon talk group."

"What's that?"

"We're a group of ladies. We get together every Friday and talk about life."

"What about life?" Out of the side of his face, he smirked for the benefit of the suits.

"The way things are going. Stuff." My mind went blank. I knew there was more to it than that. Right then, I really wanted him to interview our group. I knew we sparkled with life and intelligence. Rita had her opinions on day care, and Dorothy could rip into the abortion issue, and Phyllis believed that psychiatrists were witch doctors. Me, I could do my Bette Davis imitations.

"Here's my card," I said, whipping one out of my purse. I'd ordered these about a month ago, just for the privilege of saying that.

"It's nice to meet a fan," he said with stretched lips—not a true smile.

"Don't give me that, buddy. If it weren't for your listeners, you wouldn't be sitting here with all that fancy piping scrawled all over you."

I rejoined Jazz, who had been watching out for me. "I'd like to see Oprah nail him to the wall," I said to Jazz.

Of course, I was embarrassed. That was the trouble. I was lost somewhere between being nice and being mean. I shouldn't drink. I don't know why I was so hard on the d.j., but he was a man I had depended on to start my day, and he turned out to be a shit. From now on I'd listen to his show and think, Stuck-up turdface. Yet there I was in a French bra and an unusual amount of cleavage for this area. I didn't know what I was getting at. Jazz was smiling, touching my hand, ordering me another drink. Jazz wore patience like adhesive tape.

In bits and pieces, I've told this at the Friday talk group: My first husband, Jim Ed, was my high-school boyfriend. We married when we were seniors, and they didn't let me graduate, because I was pregnant. I used to say that I barely understood how those things worked, but that was a lie. Too often I exaggerate my innocence, as if trying to excuse myself for some of the messes I've gotten myself into. Looking back now, I see that I latched on to Jim Ed because I was afraid there'd never be another opportunity in my life, and he was the best of the pickings around there. That's the way I do everything. I grab anything that looks like a good chance, right then and there. I even tend to overeat, as if

I'm afraid I won't ever get another good meal. "That's the farm girl in you," my second husband, George, always said. He was an analytical person and had a theory about everything. When he talked about the Depression mentality of our parents' generation he made it sound physically disgusting. He had been to college. I never did go back and get my high-school diploma, but that's something I'm thinking about doing now. George couldn't just enjoy something for what it was. We'd grill steaks and he'd come up with some reason why we were grilling steaks. He said it went back to caveman behavior. He said we were acting out an ancient scene. He made me feel trapped in history, as though we hadn't advanced since cavemen. I don't guess people have changed that much, though, really. I bet back in caveman times there was some know-it-all who made his woman feel dumb.

After a while, I didn't pay any attention to George, but then my little daughter died. She had meningitis, and it was fairly sudden and horrible. I was still in shock a month later, when George started nagging at me about proper grief displays and the stages of grief. I blew up. I told him to walk. What we really should have done was share the grief. I'm sure the most basic textbook would say that. But instead he's lecturing me on my grief. You can't live with somebody who lectures you on your grief. I'll have my grief in peace, I told him. Kathy wasn't his daughter. He couldn't possibly know how I felt. That was so long ago he doesn't seem real to me. He still lives around here. I've heard that he married again and that he raises rabbits and lives out in the country, out near Bardwell—none of which I would have ever imagined. But, you know, as small as this place is, I've never laid eyes on him again. Maybe he's changed so much I just don't recognize him when I see him.

"How did you just happen to have that bra in your pocket, Jazz?" I wanted to know, but he only grinned. It was like carrying around condoms in case of emergency, I thought. The bra was just my size. I'd put it on in the rest room. The one I had worn was stretching out, and I left it in the trash can. Let people wonder.

At first, I thought Kathy just had the flu. She had a fever and she said her head was splitting—a remark so calm that she might have said her hands were dirty in the same tone. It was summer, a strange time for flu, so I hurried all the kids on out to their grandmother's that Sunday, like always, thinking the country air would make Kathy feel better. Don and Phil kept aggravating her because she didn't want to play in Mama's attic or go out to the barn. She lay around under one of Mama's quilts, and I thought later, with a hideous realization, that she somehow knew she was going to die. You never know what a child is thinking, or how scared they might be, or how they've blown something up in their imagination. She was twelve, and she'd just started her period a couple of months before. I thought her sickness might be related to that. The doctor just laughed at me when I brought that up. Can you imagine the nerve? It's only now that I've gotten mad about that. But I hear that that doctor has had a stroke and is in a nursing home. What good do bad feelings do when so much time has passed? That's what Jazz says.

George blamed me for taking her out to Mama's that day. He was gone to an engineering convention in Nashville; he was a chemical engineer at Carbide then. He said there was no reason a child shouldn't recover from meningitis. He wagged a book in my face, but I refused to read what he had found on the disease. I thought it would kill me to know that her death was my fault. I guess George wasn't such a bad guy. He just had his ways. I think we all do and none of us knows how to be sensitive enough, it seems. He probably just didn't know how to deal with the situation. It occurred to me recently that maybe he felt guilty for being away at the time, just as I felt guilty for not noticing how quiet and withdrawn she was, as though she was figuring it all out for herself. Kathy was in 4-H, and that year she was working on a Holly Hobbie display for the fair—the little girl hiding her

face in the calico bonnet. Kathy sewed the clothes herself, and
she was making a little stuffed dog and decorating a flower basket
for the scene. I still have that unfinished Holly Hobbie scene—in
the closet in a stereo box. I should probably get rid of it, because
if Kathy had lived she would have grown out of that phase, but
all I have is those little scraps of the way Kathy was, the only
reality she ever had.

Don and Phil grew up and left as soon as they got cars. Can you
believe anybody would name their sons after the Everly Brothers?
I reckon I'd still do something that silly. But I never told them
we named them for the Everly Brothers. Jim Ed, the father of all
my children, loved the Everly Brothers, and he used to play them
in his truck, back when eight-track tape decks were a new thing.
Jim Ed was loose about a lot of things, and he never criticized me
the way George did. I don't know if he blamed me about Kathy.
I have a feeling that if we'd stuck it out we could have learned to
love each other better. But he was restless, and he couldn't hang
around when we needed him most. He moved over to Cairo and
worked on the riverboats—still does. I guess he has some kind
of life. The boys see him. Don's wife ran off with one of the
riverboat guys and Don lives in a cabin over there. I don't see
him very much. He brought me a giant catfish, a mud cat, on
Mother's Day. Catfish that big aren't really good to eat, though.
He sets trotlines and just lives in the wilderness. I doubt if he'll
ever marry again. Phil is the only one of my children who turned
out normal. Now, what is there to say about that? A wife with
a tortilla face and bad taste in clothes, spoiled kids, living room
decorated with brass geese and fish. I go there and my skin breaks
out. There's no pleasing me, I guess.

Last week, Laura—my other daughter, the baby—wrote me
that she was pregnant. She's barely divorced from this museum
director she met at school—he restored old pieces of pottery,
glued them together. He made a good living but she wasn't sat-
isfied. Now she's going to be tied down with a baby and a man,

this Nick, who does seasonal work of some sort. They're living in his hometown, a little place in Arizona, in the desert. I can't imagine what would grow there.

Laura, on the telephone this past Sunday, said, "I don't want to get married again. I don't trust it anymore. And I want to be free of all that bureaucratic crap. I trust Nick more than I trust the government."

"You need the legal protection," I said. "What if something happened to him? What if he ran off and left you? I can tell you exactly how that works."

"I'd have to murder Nick to get him out of my life! Honestly, he's being so devoted it's unbelievable."

"I guess that's why I don't believe it."

"Come on, Mom. Just think, you're going to be a grandma again! Aren't you going to come out when the baby's born? Isn't that what mothers do?"

Laura was five when Kathy died. We didn't take her to the funeral. We told her Kathy had gone off to live with Holly Hobbie in New York. If I could undo that lie, I would. It was worse when she found out the truth, because she was old enough then to understand and the shock hurt her more. I thought my heart would break when I saw Jim Ed at the funeral. I saw him alone only once, for a few minutes in the corridor before the service started, but we couldn't speak what we felt. Jim Ed was crying, and I wanted to cling to him, but we could see George in the other room, standing beside a floral display—a stranger.

Jazz said, "Ever notice how at night it's scary because you feel like your secrets are all exposed, but you trick yourself into thinking they're safe in the dark? Smoky bars, candlelight—that's what all that atmosphere shit is about."

"That's what I always say," I said, a little sarcastically. Sometimes Jazz seemed to be fishing around for something to say and then just making something up to sound deep.

We were driving to see my son Don out at his cabin by the

river. It was Jazz's idea, a crazy notion that seized him. He said he felt like driving. He said I needed some air. He didn't let me finish my last drink.

I met Jazz a year ago, in traffic court. We'd both been in minor fender benders on the same road on the same day, at different times. We'd both failed to yield. I remember Jazz saying to me, "I hope that's not a reflection on my character. Normally, I'm a very yielding guy." That day Jazz had on a plaid flannel shirt and boot-flared jeans and a cowboy hat—the usual garb for a man around here. But it was his boots I loved. Pointy-toed, deep-maroon, with insets of Elvis's photograph just above the ankles. He'd found the boots in France. That night we went out for bar-becue and he gave me some peach-blush panties with a black lace overlay. We had been friends since then, but we never seemed to get serious. I thought he had a big block of fear inside him.

The cab of his truck was stuffy, that peculiar oil-and-dust smell of every man's truck I've ever been in. I lowered the window and felt the mellow river breeze. Jazz chattered non-stop until we got deep into the country. Then he seemed to hush, as though we were entering a grand old church.

We were travelling on a state road, its winding curves settled comfortably through the bottomland, with its swampy and piney smells. There were no houses, no lights. Now and then we passed an area where kudzu made the telephone poles and bushes look as though they were a giant's furniture covered up with protective sheets. At a stop sign I told Jazz to go straight instead of follow-ing the main road. Soon there was a turnoff, unmarked except for an old sign for a church that I knew had burned down in the fifties. We saw an abandoned pickup straddling the ditch. When the road turned to gravel, I counted the turnoffs, looking for the fourth one. Jazz shifted gears and we chugged up a little hill.

"Reckon why he lives way off out here?" Jazz said as he braked and shut off the engine. There were no lights at the cabin, and Don's motorbike was gone. Jazz went over into the bushes for a minute. It was a half-moon night, the kind of night that made you see things in the silhouettes. I thought I saw Don standing by the side of the cabin, peering around the corner, watching us.

Jazz reached through the truck's open window and honked the horn.

I heard an owl answer the horn. When I was little I thought owls were messengers from the preachers in charge of Judgment Day. "Who will be the ones?" I remember our preacher saying. "Who?" Even then I pictured Judgment Day as an orchestrated extravaganza, like a telethon or a musical salute. I never took religion seriously. I'm glad I didn't force my children into its frightful clutches. But maybe that was the trouble, after all.

We stood on the sagging porch, loaded with fishnets and crates of empties—Coke and beer bottles. The lights from the pickup reflected Jazz and me against the cabin windows. I tried the door, and it opened into the kitchen.

"Don?" I called.

I found the kitchen light, just a bulb and string. The cord was new. It still had that starched feel, and the little metal bell on the end knot was shiny and sharp. It made me think of our old bathroom light when Jim Ed and I first married. It was the first thing I'd touch in the morning when I'd get up and rush to the bathroom to throw up.

The table was set for one, with the plate turned face over and the glass upside down. Another glass contained an assortment of silverware. A little tray held grape jelly and sugar and instant coffee and an upside-down mug.

The cabin was just one room, and the daybed was neatly made, spread with one of my old quilts. I sat down on the bed. I felt strange, as though all my life I had been zigzagging down a wild trail to this particular place. I stared at the familiar pattern of the quilt, the scraps of the girls' dresses and the boys' shirts. Kathy had pieced some of the squares. If I looked hard, I could probably pick out some of her childish stitches.

"This is weird," said Jazz. He was studying some animal bones spread out on a long table fashioned from a door. "What do you reckon he's aiming to do with these?"

"He always liked biology," I said, rising from the bed. I smoothed and straightened the quilt, thinking about Goldilocks trespassing at the three bears' house.

The table was littered: bones, small tools, artist's brushes and pens, a coffee cup with a drowned cigarette stub, more butts nesting in an upturned turtle shell, some bright foil paper, an oily rag. Jazz flipped through a tablet of drawings of fangs and fishbones.

"He must be taking a summer course at the community college," I said, surprised. "He talked about that back in the spring, but I didn't believe it."

"Look at these," Jazz said. "They're good. How can anybody do that?" he said in amazement.

We studied the drawings. In the careful, exact lines I saw faint glimpses of my young child, and his splashy crayon pictures of monsters taped to the kitchen wall. Seeing his efforts suddenly mature was like running into a person I recognized but couldn't place. Most of the pictures were closeups of bones, but some were sketches of fish and birds. I liked those better. They had life to them. Eagerly, I raced through two dozen versions of a catfish. The fish was long and slim, like a torpedo. Its whiskers curved menacingly, and its body was accurately mottled. It even looked slippery. I stared at the catfish, almost as if I expected it to speak.

I jerked a blank sheet of paper from the tablet of drawings and worked on a note:

Dear Don,

It's 10:30 P.M. Friday and I came out here with a friend to see if you were home. We just dropped by to say hello. Please let me know how you are. Nothing's wrong. I've got some good news. And I'd love to see you.

Love,
Mom

"It doesn't sound demanding, does it?" I asked as Jazz read it.
"No, not at all."
"It almost sounds like one of those messages on an answering machine—stilted and phony."

Jazz held me as if he thought I might cry. I wasn't crying. He held my shoulders till he was sure I'd got the tears back in and then we left. I couldn't say why I wasn't crying. But nothing bad had happened. There wasn't anything tragic going on. My daughter was having a baby—that was the good news. My son had drawn some fishbones—drawings that were as fine as lace.

"Me and my bright ideas," Jazz said apologetically.

"It's OK, Jazz. I'll track Don down some other time."

As we pulled out, Jazz said, "The wilderness makes me want to go out in it. I've got an idea. Tomorrow let's go for a long hike on one of those trails up in Shawnee National Forest. We can take backpacks and everything. Let's explore caves! Let's look for bears and stuff!"

I laughed. "You could be Daniel Boone and I could be Rebecca."

"I don't think Rebecca went for hikes. You'll have to be some Indian maiden Daniel picked up."

"Did Daniel Boone really do that sort of thing?" I said, pretending to be scandalized.

"He was a true explorer, wasn't he?" Jazz said, hitting the brights just as a deer seemed to drift across the road.

Jazz thought he was trying to cheer me up, but I was already so full of joy I couldn't even manage to tell him. I let him go on. He was sexiest when he worked at cheering me up.

It was late, and I wound up at Jazz's place, a sprawling apartment with a speaker system wired into every room. His dog, Butch, met us at the door. While Jazz took Butch out for a midnight stroll, I snooped around. I found a beer in the refrigerator. I had trouble with the top and beer spewed all over Jazz's dinette. When he returned, I started teasing him about all the women's underwear he owned.

"Put some of it on," I urged.

"Are you nuts?"

"Just put it on, for me. I won't tell. Just for fun."

I kept teasing him, and he gave in. We couldn't find any garments that would fit. We hooked two bras together and rigged up a halter. With his lime green bikini briefs—his own—he looked great, like a guy in a sex magazine. It's surprising what men really wear underneath. I searched for some music to play on Jazz's fancy sound system. I looked for the Everly Brothers but couldn't find them, so I put on a George Winston CD. To be nice, I never said a word about Jazz's taste in music. Exhilarated, I sailed from room to room, following the sound, imagining it was "Let It Be Me," instead. I suddenly felt an overwhelming longing to see Jim Ed again. I wanted to tell him about Don going to school, drawing pictures, making contact with the world again. I wanted to see the traces of Don's face in his. I wanted the two of us to go out to Arizona and see Laura and the baby when it came. We could make a family photo—Jim Ed and me and Laura, with the baby. The baby's father didn't enter into the vision.

It occurred to me that it takes so long to know another person. No wonder you can run through several, like trying on clothes that don't fit. There are so many to choose from, after all, but when I married Jim Ed it was like an impulse buy, buying the first thing you see. And yet I've learned to trust my intuition on that. Jim Ed was the right one all along, I thought recklessly. And I wasn't ever nice to Jim Ed. I was too young then to put myself in another person's place. Call it ignorance of the imagination. Back then I had looked down on him for being country, for eating with his arms anchored on the table and for wiping his mouth with the back of his hand. I'd get mad at him for just being himself at times when I thought he should act civilized. Now I've learned you can't change men, and sometimes those airs I'd looked for turn out to be so phony. Guys like Jim Ed always seemed to just be themselves, regardless of the situation. That's why I still loved him, I decided, as I realized I was staring at Jazz's reflection in the mirror—the lime green against the shimmering gold of his skin and the blips of the track lighting above.

Jazz followed me into the bedroom, where we worked at getting rid of our French togs. I was aware that Jazz was talking, aware that he was aware that I might not be listening closely. It was like hearing a story at my little neighborhood talk show. He was saying, "In France, there's this street, Rue du Bac. They call streets *rues*. The last time I left Monique and the two kids, it was on that street, a crowded shopping street. The people over there are all pretty small compared to us, and they have this blue-black hair and deep dark eyes and real light skin, like a hen's egg. I waved goodbye and the three of them just blended right into that crowd and disappeared. That's where they belong, and so I'm here. I guess you might say I just couldn't *parlez-vous*."

"Take me to France, Jazz. We could have a great time."

"Sure, babe. In the morning." Jazz turned toward me and smoothed the cover over my shoulders.

"I love you," Jazz said.

When I woke up at daylight, Jazz was still holding me, curled around me like a mother protecting her baby. The music was still playing, on infinite repeat.

Elizabeth Hunnewell

A LIFE OR DEATH MATTER

(from *The Virginia Quarterly Review*)

One late afternoon in July, Minetree and I were trying to survive the ninety-four-degree heat on the screened porch. Minetree read the *Richmond News Leader* and frowned. He rubbed his temple with one finger. I rocked myself on the glider, downwind from the electric fan. Upstairs, the radio pumped out a Lawrence Welk polka. Mother was lying up there on her percale sheets, bare as the day she was born.

I was pretending to do biology homework. I'd flunked biology in the tenth grade. I was all adjusted to taking it again next year, when Minetree, my stepfather, said why don't I just get it over with at John Marshall summer school. I lasted three days out of respect for Minetree. After that, I didn't go to another single class. I took the bus every morning and got off at my friend Mary Tyler's stop. All the boys had jobs, so the two of us hung around Dr. Clement's Drug Store and read movie magazines or went out to Maymont to the public pool. Then I'd lug my bookbag home around one o'clock as if I'd had a hard morning.

I hadn't figured out yet what I'd do when Mother and Minetree got my report card. Mother would definitely make a long speech about my actions having lifelong consequences. Minetree, who took up for me whenever he reasonably could, would say something like, "Hold it, honey. When you're fifteen you don't know what lifelong means." Then he'd get on the phone with Mrs. Beazley, headmistress of my school, and arrange with her to let me retake biology. It wouldn't be a pretty scene, but it would be manageable. When Mother complained that I was getting too big for my britches and she didn't know where it was all going to end, Minetree told her that I was going through a phase and that at heart I was a good girl. When he said that, I just about melted, and for two or three days I'd try to be helpful and pleasant.

So there I was on the porch, looking studious, with my note-book and biology book propped up on my knees. It was so hot the heat had sucked up all the ice in my Dr Pepper except for one cube, which looked like spit sitting on top. The fan whirred. Minetree frowned at the newsprint every time the glider squeaked.

The sky rumbled, and a cool-down rain came on softly, just a few fat drops at a time. Minetree looked up from his news-paper and asked me to run out and see if the car windows were rolled up.

"It's hardly raining," I said.

"It'll rain more. Please go." His face was stern, and he winced when he talked.

"I'm in the middle of the circulatory system," I said. "Did you know that you have 250 million red blood cells?"

The sun shone behind the raindrops and lit up the gnats swarming the oleander bush.

"And anyway," I said, "as we all know, it's bad luck to be abroad when the devil's beating his wife."

He threw his newspaper down. "I'll go then."

I wrote 250,000,000 in my notebook under the letter I had just written to Charlie Corbin, who was away being a camp coun-selor. While I doodled faces in the zeros, I knew Minetree was putting his artificial leg in the right place to get up. "No, wait. Don't. I'll go," I started to say, but my damp shirt stuck me on the pillow cushion, and the elastic of my underpants rubbed against the sunburn I'd gotten by the pool that morning.

Thunder clapped far away, and a breeze blew in as the sun went behind a cloud.

Suddenly, I heard a sound like rain pouring through the roof onto the floor. I lifted my book and looked out under it. Minetree was still in his chair, and I could see his feet, the good one planted and the other sitting on its heel. Between them, gooey stuff, like strawberry jam, was piling up and then flattening out as it spread over the straw rug. He threw up blood in great heaves. He hung on to the arms of the chair, heaving, and red drops dribbled from his nose.

I didn't do one single thing to help Minetree except scream for Mother. When I was little and had the throw-ups, she used to hold a damp washcloth against my forehead and hold my stomach. But I just sat there, clutching my book to my chest, wishing she'd hurry up, though I didn't like to think what she'd have to say about ruining the straw rug she'd just bought at Thalhimer's last week.

The rain was picking up. The light on the porch was gray and still the red stain spread like a shadow.

"Mo-ther," I screamed again.

Minetree's hands loosened on the arms of his chair and his head fell back. His eyes were closed and blood dripped from his open mouth onto his white shirt.

I heard Mother's feet slapping the wood as she ran downstairs. Her heavy bosoms flopped as she ran across the shiny living-room floor, bare of rugs for the summer. I giggled because she looked so funny standing in the doorway, stripped stark naked, except for her nightgown, which was slung around her neck like a scarf. She couldn't see Minetree in the corner behind the lamp.

"Did you have to scream, Amelia?" she said. "You scared me to death. And why, in heaven's name, are you sitting up there?"

I was perched on the arm of the glider with my feet on the cushions. My glass of Dr Pepper fell on the brick floor and smashed. The rain was heavy now, and the air smelled like damp bark and grass and blood.

I pointed at the blood.

Her eyes followed the trail to Minetree's feet and suddenly, the way a drop of rain slides off a leaf to the ground, it reached her—what the horrible mess was all about.

"Minetree?" She ran to him and whipped her nightgown from around her neck and began to mop his mouth, kissing his face as she mopped. She whimpered his name. "Min-a-tree, Min-a-tree." Her face, slick with sweat, was as white as his.

"Amelia, call the rescue squad. Quick."

"I don't know the number." The porch screen behind my back gave as I pushed against it.

"Well, for God's sake, come here at least and hold his hand while I do it." She held his hand out to me. My knees buckled, and I weaved my way to her, trying to sidestep the bloody splatters.

His hand lay in mine like an empty glove. The veins and even the freckles were drained white. I couldn't bear to squeeze it knowing it wouldn't squeeze back, so I rubbed my thumb over the crack in the dark stone of his Virginia Military Institute ring. Minetree always said his cracked ring was the only thing he had to show for being in the war. That was just hilarious because the same shrapnel that hit his ring had torn his leg off first. Now I wondered if he had looked less dead on that Iwo Jima beach, with the flesh and bone of his leg all gritty with sand, than he did on his own porch.

Mother came flying back from the phone and stepped smack in the blood trying to get to his chest. She laid her head against his shirt and said in jerks, "Breathe. Just breathe. Until they get here." She started pounding his heart with her fist.

"You don't have any clothes on, Mother," I said. She glanced at her body and went back to her pounding, so I finally did something useful and went upstairs to get her some clothes. I grabbed the yellow sundress and underclothes from the bed. As I ran back downstairs, I heard the sirens. I got Mother dressed just as the ambulance screeched to the door. Two ambulance men rushed in with their stretcher, took Minetree's pulse, and connected him to a bottle. So he wasn't dead yet.

The men said there was a jump seat for Mother in the ambulance. She was holding on to my hand now, squishing my knuckles back and forth.

"I have to have my daughter with me too." She said. "She can sit on my lap."

"I can't sit on your lap, Mother. How can I sit on your lap? I can walk." St. Luke's Hospital was only a few blocks away.

The ambulance man frowned at me. He had a name badge pinned on his white shirt that said "Red," though his hair was coal black.

"You sit wherever your mother wants you to sit," he said. But there wasn't enough room for my head if I sat on her lap, so I sat next to her on the sticky rubber floor. We were backing out the driveway and the red light was whirling around when I remembered a life or death matter.

"The car windows. Wait."

But the driver had clicked on the siren button and Red was fooling around with the bottle contraption.

"Mother, I should have checked the car windows. Minetree asked me to."

"Amelia. It doesn't matter." Since she couldn't get to his hand, Mother was rubbing the toe of Minetree's shoe, the one that never had any life in it. The rain was really coming down now, so hard that the windshield wipers groaned and the driver had his chest against the steering wheel trying to see out.

It mattered a lot to me. I could picture the rain pouring in the windows, filling the sag in the driver's seat of the black Oldsmobile. The rain would flood the floor, cover the brake pedal and build up to the stick that jutted out from the steering wheel, the stick the United States Marine Corps had designed especially for Minetree, so he could push it to make the car go because his fake foot couldn't manage the gas pedal. The rain would rust out the little stick. It would ruin everything if Minetree couldn't just be free to get in a car and see the world when he felt like it. It seemed to me if the car went down the drain so would Minetree.

"What's wrong with him?" I asked my mother. She was watching Red listen to Minetree's heart with his stethoscope.

"What?" Her body trembled and her head jerked like she had St. Vitus' dance.

Red unplugged the stethoscope from his ears. He didn't look worried but he didn't look relieved either.

"Mr. Red," I asked. "Could you tell me please what's wrong with my father?"

"Hemorrhage," he said and started rolling the blood pressure wrap around Minetree's arm.

"Could you just tell me if a hemorrhage happens because something outside makes it happen—or whether it would just happen anyway?"

If I'd only studied my biology more I'd have known what caused a hemorrhage.

But Red was listening again through his stethoscope. I hoped he was hearing lots of blood pumping, though I didn't see how, considering the amount Minetree had left on the rug at home.

"Amelia, sugar." Mother pulled my head against her knee and patted my hair. "Just hush." My mother had taken on a funny odor, like the sour old wet bathing suit I'd stuffed in my bookbag.

The ambulance sped down Monument Avenue past Jackson, Lee, and Stuart, saddled on their horses in a shroud of mist. I said, "Thank you, Jesus," when we turned onto Allen Street at General Lee's statue because he faced south to show he'd survived the War between the States, and that was a good sign for Minetree.

Cars screeched to the curb in front of us. Whenever my mother and I pulled to the curb to let an ambulance pass, she always said, "God bless you." I rubbed a circle in the fogged-up window to see the faces that were saying a little prayer for Minetree, but all I could see was the light on top of the ambulance coloring the raindrops red.

The ambulance skidded up to the emergency entrance of St. Luke's and stopped. The driver opened the back door of the ambulance and helped Red lower a ramp. They rolled the stretcher out.

Inside the emergency room, a loudspeaker shouted "Dr. Mercer. Your patient's in emergency. Dr. Mercer to emergency." Lights glared off the white walls and bleached out the faces of an orderly pushing an empty wheelchair and a nurse who rolled a clattering medicine trolley. They looked like a pretty sick bunch and not like anybody I'd want to open my eyes to after I'd had a hemorrhage. The nurse almost collided with Minetree's stretcher, and Red muttered, "Watch it, sister." Then he yelled, "Priority admission, priority admission," and disappeared with Minetree through a swinging door with a sign that said in no uncertain terms that we couldn't go in. Mother pushed on the door anyway.

"Hey," said the nurse with the noisy medicine trolley. "You can't go in there."

Mother clamped her hand around my arm. Her skin was the color of the ivory candles on our dining-room sideboard. Perspiration ran down her face like melting wax and dropped down the front of her dress.

"Is your mother sick?" the nurse asked.

"My mother is not sick," I said. "But my father has had a hemorrhage and we have to see the doctor."

"Who is he?"

"He's Minetree Fairfax."

"There's no doctor in this hospital by that name," she said.

"No, no, no," I said. "I mean my father is Minetree Fairfax."

"What is the name of your doctor?" She stared at the bottles on her trolley as if she was counting them.

"Who's our doctor, Mother?" I said, but Mother's eyes were X-raying the swinging door.

"Mother." I peeled her hand, one finger at a time, from my arm. "Who's our doctor?" But her hearing seemed to be on the blink, and so I said, "Dr. Mercer," and hoped I was right.

The nurse directed us to a tiny little waiting room with no air and no fan and a lot of ratty magazines. Mother held my hand for dear life and played with the hairs on my arm. Her foot hammered the floor. I looked at the picture of Monticello on the wall. I tried to remember the beautiful things Mother and Minetree and I had seen when we were there last May. All I could dredge up was the bed where Thomas Jefferson breathed his last so I watched the second hand bump around the big wall clock and tried to compose the questions I'd ask Dr. Mercer.

Minetree always said he'd never known one for questions like me. He said he was going to have to give up his law practice to have time to answer them. I'd say, "Minetree, I have a question," and he'd say, "Ask and the answer shall be revealed unto you."

Minetree revealed a lot of things about my real father, who had been his brother rat at VMI. My real father died when I was three and a half, and I only had one memory of him, the day he went away to war. I had stopped asking my mother questions about him when I was little, because she'd start pushing back the skin around her fingernails, raise her eyes up, and get lost in her thinking.

But Minetree. I could ask him anything.

"Did my father ever get off the straight and narrow?" I asked, and Minetree just about keeled over laughing. He ticked off an episode for every finger of his right hand that showed me that getting into trouble was in my genes. That was last winter when Dr. Clement had called my mother to tell her that I had been begging at his soda fountain. Just a nickel here and a dime there but he said it was worrying his customers. Of course, I denied everything. I said all those powders he worked with that had turned his skin on his face gray had gotten to his brain.

Once I asked Minetree why my daddy had left an adorable baby girl and a perfectly good wife to go to war when he didn't have to. He joined the RAF before our country went to war and ferried patched-up planes from France over the English Channel, and one plane came unpatched and dropped him into the water like a bomb.

Minetree said that it didn't have anything to do with how much he loved my mother and me. Sometimes you just had to do things you didn't feel like doing because you knew they were right. I felt like saying that looked good on paper but didn't feel good in my heart. I didn't say it because tears were gathering around Minetree's eyes. Minetree was the kind of person who cried over beautiful music or just telling you the plot of a tragic story.

"Mrs. Fairfax?" A nurse stood in front of us with a clipboard. "I have just a few questions to ask you."

Mother dropped my hand and smoothed her rumpled skirt. Answering questions calmed her trembling and seemed to put new life in her, as if her answers would make Minetree well. But the kind of questions the nurse asked—name, age, color of eyes, hair, disfiguring marks—sounded like missing-person questions to me, and my stomach insides started rolling around. I picked up a thumbed-over *Photoplay* magazine with Lana Turner on the cover. She posed with her hand on the steering wheel of a white car. Her arm was draped across the back of the red leather car seat, shiny in the sun. She looked perfect and happy, like she had never done anything she didn't want to do in her whole life.

The heat in that waiting room made my hair frizz up around my face. My face tingled like it was preparing to break out in spots. My sunburn itched where I couldn't scratch it in public, and I thought about how good the fizz in a Dr Pepper would taste just then. And how I would give anything to be back out on the porch with Minetree and start the afternoon all over again.

Just as the nurse wound up her questions, Dr. Mercer turned up. He was tall, bony, white-haired, without a drop of color in his face except for a bloodshot eye. If he'd had his church suit on, I would have said he was the undertaker coming to talk over funeral arrangements. But my mother stood up and said, "John," and let him put his arms around her. She had recovered herself enough to frown at me for not standing up and shaking hands, but I felt too woozy.

"Now," he said, and his lips started moving, but my ears closed up like they did sometimes in biology class when Miss Hayes talked about body parts. I stood up, said, "I have to be excused," and ran. Down the corridor, past the swinging door, and out the exit of the hospital.

Raindrops dribbled from the bushy leaves hanging over the sidewalk, and a foggy moon had risen. I crossed over to Grove Avenue and raced up Allen Street, past Dr. Clement's Drug Store, where a dusty light lit up the bedpans and toothbrushes and Ace bandages in the window. I made it to Monument Avenue just as the spotlights lit up General Jackson, galloping in place, north towards Washington. I averted my eyes and began counting the street lanterns, guessing how many I had to pass before I'd be home.

Mist rose from the pavement like breath. The shiny wet street hissed. Like it hissed the time my father left for the war. That day, the sun beat down and made the street swim. My mother held me on her hip. My father stretched out his hand that had the fat VMI ring with the perfect stone on it, and said, "A kiss for Daddy?" But I pouted and swung away and hid my face in my mother's neck. The tires, pulling away from the curb, popped the bubbling tar in the street, and the tar hissed.

The downtown bus, the one that stopped right in front of John Marshall summer school, roared past empty, splashing up water on the sidewalk, filling my tennis shoes so that they made sucking noises as I ran. Just ahead, I saw the black Oldsmobile. Oh boy, oh boy, I crossed my fingers on both hands. The windows would be rolled up. The sag on the seat where Minetree sat would be dry, and a nurse, a cheerful one, with a pretty face like Lana Turner's, would be cranking the top of his bed down and smiling at Mother who had just pounded his pillows so that when the orderly slid him into bed, the pillows would whoosh. His room was the best corner room in the hospital. The sun would pour in like rain in the morning and at night moonlight would flood the room.

The car was parked under a maple tree. Rain dripped from the leaves and pinged against the roof. The curbside windows were up. I ran around to the other side of the car, grabbed at the door handle and rattled it. The handle didn't move. The moon behind me, bright now, lit up the drizzle on the rolled-up glass like stars, and I scooped it up and rubbed it on my face.

As it turned out, a pretty enough nurse was cranking down Minetree's bed and my mother, who had already given the pillows a workout, was fluttering her fingers in a wave as the orderly eased him onto the sheets. But I didn't know that then, so I skipped back to the hospital, careful not to step on any cracks. If they could break my mother's back, the Lord only knew what they could do to Minetree's remaining red blood corpuscles.

Larry Brown

BIG BAD LOVE

(from *The Chattahoochee Review*)

My *dog* died. I went out there in the yard and looked at him and there he was, dead as a hammer. Boy, I hated it. I knew I'd have to look around and see about a shovel. But it didn't look like he'd been dead long and there wasn't any hurry, and I was wanting a drink somewhat, so I went on out a little further into the yard to see if my truck would crank and it would, so I left. Thought I'd bury the dog later. Before Mildred got home. Figured I had plenty of time.

Birds were singing, flowers were blooming. It was just wonderful. I hated for my old dog to be dead and miss all that but I didn't know if dogs cared about stuff like that or not. I didn't have a whole lot of gas in my truck. I didn't figure I needed to get started riding and drinking. I thought I'd just ride over and get something to drink and then ride back, sit on the porch and maybe cut my toenails until Mildred nearly got home, then start burying the dog to occupy me.

Joe Barlow wasn't home. I sat in front of his house for three minutes and blowed the horn, but nobody came out. I left there and went to U. T. Oslin's house. The whole place was boarded up, looked like nobody had lived there for three years. Weeds were all up in the yard and stuff. I left there and went by Manley Musgrove's, but I figured he was asleep and didn't want to wake up, so I just spurted on past his house, didn't stop.

I'd had that old dog for a long time, from way past my first marriage. I was sure going to miss him. Mildred had always been after me to shoot him, but I never had. He was bad about catching baby opossums and dragging them up into the yard, and Mildred was always so tenderhearted she never could stand to see a thing like that. She just never had seen her cat in action, though, the one she'd let in the house to pet and sleep on the couch, get hairs all over the throw pillows. That thing had a litter of kittens last summer and I was standing out there in the yard one day while she had them stashed under the corn crib for safekeeping. I'd been out in the garden cussing and mashing cutworms off my tomatoes. I'd cuss those little fellows and pick them off and mash each one under the heel of my tennis shoe. Those little things were green and they had green guts. She went out in the garden for a minute and came back carrying a little baby rabbit in her mouth. It wasn't dead. It was still kicking. What she was doing was training her babies to be killers. She laid that baby rabbit down right in the middle of those baby cats and they didn't know what to do with it. Of course the baby rabbit was squealing right pitiful and it ran off first thing. The old mama cat run out there in the yard after it and caught it again. Brought it back. Set it back down in the middle of those kittens. They started trying to bite it and stuff, growling these little bitty baby growls. That baby rabbit jumped up and ran off again. I stood there and watched that and thought about cats in general, and about what that baby rabbit was going through. She caught it and brought it back again and laid it down in the middle of her litter. They had enough sense to bite it some then and it squealed some more and then jumped up and took off running out across the yard. Only it couldn't run too good by then. She ran out there and caught it again, brought it back. They went to gnawing on it again. It jumped up and ran off again. She brought it back again. It was getting slower each time. I thought, Yeah, I ought to just go in the house here and get me about four rounds of number six shot and load up my Light Twelve and clean these sadistic creatures out from under my corn crib. The only thing was they kept the rats away and I guess a man has to give up one or two things to get another thing or two, but I went and got me a hammer handle and put that baby rabbit out of its misery. I used to raise them a long time ago, rabbits. I was pretty familiar with them. They were so cute when they were little. Just little balls of fur. They'd hop around there in the cage, eating lettuce, plus I fed them Purina Rabbit Chow, and they grew pretty fast on that and it wouldn't be but about eight weeks before they'd be ready to kill. They'll dress out about two pounds of meat at that age. By then your doe's bred again and expecting some more or maybe even having them by then and they'll eat you out of house and home if you don't harden your heart and take eight or ten of them out behind the corn crib and knock them in the head. I had some neighbor kids then. They played with those rabbits all the time. They'd hold them up beside their cheeks and just smile and smile and rub that fur with their faces. And here I was out behind the corn crib while the kids were in school knocking rabbits in the head and dressing them and then telling the kids they got out of the cage and ran away. It finally made me so uneasy and torn in different directions I had to quit it. I gave my doe away and turned the buck loose, I guess the coyotes ate him. I was thinking about all that while I was riding around, looking for a drink. I knew Mildred wouldn't be happy to see that dead dog in the yard. I knew she'd be happy to see it dead, only not in the yard.

I ran up on a Negro fishing by a bridge and stopped and hollered at him and asked him did he have anything to drink. Turned out it was Barthy, or Bartholomew, Pettigrew, a Negro I'd been knowing for most of my life. I had even picked some cotton with him a long time before, in my teenaged years. He didn't want to let on like he had anything but I knew he did because he always did. He was an old-timey Negro, one that wouldn't give you any sass. Of course I don't think one man ought to have to bow down to another because of the color of his skin. But I had to get down in the creek with him and squat down talking to him before he'd

even let on that he might have *anything* to drink. And what he
had wasn't much. Three Old Milwaukees in some cool water that
his minnows were swimming around in. We talked about cotton
and cows for ten minutes and corn some, then I finally gave him
a dollar and got one of his beers. He didn't know where U. T.
Oslin was.

By the time I'd gone about a mile I'd finished half of that one.
I knew that wasn't going to get it. I had a dog to bury, and I
knew it would take more than one half-hot Old Milwaukee. I
checked my billfold and I think I had four dollars. I kept driving
slower and slower. I tried to take little sips out of that beer. But
the closer I got to the bottom, the hotter it got. Finally I drank
all of it and chunked the can out the window. I would have loved
to've had about a cold six-pack iced down, and about ten dollars
worth of gas in my truck. I could have rode and rode and drank
then. I decided I might better get back to the house and see if I
could find my checkbook.

Mildred wasn't in yet. My old dog hadn't moved any. I poked
him a little with my tennis-shoe toe. He just sort of moved inside his skin and came back to rest. I estimated the time before
Mildred would be home. I judged it to be about forty-five minutes. That was enough time for a shower, piss on burying the
dog. I figured I could do it when I came back in. I'd already taken
that first drink and I wanted another one. And I told myself it
wasn't every day a man's dog up and died.

I ran inside and showered and shaved and slapped some shit
on my hair. I drove uptown and wrote a twenty-dollar check at
Kroger's, picked up a hot sixer and a one-twenty-nine bag of ice.
I knew Mildred would be perturbed when she saw that I was out
loose again. Lord love her, she had trouble keeping me home;
her puss was just not that good. And so I would have to strike
out occasionally, for parts and places unknown.

There was a nice place on the other side of town that didn't
mind country people coming in there simply because they didn't
have a whole lot of class. The only thing wrong with it was that

sometimes the people who came in there had so little class that occasionally they would get to arguing and begin to shoot and cut one another. They wouldn't do it when they were sober, it would just be after they were drinking. I figured it would be a good place to be sitting on a bar stool right about that time, before they all got to drinking heavy.

I parked my truck under a tree and went inside that establishment and it was dark and cool, like under a corn crib would be. I knew I had that six-pack to drive me all the way home. Mildred was sexually frustrated because of her large organ and it just wore me out trying to apply enough friction to that thing for her to achieve internal orgasm. So, it was titillating for me to sit on a bar stool and talk to the young waitresses who served drinks and just generally fantasize about their young tight organs and wonder what they would be like, although it was guilty work and unsettling and morally not right.

I ordered a beer, spoke to everybody in general, lit a cigarette. I felt quite at home. I had on a clean shirt and my teeth had been brushed. I saw by my wristwatch that Mildred would be arriving home in about five more minutes. My beer arrived and I held it up high in the air and, saluting, said: "Here's to Mildred?" Several people looked at me funny.

This particular bar had a lot of red velvet in it. It also had numerous mirrors that looked like they had been splattered with gold paint. It was quite classy, for a place that had so many people with little or no class come into it.

After I got a few nice sips of my beer, I went over to the jukebox and put some money in to help pass the time and help take my mind off thoughts of Mildred. They had fourteen Tom T. Hall songs and I played every one of them. It seemed to put everybody in a good mood. I noticed several people looking at me kindly, as if to say thanks for playing all that Tom T. I knew that by then, Mildred had seen my dead dog. I didn't want to think about it, and I didn't know what she would think about it. I knew that she would be unhappy with me for not going ahead and burying the dog, and also for being out late drinking and riding. We had been over this thing many times before, and we weren't getting any closer to a solution. I just couldn't do anything with her big Tunnel of Love. I could hit one side at a time, but not both sides. I didn't feel like this was my fault, since I, like many other men or nearly all men, played high-school basketball and football and baseball and hockey and have taken many showers with naked boys and know by casual observance that I am adequately hung. Perhaps even well hung. I have seen boys whose peters looked like acorns. Mildred would not have even known one of those boys had it in. She would have just thought they were lying on top of her jerking. I would have had to be the Moby Dick of love to adequately satisfy Mildred. But I had sworn before God and Church to always cherish her and I supposed I would always have to. I did not cherish my first, other wife; I threw her over for Mildred. But it did not keep me from wanting something a little tighter than a feeling of sticking my equipment out the window and having relations with the whole world.

I got back on my bar stool and got another few nice sips of my beer and thought about the time Mildred and I discussed corrective surgery for her deformity. Mildred, I should point out, had the most wonderful ass. That was the original point of interest that attracted me to her. I have seen men pant, looking at her in a bathing suit. Mildred was always naturally hot-sexed. I knew it had to be frustrating for her to be like that. But she said she would be absolutely mortified to have to undergo an operation of that nature or even discuss it with a doctor or a nurse. So, sitting there on that bar stool, I didn't know much other way to turn. I knew she wasn't going to like that dead dog lying in our front yard. I thought, Hey, baby, what about your cruel cats?

By the time I'd had my second beer I thought about going home and hauling the shotgun out and killing every cat on the place. The last time I had counted them, there were lots of them.

Rats had ceased to be a problem. I was sure rats came up on the edge of the yard, took one look at all those cats, and said: No way, José.

Often people in bars don't speak to one another and often this is what happens to me. I am extremely friendly. I just don't know what to say to people. I didn't know what to say to Mildred the first time I met her. I met her in Destin, Florida, and saw that wonderful ass she had. She did all the talking. I was down there recuperating from my divorce that was almost pending. I was separated from my first wife, but the divorce was not pending. It was just almost pending, and I was trying to recuperate from that and was going home to try and patch things up in a few days. When I saw Mildred, everything went out the window, good intentions, everything, the divorce became pending. Mildred represented herself as a virtuous woman with naturally hot tendencies, and she showed me in several ways that she was not technically a virgin except for the remnants of her maidenhead which she wished to preserve until her wedding night, but later I found out that this was simply not the case. As a matter of fact, much to my chagrin, I thought on our wedding night that Mildred's puss had simply been worn out from massive thrustings over a period of many years with some enormous number of men, which caused me and Mildred to almost divorce the next day, until she broke down crying at the Continental Breakfast and confessed that I was only the first and one-half person to ever penetrate her. I took that as a compliment to mean the other person had only got in halfway.

By the time I started drinking my third beer I had thought a lot about Mildred's womb and had begun to wonder if by some lucky chance she ever got pregnant would the baby fall out prematurely. I wondered if any of the other men in that bar were facing that particular problem and didn't figure they were. What I figured was it was a unique problem but not quite out of line with the rest of my life. It seemed for some reason or another I had always been given the short end of the stick. I knew that it had nothing to do with my nature or character and was just an unlucky streak of fate, just like when I had fallen off the persimmon tree limb four feet off the ground at my grandmother's house and broken my arm and missed my own birthday party, then got back home with the cast on and there were only crumbs of cake in puddles of ice cream that flies were walking over on the picnic table, with all my friends gone and all the toys and presents unwrapped and already played with.

By the time I started drinking my fourth beer I did not give much of a damn whether I ever got any more of Mildred's puss or not. I knew that she had been home for quite a good while by then and was probably wondering where I was. I knew that she had probably already fixed supper and had noted my dead dog in the yard and was probably sitting out on the front porch looking for me to come in. I began talking to some young women shooting pool and took up a stick myself and shot about three racks of eight ball with them, losing all three for a dollar. I was merely hustling these young ladies and trying to get a line of trash going. I thought I could lure some of them off with the cold sixer in my truck later.

By the time I started drinking my fifth beer there were several longhaired tattooed muscled young men who had come into the place and they had scabs on their arms and boots and overalls on. They didn't appear jocular and they looked like they had been out in the sun all day, working very hard. My skin was milk white and I had seven dollars left in my pocket. I knew it was about time for me to get on the road.

I went outside and got in my truck and got out of town quickly. I hated to think about my old dog lying there in the yard, unburied. I thought I might ride around for a while and think about him, and Mildred, but I didn't know what good it would do. I had considered sending off for one of these pump-up penis deals, but I thought they might be dangerous or at the least would not work.

Within ten minutes I was away from town and out on a back

road that didn't have lawmen patrolling it and I felt free there
to open the suds I had iced down earlier and partake of them. I
knew that Mildred would want me in the bed beside her as soon
as I got home and I wasn't looking forward eagerly to that. I felt
like all our ministrations to each other were headed to a dead end
and that nobody would care fifty years from now what we had
gone through. It left me feeling a little bit depressed and fearful
and I started drinking even more, faster.

I rode for quite a while. I saw some cows loose from a pasture
and weaved in among them. The locusts had crawled out of the
ground after thirteen long years and when I stopped to pee on
a bridge I thought my truck was still running because of them.
They were beyond any loudness of bugs I had ever heard.

I had had about eight beers by that time. My blood alcohol
content was probably in the .10 range or maybe a little lower
or higher. It didn't actually matter. Squeezing her legs together
didn't help matters any at all. It was hopeless. I didn't know what
to do and I didn't want to go back home. I kept riding, drinking,
riding. I thought maybe I might run into somebody. I knew I'd
eventually have to bury that dog. I knew she was sitting out on
the porch, waiting on me. Watching all the lights coming down
the road. Wondering if each one was me. I felt sad about it. I
opened another beer and realized the folly of not stopping by the
liquor store while I was in town and purchasing a half pint of
peach schnapps to go along with my nice cold beers. I deliberated
for several minutes over this dilemma and found it was probably
an oversight on my part. I did not want to go home, neither did
I want to be indicted by the Mississippi Highway Safety Patrol
for Driving Under the Influence of alcohol. I observed that I was
driving fairly straight and I had not slurred any words yet to my
knowledge. My eyes were not red and my blood pressure did not
feel elevated. I felt that a short run back to town would not have
astronomical odds in favor of my being overtaken after a high-
speed pursuit. I turned around at a small place on the road and
began to retrace my route back to civilization.

I returned to and from town without incident and once more resumed my erratic wanderings over country roads near my home. The evening hour had begun to wane and it was nearly dark. I knew if I stayed out much longer there would be some dramatic scene with Mildred upon my arrival home and I wished to postpone that as much as possible. Mildred could never understand my wanderlust and my anxiety over her never-ending overtures of love and affection and requests for sexual gratification which she constantly and at all hours of the night pressed upon me while I tried to sleep. However, I knew that however late I was, Mildred would probably only raise a token protest in lieu of the fact that I was home and could begin once more plunging fruitlessly into the depths of her passion. The only defense available to me was to consume quantities of alcoholic beverages that would allow me to arrive home in a state of lethargic consciousness in which a stupor might then be attained.

I did not know what I was going to do with Mildred or how I was ever going to be able to come to a life of harmonious tranquility where matrimonial happiness was a constant joy. The only good thing about it was it gave me a subject of constant worry that I was able to slide endlessly back and forth in my mind during my various ruminations and ramblings over blacktopped back roads. We were not social people and were never invited to parties, nor did we give parties where we invited people to them. We basically lived alone with each other on ten acres of land that was badly eroded in a house of poor quality. I was not drunk but I did not feel sober. The needle on my gas gauge was pointing toward E and had been pointing that way for quite a while. There did not seem to be anything else to do but return home with my remaining beer and schnapps and face the prospect of burying my dog/dealing with my wife. I could see her face just as well and her small ears, and I could see kissing her nose and her chin and her cheeks and the small hollow place inside her soft little elbow, and I felt like disaster was on the way, since it felt like one of those evenings that I'd already had too many of. I wanted to do all I could for her and it didn't seem like I could do anything for her at all.

Upon entering my yard there were no lights on at my house and my dog was lying just as I had left him. Mildred's car was not in the carport, which was a most unusual occurrence. I was not extremely steady entering my house and stumbled around a bit before I found the light switch and turned it on. There on the coffee table, held down by an empty beer bottle, was a note that was addressed to me. . . . It said:

Dear Leon,

I have met another man and I have gone away with him. He has the equipment to take care of my problem and we have already "roadtested" it, so to speak. Forgive me, my darling, but he is the one man I have been searching for all of my adult life. I have taken the cats but of our house and property I want nothing. My attorney will be in contact with you but as for me I must bid you adieu and wish for you that you will someday find your own happiness.

XXX,
Mildred

It took a while for the words to sink in, for the reality of what I was reading to hit me. Mildred was gone, apparently, with another man with a huge penis. I went out to my truck and got another beer and walked back over to my dog. He was still there, still dead, only by then he had begun to stiffen a little as rigor mortis set in. I knew I needed to get a shovel and bury him but I could feel the emptiness of it already. I went up on the porch and sat down. I sipped my nice cold beer. I could imagine Mildred in a hotel room somewhere with the man she had taken, and I could imagine them moving together and Mildred's happiness and total fulfillment and joy with her new-found sexual gratification. I hated that I had never been able to give her what she wanted. I knew that I would just have to try and find another wife. I didn't know where to start looking, but I decided that I would start first thing in the morning, as soon as the dog had been given a suitable burial. There were plenty of women out there, and I knew that somewhere there was one that was right for me. I hoped when I found her, I would know it. I felt like one part of my life was over but that another, just as important part, was beginning. I felt a lot of optimism, and I knew I could get another dog. But I was already beginning to feel a little lonesome, and I could feel it surrounding the house, closing in. I tried not to think about it, but I sat out there on the porch for a long time that night, doing just that. I looked around for the cats but it was true, she had taken every last one, looked like. It would have been nice to have had maybe just one, a small one, to sit and pet and listen to it purr. I knew they could be cruel and vicious, but I knew they needed love just like everyone else. I thought about Mildred in that other man's arms, and how fine her ass looked in a bathing suit. Right about then I started missing her, and the loneliness I have been speaking of really started to set in.

SOUTH OF KITTATINNY

(from *Story*)

S outh of Kittatinny the road just keeps going down and settles into the hollers between the ridges. The Pittsburgh radio stations fade out here—it's mostly West Virginia and at night the big clear-channel from Nashville. Between Outerbridge and Porter there isn't but one weigh station and the stop at Ford's Corners.

Back before the war there was a dozen little towns along this stretch, two or three houses and what-have-you. Even a coal tipple or two when that still paid—my uncle was a small operator. His was a big house for then and we used to go up to his place Christmases, the Perrys and my ma and me and the Whitesides, maybe forty of us.

The boy cousins would go down into the trees and shoot squirrel and dress it for the table and the women would say they were too busy to cook them but they did anyway. We all ate at planks laid out on trusses in the yard.

I remember Earlene, leaning in one of the doorways, just out of the light. Her black hair was long then, nearly to her waist. She was fresh and lazy and her hand was at her throat, stroking the little soft spot there. "What you watchin', boy?" She smiled.

Fifteen years ago the house was already busted down the mountain.

* * *

There was eight who went to fight out of the Whitesides alone,
but I was too young. I slept in town at my Granny Streeter's
winters so that I could catch the schoolbus to the new union
high school in Porter, and I swept out her store and kept up the
woodpile.

Nights, we pulled the big blackout shades in the store's windows and listened to Edward R. Murrow. There would be five or
six old men around the stove, and Gran would deal out solitaire
on the counter. Paris was burning.

"I hadn't ought to be here!" I'd say, and slam the door as hard
as I dared on my way out. But there was nothing on the porch or
in the road but the moon, and though I walked up and down the
town that year, every which way, there wasn't anyplace to go.

Archer Whiteside came by for Thanksgiving and he had Earlene
in tow. He was skinny and dark and mean like always, but he
looked know-it-all in a way he hadn't before. When he hunkered
down on the porch he did it carefully, rocking on the toes of his
spit-polished oxfords, and when he stood up he ran his fingers
along the creases in his khakis to sharpen them. He had a medal
for marksmanship.

"I'll just pick 'em off," he said, sighting along his finger. "Like
turkeys. They ain't much different."

"Turkeys don't pack guns." That was Earlene, and Archer
laughed—she could make him laugh over anything. Over my bed
I had a picture of Veronica Lake cut from *Life* magazine and
Earlene wore her hair like that, always falling into her face and
always having to be pushed back, but you knew it was supposed
to happen that way over and over again.

Archer and Earlene danced in the store in the middle of the
night. WGN from Chicago, turned down low. I'd watch sometimes from the top of the stairs, until they nearly stood still and
he'd start to slide his hands up the back of her legs under her
skirt and then I couldn't watch anymore.

Christmas day we were less than a dozen of us in my uncle's

big house, just the aunts and uncles and two or three girl cousins and Gran and me. That year we had just squirrel and corn bread, and after we ate we sat around and cracked butternuts and the old folks talked about how next year everything would be back the way it had been.

At sunset Earlene and I went down the mountain to fetch uncle's skinny jersey. The sky was high and milky, streaked with pink, and it was just warm enough to work up a little sweat. She had on a cherry red dress with little half-moons of damp under the sleeves. I lifted her up for the fences and once I didn't put her down quick.

"What do you think you're doin', Cole?"

"I don't know." And I didn't. Just that I was struck with that first knowledge of a woman's body—heavier than I had thought, rounder and even more wildly desirable.

"You're just a baby, sweetie. And my cousin to boot."

"So's Archer."

She just laughed. She said, "I got a letter. I think he's in Europe. Ain't that somethin'?"

"I guess," I said. But she had wound her fingers in my own and it was fair to say I didn't envy Archer anything. We took off down the mountain, running and whooping. She shouted, "It's Christmas, Cole! Christmas!" And when I stopped, she went on, and I watched, scared she would break herself open on some rock and knowing she would never forgive the one who halted her.

In February, she came to live at the store. I came home from school one day and there she was. "I guess you all will have to put another potato in the soup," she said. "My folks have run me off my place."

"That's great!"

She smiled. "Is it?"

Gran said, "Earlene's here to help out for a while, Cole. You can put her things in the spare room."

The two of us stayed up till two or three that night, playing cards at the kitchen table, laughing. Around midnight, she had me sneak into the store and get us a couple of Cokes. When I got back she held up a Mason jar. "From my daddy's hidey-hole," she said.

"Is that real bourbon?"

"Real enough. Bottoms up."

We sat on the floor and passed the jar between us until the lamp guttered out for good. Then she helped me into my bed, and I remember that she sat on the end of it and cried, and that I knew I should give comfort but couldn't think of how before I slid into sleep.

In the morning Gran came into my room before I left for school. She stood in the doorway, her hands gnawing at the insides of her apron pockets. She said, "Earlene ain't here for no parties, Cole."

"No, ma'am."

"Direckly she has the child, she'll go back to her folks."

"Yes, ma'am."

I didn't take the schoolbus that day but walked in the woods, and when I went back home I didn't go inside but chopped wood for an hour until Earlene came to the door. She hung a dishrag on the line. I said, "Why didn't you tell me?"

"Maybe I was tired of tellin'."

I sank the ax in the block. "Damn it all, Earlene!"

"I ain't obliged to you, Cole. Supper's ready when you want it." She let the screen door slam behind her.

The cold came late that year and then squeezed hard for only two or three weeks before it let go. A yellow fuzz grew up on the trees, and it was the last of the basketball season.

That year the big game was in Porter. The two Pell boys and I walked down to the junction, shoving each other and laughing and running in circles, and by the time Coach picked us up in his old Ford we were crazy high—though sometime after we got to the school locker room we got quiet because a funny sort of knowing settled down on us the way it now and then does and we knew we were going to win the game. When the other team came out on the floor they knew it too—it wasn't going to be their night. I remember that the gym was bright and hot and almost empty because folks didn't use a ration of gas to go to a ball game.

It was half over before I saw Earlene. She was on a bench about halfway up, wrapped in her old green coat, her dark hair spread out on her shoulders. She waved and smiled, and when I turned back to play, everything was complete. Every move I made, I made in my body and in her eyes—I caught the ball and put it over the top in one slow leap and I could see how she saw me, hanging like that.

It was all over by nine o'clock. The mothers and a couple of dozen people from the town came crowding in. "Jesus," Coach said. "A one-horse town in the middle of nowhere. There's a war on. And they're good, can you beat that?" The whistle down at the mine went off and everybody hollered and somebody poured home-brew over our heads.

Earlene came through the crowd. "Well, I guess you're really somethin', ain't you?" She kissed my cheek and I put my arm around her waist.

"We were good, weren't we?"

She laughed. "You were awful good."

I leaned over and put my mouth over hers and could feel the swell of it, but only for a moment. "Cole," she said. "Just behave."

We all of us went to Buck's Café out on the highway and Coach treated us to ham and eggs. We were jammed into half a dozen booths, and we kept ordering until Buck said that was it, the kitchen was closed. Then we bought Cokes out of the cooler and Jim Holly spiked them with white lightning while Coach looked the other way. Beryl Ready and a boy from up the mountain jitterbugged on the counter. I kept my arm around Earlene in a corner booth and spread jam on biscuits for her, which she ate one after another. "Oh, Lord Jesus stop me." She sighed and licked her fingers one by one. "I'm going to be big as a house."

"A pretty, pretty house."

"You're drunk as a lord, Cole Streeter."

It was a long pull up the mountain. The moon had come up like a flood into the windows of the car. Coach sang "Barbry Allen" and "The Minister's Farewell" and the Pell boys kept him company.

Earlene sat between my knees. "God, I need a cigarette," she said. I could feel the warmth of her back against my belly and the solid round spread of her in my thighs. My fingers could make the span from her elbow to her wrist—she was that small—and there was a fine down on her forearms that just barely tickled the palms of my hands. I slipped my hands down her arms and thought I could feel her breasts with the tips of my fingers.

She said, "That little red-headed girl who talked to you—she fancies you."

"Does she?" I slid my hands down over her rounded belly and felt the surprise of it in my fingers. "It's hard. I didn't know it would be hard."

"Leave me be, Cole."

But that was something I could not do. I pulled her in tight and felt the warmth in my hands and up my arms and chest. I said, "You're beautiful."

She pulled away and took out her cigarettes and lit one and let the match burn a second too long before she threw it out the window. She said, "If Gran sees you like this, we're both in for it." But she settled back against me, and I hoped all the way up the mountain that she would fall asleep in my arms, though she never closed her eyes and her heart was never steady.

One Saturday night after supper we all played hearts and listened to the Opry. Earlene said, "You reckon my blue-check dress would be good enough for Sunday meetin'?"

Gran said, "Don't start, Earlene."

Earlene winked at me. "I ain't startin'."

"You are."

We played out the hand and Gran went up to bed. Earlene dealt out two-handed rummy. She said, "I guess I'm willful. Am I willful?"

I smiled. "Maybe. A little."

"Will you go with me?"

"I'll go."

In the morning we were Sunday-dressed by nine. Gran looked like thunder but all she said was, "Earlene, if you're comin' you got to wear a hat."

The church was the old one then, the one at Four Corners. The three of us walked, Gran in front, on the edge of the road where it wasn't churned up, and I carried Gran's Bible and Sacred Harp and seat pillow. By the time we were at the junction we could see people in knots on the steps and scattered out into the road. Gran said, "It's mostly Huxtables and Lees. Just keep your head up and speak when you're spoken to."

At the foot of the steps were a clutch of Lees and the Yarborough brothers and their wives. Gran nodded. "Unseasonable hot, ain't it?" And they most of them nodded back but for Gracie Lee, a pale, flimsy woman from down the holler who had a small child in her arms. Earlene said, "Why, Gracie Lee—is that your baby? She's got so big!" But the woman turned away. I gave Earlene and Gran each an arm and got them up the steps. "Lord," Earlene said. "I went to school with Gracie Lee." And I said, "The woman is borderline foolish." And Gran said, "Hush."

Sister Beulah Hennessey was in the vestibule. She sat on a folding chair, red-faced and big, fanning herself with a fan from Higby's Funeral. "Why, Earlene," she said. "You ain't come a moment too soon, have you?"

"There's things I could say, Beulah Hennessey," Gran said, but she didn't. She pulled Earlene and me up to maybe the third or fourth bench from the front.

I've spent more Sundays than I can count like that, in the dim light and the smell of dust and old wood and damp rising, all of it blown across by wafts of sweet grass and sun from the open windows. And there's a good drowsiness comes out of the hymns and all—when you come to yourself you wish to be a better man. But that morning I knew before we sat that we had run the wrong way.

The preacher was on the circuit, young and timid and without a grip on things. And he had scarcely started when the Calderses moved onto the bench in front of us. Molly Calders shooed her children in and then saw Earlene. "Well," she said, and yanked on her oldest boy's shirt and steered him out and across the aisle. The nine of them rustled by, straw-haired and blue-eyed, most of them sucking on something, fingers or a thumb.

Earlene put her hands over her belly. "It ain't like they never seen such a thing." And then, more loudly, "It's said Molly Calders drowned two of her own."

Gran said, "Be still, child."

"She just didn't get caught."

The preacher petered out. Two or three people stood to their feet and old Alexander Conroy began to line out in his high, quaking voice. *When the midnight cry began, O what lamentation . . .*

And then the congregation, a few at a time, like bees swarming, "Way-unnn . . ."

Earlene said, "My grandad's the one put the roof on this place. With his very own hands."

Thousands sleeping in their sins, neglecting their salvation . . .

"Thow-zzands . . ."

All I could think of was how to get Earlene out fast. I pulled her to her feet. She said, "My daddy's tithed her for thirty years," and I said, "Shut up," and took her by the arm and we headed up the aisle with Gran in the train.

Lo, the bridegroom is at hand . . .

I pushed open the heavy doors.

Who will kindly treat Him?

Under the big pin oak in front were five or six men, one of them Jem Huxtable. He was a deacon, tall and dark, leather-skinned, about the age my daddy would have been. He now and then paid me hire to cut wood with him in his lot, and he took me coon hunting. I'd never known him to raise his hand or voice to anyone.

As we came nigh the men, each of them turned away from us but Jem. I don't know what I thought I was going to do, but I lunged for the nearest of them. Jem stepped between. "Not at meetin', Cole."

I shouted, "You bastards!"

"Keep your peace."

"Sonsabitches!" And then to Jem. "Don't let them do this. Please."

He put his hand down gently on my shoulder. "She's been whorin', son."

I cold-cocked him. He fell, sprawled across the ropy roots of the old tree. I heard Earlene say, "Sweet Jesus, Cole," and a part of me prayed that he would sit up but I didn't wait to see it. I said, "Just walk. Get Gran and start walkin'."

The day had settled into a still heat. In town, the houses were Sunday-quiet—there was no one around but old Jimmy Keene and a dog or two. When we got to the store, Gran sat down heavily in her rocker on the porch, her hat on her head and her pocketbook in her lap.

I went inside and got a Coke from the cooler and drank it so fast that the spray at the back of my throat made me dizzy, and then I rolled the cool bottle across my forehead. Through the screen door I heard Gran say, "Earlene. Child. What did you expect?" And then their voices back and forth.

I sat on the floor with my back against the wall, in the cool dark that smelled of vinegar and wood ashes and molasses candy. I watched a narrow wedge of sun crawl up the far wall.

Gran came in. She rattled the damper in the stove and then straightened four or five boxes on a shelf. She was still wearing her hat. She said, "Earlene's run off. But she'll be back." Then she went on into the kitchen and closed the door behind her, and

I said fiercely, "Now look what you gone and done!" Though I knew she didn't hear me and I didn't know who I was saying it to anyway.

Earlene was gone for nine, ten hours. Gran and I ate crackers and milk for a late supper, and when Gran went out to throw the dishwater on her beans she came back in and said, "There's a light in the barn loft."

I let out my breath.

Gran said, "You might want to bring her out some pot cheese or bread. She'll be needin' somethin'."

"Yes, ma'am."

She took the handkerchief from her apron pocket and blew her nose loudly. "I'm goin' up to bed then. Don't forget to douse the lamp."

The barn was dark, and the ladder to the loft was splintery and had too much give in it. Halfway up I called, "I need some help here." And when Earlene leaned over the edge I handed her up cheese wrapped in paper and a jar of blackberry jam.

She said, "How'd you find me?"

"You can see that candle in the next state." I climbed over into the loft and pulled her Mason jar out of my shirt.

"And where'd you find that?"

"In your suitcase."

"Well. Looks like we're sharin' then, don't it?"

We sat cross-legged in the dry, winey-smelling bed of last year's hay and ate jam off of our fingers and passed the bourbon back and forth.

She said, "Did you think I was gone for good?"

"Sort of."

"I was. Almost." She took a stiff swallow. "God, this is awful stuff."

"Is it?"

"If you don't know, you shouldn't be drinkin' it." She handed the jar to me. "You ever miss havin' a daddy?"

"I don't know. Maybe."

"You recollect him at all? Your daddy?"

"Not much."

"He was a pretty, Black Irish son of a bitch. He broke your mama's heart."

I smiled. "Do I favor him?"

"I ain't sayin'." Earlene emptied the jar and threw it in a large arc over the edge of the loft. It flashed once in the candlelight and then fell without any noise at all.

I said, "I love you."

"Aw Lord, Cole."

"I do."

"I ain't anyone to love."

"They're fools, the church and all."

"Maybe I got it comin'."

"You don't." With my finger I traced the line of light on her cheek and arm. "I swear you don't."

She closed her eyes and whispered. "I'm just so tired, baby. I'm just so damned tired."

"I know. I know." I slid her down easy. I kissed her eyes and mouth. I cupped her breasts through the soft cloth of her dress and then I unbuttoned her dress and sucked. I knelt over her and eased her skirt up, and when I saw her belly I was scared for a second and said, "I won't hurt you," hoping it was true, but even before the words were out I didn't care about that or anything else but her hand helping me into her and then the push down and through and over onto the other side.

The last of the leaves lost their spring yellow and the creeks settled into their summer banks. Mornings, before school, Earlene and I sat at the kitchen table and ate toast and jam and talked quiet and not about anything in particular. I would out-line her hand on the tabletop like a child's play-picture or she'd let me sit with my head in her lap. "You're gettin' brown as a gypsy," she'd say and smooth my cheek and my hair until I was half-asleep.

I went to her bed only now and again, late, when there was no one around and no light anywhere, or sound. There was only the feel of her warm, solid flesh, the taste of her sweat, and the smell our bodies made together. I knew better than to speak—then or in the mornings. I just put myself into her hands when she'd have me and how.

School wound down for the year and I asked Gran if I could stay in town for the summer. She said, "Don't your mama need you home?"

"Ty's old enough to hoe." Tyson was my cousin down the road and I had no idea how he or my mama would feel about him doing her hoeing.

"This will be a hard summer, Cole. Just as long as you know."

"I do. I do know." So I stayed. And weekdays I took Old Man Pell's horse and wagon up the mountain and down again to fetch molasses and eggs from the back roads. The farmers would hand over the heavy cans and crates and bite the coins I paid them with and then ask, "What's the news, son?"

"They say Ike is goin' to push back soon."

"He don't push and we'll all be talkin' Dutch."

The store stocked syrup and eggs and a whole lot of rye flour sent down from Chicago that no one ever bought, and milk and cheese and buttermilk. There were usually a couple of dozen jars of home-canned chicken and string beans and four cans of sweet-and-sour beets that had been in the store as long as I could remember.

We sold less and less, but every evening more people came into the store for the radio news. Gran's Philco sat on a half-barrel in front of the stove, facing Louisville, which gave the best signal through the mountains that time of year. Art Sansom was in charge and he'd switch on the juice that was run off an old Model A and there would be a sound like wind and hail. "Now we're goin'," he'd say, and tinker with the dial till we heard a man's voice, faraway and small. "Today the Allies were fighting their way up the boot of Italy. . . ."

Earlene always sat across the road on Smalley's fence, smoking, while we listened. I'd find her when people were wandering out. "We're in Rome," I might say.

"Are we?"

"We're kickin' ass."

Once as we spoke, she reached out and touched the front of my trousers. Then she unbuttoned me and in the dark, with people scarcely a stone's throw away, she handled me and brought me over the edge. After, she covered my mouth with her hand. "Don't say anything," she said, and walked away.

It wasn't more than two or three days later that she said I couldn't come to her anymore at night. She said, "It just ain't right," and I thought there would be no living through it, the longing and the grief were that great at first. But quicker than I would have believed, I settled. Because anything she would give me was better than anything else.

Sometimes she rode with me on the wagon. Halfway up the mountain was a place with a waterfall and a flat spot that got the sun at noon, and I'd put down an old quilt and we'd sit and eat cheese or maybe a handful of berries from the side of the road.

She had an old comb made of horn with all the teeth smoothed round, and after we ate I sat behind her and combed her hair. It was just past her shoulders and the color of coal. She said, "My great-grandmaw Wilkes give me that comb when I was just one years old. I remember when she did. My mama says I don't, but I do."

"Is that right?" Blowaway threads of her hair were so light they rested on the air.

"She was sittin' in the parlor of our old house, and she was dark as an Indian."

I gathered up all her hair in my two hands and then let it fall. She said, "You ain't listenin'."

"I'm listenin'."

Now and then she would sleep, and I would lie on my side and watch her and wait for her to wake so that I could lift her in my arms into the wagon.

The days stretched longer and longer into the night at both ends. The early summer skies were wide and blue and clear and hardly changed from one morning to the next.

A telegram came from Memphis. Doke Graham drove it up from Porter. He handed me a yellow envelope out his car window and said, "I don't suppose you carry hairpins no more? I always ask for the wife."

Gran came out onto the porch and then Earlene.

I said, "No, sir."

"Well, then." He put his car in gear and rolled out of the yard.

I said, "It's probably nothin'."

"It's Archer," Earlene said, and turned back into the store.

Gran said, "Give it here, child." She unfolded the square of paper and read it. "He's missin'," she said, and went in after Earlene. I could see how she dragged a little, as though the porch floor had all of a sudden gone soft.

The next few days were all of a piece. We slept when we couldn't stay awake and we ate whatever we found whenever we remembered. At first Earlene walked—she walked around the store and the yard and the barn, then down the road to the junction and back. Gran said, "You got to sit. And you got to eat."

"I ain't hungry."

"There's coconut white cake Sister Beulah Hennessey brought."

I said, "She don't need nothin' from that sorry crowd."

And Gran said, "Hush, Cole. Take mercy where it's given. Earlene?"

"I ain't hungry." But she finally came to rest in the porch rocker and then she wouldn't move.

During the day, people coming and going into the store were quiet. The men took off their hats. Half a dozen women from the town and even the church did turns just sitting on the porch with Earlene, fanning and rocking.

Nights, Gran and I tucked quilts around Earlene in the rocker and I slept on the porch floor. I would lie as close to her as I could, pulling her feet inside my shirt and against my belly to warm them. She'd say, "Oh, baby, you don't want to do that."

"Yes, I do." I couldn't tell her that I was afraid to sleep, afraid that she would grow cold and die while I wasn't paying mind. I just held her feet until it got too dark to see or feel and I dozed in spite of myself.

As far as I know, she didn't sleep at all. Once when I woke at two or three in the morning, she said, "Will you comb my hair?"

I knelt behind her. Her hair was warm under my hands in the cool night. She said, "I remember when I got that comb from my great-grandmaw."

"I know."

"I was just a baby."

"I know."

"Do you believe I remember?"

"Sure I do."

The second telegram came on a Tuesday morning. Doke brought it up with a used incubator for Smalley and a litter of six-week hounds. We were all of us out on the porch and Earlene took the envelope and opened it and spread the telegram out on her lap. She read it and folded it up again carefully, keeping the creases, and put it in her pocket. She leaned forward and I saw sorrow roll up her back like wind over grass. "Oh, God," she said, and she wept then, and I wanted to holler or pray or shoot somebody, I didn't know which—my heart was that hard put deciding what way to go.

Gran said, "Jesus help us. Cole, get the Jack Daniels."

But Earlene had already wound down and, shaky, she said, "I don't need no whiskey." She stood, her face all lit up and wet at the same time, and she started to laugh. She said, "Baby, come here and give me a hug," and she pulled me in close and swung me around like we were dancing. "Oh, Cole," she said, and I could feel the ease in her, the joy. "He's comin' back. He's comin' home."

It turned out that Archer's right leg was all but gone—they would take it off in Richmond by October of that year. He came home the last week in May. We hung the store with red crepe-paper streamers, and a lot of people from the town gathered on the porch and in the store.

It was a cool, wet morning with a sky gray as a washed slate. He came up with Doke, and when he got out of the car—two men had to help him with his crutches—I remember that he looked tired and wary and a little surprised, as if the town and the people had sprung up new while he was gone.

Once Earlene got hold of him, she wouldn't let go, and he laughed and put a hand on her belly. "So this is junior, is it? Is he a pistol, like his daddy?" But some edge had gone off him. We had made up a bed downstairs in the kitchen, and in the next few days he moved back and forth from there to a place near the stove and never seemed to miss more.

On the sixth of June we all listened to the reports as the Allies took the beach in Normandy. Everything was turning, we could feel it even there on the mountain—nothing would be the same again. Archer sat in a chair close by the radio with his bad leg up on a crate, and Earlene stood behind him and smoothed his hair. "Damn it all if they ain't movin' in without me," he said. But I could see how all of him was caught up beneath her hand and how he was content. They were going down to Roanoke in a week, to the veteran's hospital, and they were getting married on the way.

Mama sent word that she needed me after all and I was happy to hear it. I made a deal with Clayton Pell to do Gran's egg route, and I packed up my clothes and basketball and the pictures from magazines I'd hung.

The day Archer and Earlene were leaving, I got up before

sunup and ran the road up the mountain—six, maybe seven miles. When I left town it was still dark, there wasn't a light anywhere but in the yard of the 66 station. I remember Burky's red-and-white spaniel came out and kept me company to where the macadam gave out and then she dropped away and there wasn't anything but the dark road and the darker trees and everything in me that wanted to stop.

I got as far as Stepp's old barn. I got there when the mountaintop was starting to get light, and the east was a blue as frail as a robin's egg.

I leaned with both hands on one knee and tried to catch my breath but I didn't seem able to, and somewhere in there I started to bawl like a baby. I cried for everything I'd ever known of her— for her black hair and her smile, for the way she jiggled one foot when she was edgy, for the taste of her mouth, for the smell of her skin and the way it stayed on my own. And one by one I gave each thing over into Archer's hands because I knew she wanted it that way. I think now it's the sort of thing the heart is strong enough to do only once.

Gran and I saw them off at Porter. The bus stop was just a bench outside The Tulip Shop then, you had to let them know you were coming or the bus didn't stop at all. It was a hot, hazy day. We stood just off the road next to three or four cartons tied with string—stuff Gran had gotten together to help them set up housekeeping. We none of us could think of anything to say until we saw the bus come over the rise and then there was no time left. Gran said, "Now don't forget there's fried chicken and doughnuts in the suitbox. It's no sense spendin' good money for food on the way."

Archer punched me in the arm. "Take care of the cows and the womenfolk, son."

"I'll do that."

The bus pulled into the yard and dust rose and stayed like

smoke in the hot air. Gran said, "Cole, help with the parcels. I should've put the blue dishes in after all, Earlene."

"Gran, we got more dishes than we'll ever use."

I had to half-carry Archer onto the bus. By the time I got him settled in the back, there was sweat out on his forehead and a white circle around his mouth. He pulled a flask out of his uniform pocket. "To the U.S. of A. and tits everywhere." He took a pull. "You want a belt? It's good Frenchie stuff."

"Thanks anyway."

I had gone over in my mind how I would last hold her, but it didn't work out that way. We met in the aisle of the bus and hugged just long enough for her to say in my ear, "Don't hate me, baby."

"I don't hate you."

And then I was off the bus and standing in the roadbed with Gran. The doors closed and the air brakes hissed, and the last thing I saw was the bus going down and around the curve at the bottom of Meekinville Road, and in the back window something like a bird's wing that could have been her hair.

Mark Richard

THE BIRDS FOR CHRISTMAS

(from *The New Yorker*)

We wanted "The Birds" for Christmas. We had seen the commercials for it on the television donated thirdhand by the Merchant Seamen's and Sailors' Rest Home, a big black-and-white Zenith of cracked plastic and no knobs, a dime stuck in the channel selector. You could adjust the picture and have no sound, or hi-fi sound and no picture. We just wanted the picture. We wanted to see "The Birds."

The Old Head Nurse said not to get our hopes up. It was a "Late Show" after Lights Out the night before Christmas Eve. She said it would wake the babies and scare the Little Boys down on the far end of the ward. Besides, she said, she didn't think it was the type of movie we should be seeing Christmas week. She said she was certain there would be Rudolph and Frosty on. That would be more appropriate for us to watch on the night before Christmas Eve.

"*Fuck* Frosty," Michael Christian said to me. "I seen that a *hunrett* times. I want to see 'The Birds,' man. I want to see those birds get all up *in* them people's hair. That's some real Christmas TV to me."

Michael Christian and I were some of the last Big Boys to be claimed for Christmas. We were certain *someone* would eventually come for us. We were not frightened yet. There were still some other Big Boys around—the Big Boy who ran away to a gas station every other night, the Human Skeleton who would bite you, and the guy locked away on the sun porch who the Young Doctors were taking apart an arm and a leg at a time.

The Young Doctors told Michael Christian that their Christmas gift to him would be that one day he would be able to do a split onstage like his idol, James Brown. There never seemed to be any doubt in Michael Christian's mind about that. For now, he just wanted to see "The Birds" while he pretended to be James Brown in the Hospital.

Pretending to be James Brown in the Hospital was not without its hazards for Michael Christian; he had to remember to keep his head lifted from his pillow so as not to *bedhead* his budding Afro. Once, when he was practicing his singing, the nurses rushed to his bed asking him where it hurt.

"I'm warming up 'I Feel Good,' stupid bitches," said Michael Christian. Then his bed was jerked from the wall and wheeled with great speed, pushed and pulled along by hissing nurses, jarring other bedsteads, Michael Christian's wrists hanging over the safety bedrails like jailhouse-window hands; he was on his way to spend a couple of solitary hours out in the long, dark, and empty hall, him rolling his eyes at me as he sped past, saying, "Aw, man, now I feel BAD!"

Bed wheeling into the hall was one of the few alternatives to corporal punishment the nurses had, most of them being reluctant to spank a child in traction for spitting an orange pip at his neighbor, or to beat a completely burned child for cursing. Bed wheeling into the hall was especially effective at Christmastime, when it carried the possibility of missing Christmas programs. A veteran of several Christmases in the hospital and well acquainted with the grim Christmas programs, Michael Christian scoffed at the treasures handed out by the church and state charities—the aging fruit, the surplus ballpoint pens, the occasional batches of recycled toys that didn't work, the games and puzzles with missing pieces. Michael Christian's Christmas Wish was as specific as mine. I wanted a miniature train set with batteries so I could lay out the track to run around on my bed over the covers. Not the big Lionel size or the HO size. I wanted the set you could see in magazines, where they show you the actual size of the railroad engine as being no larger than a walnut.

"You never get that, man," Michael Christian said, and he was right.

James Brown in the Hospital's Christmas Wish was for "The Birds" for Christmas. And, as Michael Christian's friend, I became an accomplice in his desire. In that way, "birds" became a code, the way words can among boys.

"Gimme some BIRDS!" Michael Christian would squawk when the society ladies on their annual Christmas visit asked us what we wanted.

"How about a nice hairbrush?" a society lady said, laying one for white people at the foot of Michael Christian's bed.

"I want a pick," Michael Christian told her.

"A pick? A shovel and pick? To dig with?" asked the society lady.

"I think he wants a comb for his hair," I said. "For his Afro."

"That's right: a pick," said Michael Christian. "Tell this stupid white bitch something. *Squawk, squawk,*" he said, flapping his elbows like wings, as the nurses wheeled him out into the hall. "Gimme some BIRDS!" he shouted, and when they asked me, I said to give me some birds, too.

Michael Christian's boldness over the Christmas programs increased when Ben, the night porter, broke the television. Looking back, it may not be fair to say that Ben, the night porter, actually broke the television, but one evening it was soundlessly playing some kiddie Christmas show and Ben was standing near it mopping up a spilt urinal can when the screen and the hope of Michael Christian's getting his Christmas Wish blackened simultaneously. Apologetic at first, knowing what even a soundless television meant to children who had rarely seen any television at all, Ben then offered to "burn up your butt, Michael Christian, legs braces and all" when Michael Christian hissed "stupid nigger" at Ben, beneath the night nurse's hearing. It was a sombre Lights Out.

The next night, a priest and some students from the seminary came by. Practice Preachers, Michael Christian said. While one of the students read the Christmas story from the Bible, Michael Christian pretended to peck his own eyes out with pinched fingers. When the story was finished, Michael Christian said, "Now, you say the sheepherding guys was so afraid, right?"

"*Sore* afraid," said the Practice Preacher. "The shepherds had never seen angels before, and they were *sore* afraid."

"Naw," said Michael Christian. "I'll tell you what—they saw these big white things flapping down and they was big *birds,* man. I know *birds,* man, I know when you got bird *problems,* man!"

"They were *angels,*" said the young seminary student.

"Naw," said Michael Christian. "They was big white birds, and the sheepherding guys were *so* afraid the big white birds was swooping down and getting all up in they *hair* and stuff! *Squawk, squawk!*" he said, flapping around in his bed.

"*Squawk, squawk!*" I answered, and two of the Practice Preachers assisted the nurses in wheeling Michael Christian into the hall and me into the linen cupboard.

One night in the week before Christmas, a man named Sammy came to visit. He had been a patient as a child, and his botched cleft-palate and harelip repairs were barely concealed by a weird line of blond mustache. Sammy owned a hauling company now, and he showed up blistering drunk, wearing a ratty Santa suit, and began handing out black-strapped Timex junior wristwatches. I still have mine, somewhere.

One by one we told Sammy what we wanted for Christmas, even though we were not sure, because of his speech defect, that that was what he was asking. Me, the walnut train; Michael Christian, "The Birds." We answered without enthusiasm, without hope: it was all by rote. By the end of the visit, Sammy was a blubbering sentimental mess, reeking of alcohol and promises. Ben, the night porter, put him out.

It was Christmas Eve week. The boy who kept running away finally ran away for good. Before he left, he snatched the dime from the channel selector on our broken TV. We all saw him do it and we didn't care. We didn't even yell out to the night nurse, so he could get a better head start than usual.

It was Christmas Eve week, and Michael Christian lay listless in his bed. We watched the Big Boy ward empty. Somebody even came for one of the moaners, and the guy out on the sun porch was sent upstairs for a final visit to the Young Doctors so they could finish taking him apart.

On the night before Christmas Eve, Michael Christian and I heard street shoes clicking down the long corridor that led to where we lay. It was after Lights Out. We watched and waited and waited. It was just Sammy the Santa, except this time he was wearing a pale-blue leisure suit, his hair was oiled back, and his hands, holding a red-wrapped box, were clean.

What we did not want for Christmas were wristwatches. What we did not want for Christmas were bars of soap. We did not want any more candy canes, bookmarks, ballpoint pens, or somebody else's last year's broken toy. For Christmas we did not want plastic crosses, dot books, or fruit baskets. No more handshakes, head pats, or storybook times. It was the night before Christmas Eve, and Michael Christian had not mentioned "The Birds" in days, and I had given up on the walnut train. We did not want any more Christmas Wishes.

Sammy spoke with the night nurse, we heard him plead that it was Christmas, and she said all right, and by her flashlight she brought him to us. In the yellow spread of her weak batteries, we watched Michael Christian unwrap a portable television.

There was nothing to be done except plug the television into the wall. It was Christmas, Sammy coaxed the reluctant night nurse. They put the little TV on a chair, and we watched the end of an Andy Williams Christmas Special. We watched the eleven-o'clock news. Then the movie began: "The Birds." It was Christmas, Sammy convinced the night nurse.

The night nurse wheeled her chair away from the chart table and rolled it to the television set. The volume was low, so as not to disturb the damaged babies at the Little Boy end of the ward—babies largely uncollected until after the holidays, if at all. Sammy sat on an empty bed. He patted it. Michael Christian and I watched "The Birds."

During the commercials, the night nurse checked the hall for the supervisor. Sammy helped her turn any infant that cried out. The night nurse let Sammy have some extra pillows. Michael Christian spoke to me only once during the entire movie: quietly, during a commercial when we were alone, he said, "Those birds messing them people *up*."

When the movie was over, it was the first hours of Christmas Eve. The night nurse woke Sammy and let him out through the sun porch. She told us to go to sleep, and rolled her chair back to her chart table. In the emptiness you could hear the metal charts click and scratch, her folds of white starch rustle. Through a hole in the pony blanket I had pulled over my head I could see Michael Christian's bed. His precious Afro head was buried deep beneath his pillow.

At the dark end of the ward a baby cried in its sleep and then was still.

It was Christmas Eve, and we were sore afraid.

Robert Morgan

POINSETT'S BRIDGE

(from *Epoch*)

Son, it was the most money I'd ever had, one ten-dollar gold piece and twenty-three silver dollars. The gold piece I put in my dinner bucket so it wouldn't get worn away by the heavy silver. The dollars clinked and weighted in my pocket like a pistol. I soon wished they was a pistol.

"What you men have done here this year will not be forgotten," Senator Pineset said before he cut the ribbon across the bridge. "The coming generations will see your work and honor you. You have opened the mountains to the world, and the world to the mountains."

And he shook hands with every one of us. I still had my dirty work clothes on, but I had washed my face and hands in the river before the ceremony. The senator was as fine a looking man as you're ever likely to see. He wore a striped silk cravat and he had the kind of slightly red face that makes you think of spirit and health.

The senator and all the other dignitaries and fine ladies got in their carriages and crossed the bridge and started up the turnpike. There was to be a banquet at the King House in Flat Rock that evening to celebrate the road and the bridge. I shook hands with the foreman Delosier and started up the road myself for home.

Everything seemed so quiet after the ceremony. The warm fall woods was just going on about their business, with no interest in human pomp and projects. I carried my dinner bucket and my light mason's hammer, and I thought it was time to get home and do a little squirrel hunting. I hadn't spent a weekday at home since work started on the bridge in March. Suddenly two big rough-looking boys jumped out from behind a rock above the road and ran down into the turnpike in front of me.

"Scared you?" one said, and laughed like he had told a joke.

"No," I said.

"We'll just help you carry things up the mountain," the other said. "You got anything heavy?" He looked at my pocket bulging with the silver dollars. I had my buckeye in there too, but it didn't make any sound.

"Yeah, we'll help out," the first one said, and laughed again.

Now I had built chimneys ever since I was a boy. Back yonder people would fix up on their own a little cabin and make a fireplace of rock, then the chimney they just built of plastered mud and sticks. Nobody had the time or skill for masonry. Way back yonder after the Indians was first gone and people moved into these hollers a wagonload at a time, coming to grab the cheap land, they'd live in any little old shack or hole in the ground with a roof over it. The first Jones that come here they said lived in a hollow tree for a year. And I knowed other families that hid theirselves in caves and lean-to's below cliffs. You just did the best you could.

My grandpa fit the British at King's Mountain and at Cowpens, and then he come up here and threw together a little cabin right on the pasture hill over there. You can see the cellarhole there still. And where we lived when I was a boy the chimney would catch fire on a cold night, or if pieces of mud fell off the sticks, and we'd have to get up on the roof and pour water down. You talk about cold and wet, with the house full of smoke. That was what give Grandpa pneumony.

That was when I promised myself to build a chimney. Nobody

on the creek knew rockwork then, except to lay a rough kind of fireplace. Only masons in the county was the Germans in town, the Doxtaters and Bumgarners, the Corns, and they worked on mansions in Flat Rock, and the home of the judge, and the courthouse and such. I would have gone to learn from them but I was too scared of foreigners to go off on my own. People here was raised so far back in the woods we was afraid to go out to work. So I had to learn myself. I'd seen chimneys in Greenville when Pa and me carried to market there, and I'd marveled at the old college building north of Greenville. "Rockwork's for rich folks," Pa said, but I didn't let that stop me.

After the tops was cut and the fodder pulled one year, I set myself to the job. First thing that was needed was the rocks, but they was harder to get at than it might seem at first. They was rocks in the fields and pastures. Did you just pry them up with a pole and sled them to the house? And the creek was full of rocks, but they was rounded by the water and would have to be cut flat. That was the hardest work I'd ever done, believe me, getting rocks out of the creek. It was already getting cold, and I'd have to get out there in the water, finding the right size, and tote them up the bank, prying some loose from the mud, and scrape away the moss and slick.

They was a kind of quarry over on the hill where the Indians must have got their flint and quartz for arrowheads. The whole slope was covered with fragments of milkquartz, and I hauled in some of those to put in the fireplace where the crystals could shine in the light.

I asked Old Man Davis over at the line what could be used for mortar and he said a bucket of lime mixed with sand and water would do the trick. And even branch clay would serve, though it never set itself hard except where heated by a fire.

Took me most of the fall, way up into hogkilling time, to get my stuff assembled. I just had a hammer and one cold chisel to dress the rock. Nobody ever taught me how to cut stone, or how to measure and lay out. I just learned myself as I made mistakes and went along.

Son, I remember looking at that pile of rocks I'd carried into the yard and wondering how I'd ever put them together in a firebox and chimney. My brother Joe had already started to play with the rocks and scatter them around. Leaves from the poplars had drifted on my heap and already it looked half-buried. I waited until Ma and Pa and the other younguns had gone over to Fletcher to Cousin Charlie's. In those times people would visit each other for a week at a time once the crops was in. I stayed home to look after the stock. One morning at daylight I lit in and tore the old mud chimney down. I knocked most of it down with an ax, it was so shackly, and then I knocked the firebox apart with a sledgehammer.

Well there it was, the cabin with a hole in the side and winter just a few short weeks away. That was when I liked to have lost my nerve. The yard was a mess of blackened mud and sticks, and my heaps of rocks. I thought of just absconding, of heading west and never coming back, of taking the horse and going. I stood there paralyzed, you might say, with indecision.

But then I seen in my pile a rock that was perfect for a cornerstone, and another that would fit against it in a line with just a little chipping. So I shoveled out and leveled the foundation and mixed up a bucket of mortar. I put the cornerstone in place, and slapped on some wet clay, then fitted the next rock to it. It was like solving a puzzle, finding rocks that would join together with just a little mud, maybe a little chipping here and there to smooth a point or corner. But best of all was the way you could approximate a line, running a string or a rule along the edge to see how it would line up, so when you backed up you saw the wall was straight in spite of gaps and bulges. I worked so hard selecting and rejecting rocks from my pile, mixing more clay and water, setting stone against stone, that I never stopped for dinner. By dark I had the hole covered with the fireplace, so the coons couldn't get inside. I liked the way I made the firebox slope in toward the chimney to a place where I could put a damper. And I set between the rocks the hook from which Ma's pot would hang.

It wasn't until I was milking the cow by lanternlight I seen how rough my hands had worn. The skin at the ends of my fingers and in my palms was fuzzy from handling the rock. The cow liked to kicked me, they rasped her tits so bad.

But by the time Ma and Pa had come home from Cousin Charlie's I had made them a chimney. I made my scaffold out of hickory poles and hoisted every rock up the ladder myself and set it into place. It was not the kind of chimney I'd a-built later, but you can see the work over there at the old place still, kind of rough and taking too much mortar, but still in plumb and holding together after more than sixty years. I knowed you had to go above the roof to make a chimney draw, and I got it up to maybe six inches above the comb. Later I learned any good chimney goes six feet above the ridgepole. It's the height of a chimney makes it draw, that makes the flow of smoke go strong up the chimney into the cooler air. The higher she goes the harder she pulls.

People started asking me to build chimneys, and I made enough so I started using fieldstone, and breaking the rocks to get flat edges that would fit so you don't hardly have to use any mortar. They just stay together where they're laid. And people asked me to steen their wells, and wall in springs and cellars. It was hard and heavy work, taking rocks out of the ground and placing them back in order, finding the new and just arrangement so they would stay. I had all the work I could do in good weather, after laying-by time.

Then I heard about the bridge old Senator Pineset was building down in South Carolina. Clara—we was married by then—read about it in the Greenville paper which come once a week. The senator was building a turnpike from Charleston to the mountains, to open up the Dark Corner of the state for commerce he said. But everybody knowed it was for him and his Low Country kind to bring their carriages to the cool mountains for the summer. They found out what a fine place this was and they started buying up the land around Flat Rock. But there wasn't hardly a road up Saluda Mountain and through the Gap except the little wagon trace down through Gap Creek. That's the way we hauled our hams and apples down to Greenville and Augusta in the fall. That same newspaper said the state of North Carolina was building a turnpike all the way from Tennessee to the line at Saluda Gap.

The paper said they was building this stone bridge across the North Fork of the Saluda River. It was to be fifty feet high and more than a hundred feet long, "the greatest work of masonry and engineering in upper Carolina," the paper said. And I knowed I had to work on that bridge. It was the first turnpike into the mountains and I had to go help out. The paper said they was importing masons from Philadelphia and even a master mason from England. I knowed I had to go and learn what I could.

Senator Pineset had his own ideas about the turnpike and the bridge, but we knowed there'd be thousands of cattle and hogs and sheep drove out of the mountains and across from Tennessee as well as the rich folks driving in their coaches. That highway would put us in touch with every place in the country you might want to go.

I felt some dread, going off like that not knowing if they would hire me or not. I had no way of proving I was a mason. What would that fancy Englishman think of my laying skill? And even if he took me on, it was a nine-mile walk each way to the bridge site. I knowed the place all right, where the North Fork goes through a narrow valley too steep to get a wagon down and across. There's something about the things a man really wants to do that scares him. He's got to go on nerve a lot of the time. And nobody else is looking or cares when you make your choices. That's the way it has to be. But it was a kind of fate too, and even Clara didn't try to stop me. She complained, as a woman will, that I'd be gone from sunup to sundown and no telling how long it would take to finish the bridge through the summer and into the fall. And she wouldn't have no help around the place except the kids. "They may not do any more hiring," she said. But I knowed better. I knowed masons and stonecutters of any kind was hard to come by in the up country, and there would be thousands of rocks to cut for such a bridge. And when I set off she give me a buckeye to put in my pocket for luck. She didn't normally hold to such things, but I guess she was worried as I was.

Sometimes you get a vision of what's ahead for you. And even if it's what you want most to do, you see all the work it is. It's like foreseeing an endless journey of climbing over logs and crossing creeks, looking for footholds and negotiating mud and swampland. And every little step and detail is real and has to be worked out. But it's what you are going to do, what you have been given to do. It will be your life to get through it.

That's the way I seen this work. Every one of that thousand rocks, some weighing a ton, I guessed, had to be dressed, had to be measured and cut out of the mountainside, and then joined to one another. And every rock would take hundreds, maybe thousands of hammer-and-chisel licks, each lick leading to another, swing by swing, chip by chip, every rock different and yet cut to fit with the rest. Every rock has its own flavor, so to speak, its own grain and hardness. No two rocks are exactly alike, but they have to be put together, supporting each other, locked into place. It was like I was behind a mountain of hammer blows, of chips and dust, and the only way out was through them. It was my life's work to get through them. And when I got through them my life would be over. It's like everybody has to earn their own death. We all want to reach the peacefulness and rest of death, but we have to work our way through a million little jobs to get there, and everybody has to do it in their own way.

The Englishman was Barnes, and he wore a top hat and silk tie, though he had a kind of apron on. "Have you been a mason long?" he said.

"Since I was a boy," I said.

"Have you ever made an arch?"

"Yes sir, over a fireplace," I said.

"Ours will be a little bigger," he said and looked me up and down.

"Let me see your hands," he said. He glanced at the calluses the trowel had made and sent me to the clerk, who he called "the clark."

I was signed on as a mason's helper, which hurt my pride some, I'll admit. All morning I thought of heading back up the trail for home, and letting the fine Englishman and crew build whatever bridge they wanted.

And if I thought about leaving when the clerk signed me on as an assistant, I thought about it twice when Barnes sent me away from the bridge site up the road to the quarry. It was about a mile where they had picked a granite face on the side of the mountain to blast away. One crew was drilling holes for the black powder, and another was put to dressing the rock that had already been blasted loose.

I had brought my light mason's hammer and trowel, but I was give a heavy hammer and some big cold chisels and told to cut a regular block, eighteen inches thick, two feet wide, and three feet long. The whole area was powdered with rock dust from the blasting and chipping.

"Surely you don't want all the blocks the same size?" I said to Delosier, the foreman from Charleston.

"The corner stones and arch stones will be cut on the site," he said. "In the meantime we need more than five hundred regular blocks, for the body of the bridge." He showed me an architect's plan where every single block was already drawed in, separate and numbered.

"You're cutting block one aught three," he said.

Some of the men had put handkerchiefs over their noses to keep out the rock dust. They looked like a gang of outlaws hammering at the rocks, but there was nothing to protect their eyes. I squatted down to the rough block Delosier had assigned me. After the first few licks I felt even more like going home. It would take all day to cut the piece to the size Barnes required. I wasn't used to working on rocks that size and shape.

After a few more licks I saw where the smell in the quarry come from. I thought it was just burned black powder, but it was also the sparks from where the granite was hit by the chisels. Every time the steel eat into the granite it smoked and stunk a little. With a dozen people chipping, the whole place filled up with dust and smell.

But I kept at it. I had no choice but to keep working because I would never have another chance like that. And even then I knew that if you don't feel like working in the morning it will get better if you just keep at it. You start out feeling awful and if you work up a sweat the job will begin taking over itself. You just follow the work, stick to the job, and the work will take care of you. I put my handkerchief over my nose and started hammering along the line I'd measured and scratched on the side of the block. I was already behind if I was going to finish that block in one day.

"You want a drink, boss?" The slave held a dipper from the bucket of water he'd just carried from the spring on the mountainside.

I pushed down the handkerchief and wiped the dust from my lips. The cold water surprised me. I had been concentrating so hard on work I'd forgotten I was thirsty. And I wasn't used to being waited on by no slave or called boss.

When we stopped for dinner everybody washed their hands in the creek and we set in the shade and opened our lard buckets. Clara had packed me some shoulder meat and biscuits. My arm was a little sore from the steady hammering. My block was cut on only one side. Delosier inspected my work and spat without commenting. I had made a clean face, but I'd have to speed up to finish that evening.

The slave that carried water had a harmonica in his pocket which he began playing. There was a slave boy named Charlie that carried tools and messages between the quarry and bridge. "Hey, Charlie," somebody was always calling, "Hey, Charlie, get this bit sharpened."

Charlie started dancing right there in the clearing to the harmonica music. He started to move the toes on one foot, and then the foot. You could see the music traveling up his leg, up to his waist, and then travel out one shoulder and around till he had his hand dancing. You never saw such a sight as when he started dancing all over. The harmonica played faster, and the boy started dancing around in circles and the first thing you know he was doing somersaults all over the clearing.

Then the harmonica player moved back in the shade and slowed down and the boy slowed down too. He danced backwards, getting slower, like he was winding down, slower and slower, until he stopped and the music went down one arm and through his body and down a leg until only the foot was moving, and then the toes. And he stood still all over when the music stopped.

Now the funny thing was Delosier had been watching and enjoying the dancing as much as any of us. But as soon as the music stopped he said, "That's enough of that. You're wasting energy on my time. You boys can play and dance on your own time."

I didn't see no call for what he said, since it was dinner hour. But we all put our dinner buckets down to go to work, and the boy, sweating something awful from the dancing, ran to sharpen more chisels. I hunkered down over my block.

"Never mind what our names are," the older boy said.

"No, I won't mind," I said.

"We'll just walk along with you a little ways, to keep you out of trouble."

I tried to remember if I'd seen them anywhere before. Chestnut Springs even then had a lot of rough people, liquor people and all. Names like Howard or Walker kept coming to mind, but I couldn't place them. Our folks had come from South Carolina and I knowed a lot of people from Landrum and Tigerville, but I couldn't place them.

"You just got paid down at the bridge," the older boy said.

"I worked on the bridge," I said. I could have said I walked this road every morning and evening for nearly five months, and I'd never seen them.

"You wouldn't fool us," the younger one said. "We watched

all them big shots from up on the mountain. And we seen all of you-uns standing around before they cut the ribbon."

"You should have come down and had some punch, and some sweetbread," I said. "One of the carriages from Greenville brought a basket of sweetbread and a keg of punch, along with a big bottle of champagne for the dignitaries."

"We got our own bottle," the older boy said.

"Can't we help you carry something," the younger brother said. He lifted a side of his vest and I seen the pistol in his belt.

"I'm doing fine," I said.

"Ain't you got something just a little too heavy for you to carry," the older one said. I noticed he had a knife about eighteen inches long stuck in his belt.

If only another carriage would come along, or if we'd meet a wagon coming back from mill, I could ask for a ride. I prayed that somebody I knowed would be walking down the mountain. But there was nothing ahead but the road through the holler, built while we was building the bridge, winding up toward Saluda Gap.

"What you got in there, boss?" the older brother said, and prodded my pocket with the pistol.

"You got something a-ringing a regular tune," the younger one said.

"You wouldn't lie to us?" the other one said.

I stepped back, and just then I seen the rock in the younger one's hand.

After the first day I was almost too tired to walk back up the mountain. And the next day I was nearly too sore to lift a hammer. But I made myself keep going, and after a while I worked the soreness out. It took about a week for me to learn to cut a block a day, getting surer and ever closer to the measurements. It took ten men to slide one of those blocks up on an ox cart to carry to the bridge site. Delosier showed us how to do things with rollers and skids and pulleys you never would have dreamed of. I had never handled big stuff like that before. It looks like there ain't nothin a man can't do if he just takes time to study it out.

I got a little bit of a cough from breathing the rock dust, but after seven or eight weeks we had most of the blocks cut and moved down to the bridge itself. They had put up a frame of poles and timbers to build the arches on, and I looked close to see exactly how Barnes and Delosier done it. If a giant could pick up all the rocks of an arch and drop them into place at once you wouldn't need a frame underneath. But with regular men moving in a rock at a time there was no other way. Delosier built a big A-frame with pulleys to hoist the stones into place. It was something to watch.

They had a spot right down by the river where we did the final dressing of blocks before they was lifted into place above. Once the arches were built we could roll everything out onto the bridge as we went, but the arches had to be put in place first. It was convenient, and cooler by the water. We wet the drills and rocks to keep down the dust.

"Everything will be fine unless there's a flash," I said to Delosier.

"What do you mean a flash?"

"A flash flood," I said. "On ground this steep it can come up a flash tide pretty quick."

"It's not the season for flash floods," Mr. Barnes, who had overheard me, said.

"A flash can come anytime," I said. "All you need is a cloudburst on the slope above."

"You mountain folk are so superstitious," Mr. Barnes said. "All you ever do is worry about lightning, panthers, snakes, floods, winds, and landslides."

I knew there was truth in what he said, but it was like he was saying that I, as an assistant mason, didn't have a right to an opinion either. But I let it go and went back to work.

But along in July it come up the awfullest lightning storm you ever seen. You know how it can thunder in South Carolina, there at the foot of the mountain, after a hot day. It was like the air was full of black powder going off. We got under the trees, until we saw a big poplar on the ridge above turn to fire and explode. Splinters several feet long got flung all over the woods. We got under the first arch then, knowing the rock wouldn't draw the lightning.

"When the Lord talks, he talks big," Furman, another mason's assistant, said.

The slaves got in under the cover of the arch, saying nothing. Lightning struck up on the ridge again, and it was like the air had jolted you.

"The Lord must have a lot on his mind," the harmonica player said.

"Maybe telling us how sick of us he is," another slave said.

The storm passed over for a minute and then come back, the way a big storm will. Lightning was dropping all around on the ridges above. It was so close you could hear the snap, like whips cracking, before there was any thunder. Snap-boom, snap-boom. The air smelled like scorched trees and burned air.

"This old earth getting a whipping," the harmonica player said.

After about twenty minutes the worst of it passed, and we could hear the thunder booming and rattling on the further mountains. While it was still raining a little we got out and stood in the drizzle and the drip from the trees.

"What is that roar?" Delosier said.

"Just wind on the mountain, boss."

"No, it's coming closer."

It did sound like wind on a mountainside of trees, and my first thought was we was having a little twister. They don't come often to the mountains, but they have been known to bore down out of the sky, twisting up the trees.

And just then it hit me there was a flash tide coming down the valley. "It's the creek," I hollered, but no one seemed to notice.

"It's the river," I hollered again. "Let's get the tools." There must have been a dozen hammers and chisels, several T-squares and rulers, levels and trowels under the bridge. And there was an extra set of block and tackle. Only Charlie and the harmonica player seemed to hear me. They ran down and got five or six of the sledgehammers, and I got one end of the big block and tackle and started to drag it up the bank.

Then everybody all at once saw the water coming. It was gold colored from the red clay and frothy as lather. The river was just swollen a little bit, as was normal after a hard rain as nearby run-off spilled into the stream. But somewhere higher up, a valley had been drenched all at once with the cloud's insides dropping into a narrow branch holler. It was not like a wall of water exactly. It was more like a stampede of furry paws rolling over each other, slanted down to a frothy front that swerved and found its way through trees and bends. Besides the foam you could see sticks and leaves and all kinds of trash tossed up and tumbled around.

Everybody pulled back from the banks at once and I had to let go the big block and tackle after wrapping it around a tree. I let go and run back up the hill with the rest.

That big cowcatcher of water come through the narrow valley tearing saplings loose and bending trees over till they pulled out by the roots. There was a wind with it too, a cold breeze swept down with the tide. I thought at first the bridge was going to go, the frames we had put up for the arches. But I guess there was enough weight on them now to hold them down. The bridge was far enough along to hold intact.

"The Lord have mercy," the harmonica player kept saying.

"Oh blast, oh blast it all," Mr. Barnes said, and took off his hat as he watched the charge of water swirl through his frames and pilings and suck through the arches.

"Oh blast it all," he said.

"Everybody safe?" Delosier called.

We looked around and everybody seemed to be there, wet from the rain and white-faced with shock. The body of a mule shot by in the current, and then a chicken coop. A cart that had been used at the quarry came down. And a big black snake passed, spun around as it tried to swim.

"The Lord almighty."

The water rose to the groin of the biggest arch, and slapped at the stones a while, then began to recede. Once the high mark was reached the flood began to drop quick, pulling back from the banks, drawing most of the debris with it, letting go of roots and stumps. As fast as it had come the flash shrunk back to the river bed, leaving sticks and trash caught in the tops of bushes and the banks scoured. You could tell how high it went because the ground there was bare as a plucked chicken. Roots and rocks were exposed in the dripping slope.

Many tools had been washed away, and some of the blocks we was cutting had been carried down by the tide. Several logs and saplings had been lodged against the pillars of the bridge.

"Why, look at that," Charlie said, and pointed to what looked like a seedbox. "Boss, I don't want to look at that," he said to Delosier. It was not a seedbox, but a pine casket, half-rotted away. Everybody crowded to the box, but there was nothing in it except some rotten rags and bones.

"Don't that beat all," Delosier said.

Mr. Barnes directed four men to carry the box up the hill and bury it above the road.

"Shouldn't we find out who it was and return it to the family?" Delosier said.

"And how do you propose to do that, sir?" Mr. Barnes said. "This could have come from anywhere upstream, and we have work to do."

As soon as they had started up the hill Mr. Barnes turned his glare on me. "Jones," he said, "you could have warned us."

"I told you it might flood," I said.

"Jones, you might have warned us effectively," he said. "From what you said I understood there was only the remotest chance of a flood, and that after days of rain."

"A flash can come up quick," I said.

"So I notice," he said. "You folk never know how to say what you mean."

The other time I saw Mr. Barnes lose his temper at me was when I put on the hoist a block that had been overchipped. The rock was already cracked a little, and when I tried to smooth it up, a chunk two inches wide come off. But in a big block that didn't seem to matter. We could turn it inside and no one would know. I didn't see Mr. Barnes come up behind me as I was fixing the ropes.

"You know *perfectly* well that won't do," he said. He tapped the rock with his cane.

"We can turn that side in," I said.

"Jones," he said, "I'm disappointed in you. Hiding shoddy work. Very disappointed."

I was taken by surprise. Nobody had talked to me like that since I was a little boy. It was not what he said but the tone of his voice that was so shocking and humiliating. I had heard him scold others but it was different when he turned his scorn on me.

"Jones, if you can't meet our standards you can go back to your chimneys," he said. "Go back to your stick and mud. No one requires your presence here."

"I'm sorry, sir," I said. And immediately I was more humiliated to have apologized. It was as though his manner and his rage had pulled the apology out of me with no decision on my part, as if I had been hypnotized by his glare and his anger and had no choice.

"Well then," he said. "You'll get rid of that block and go back and cut another."

It was after he strode away that the anger and hate began rising in me, pushing aside the surprise and embarrassment. He has no right to talk to me that way, I kept saying to myself. Everybody on the job, including the slaves, heard him tell me off for almost nothing. It was like a public whipping. And not only had I felt helpless to defend myself, I had actually apologized to that limey lord-over-creation. That's why my grandpappy fit the Revolution, to get rid of such strutting peacocks, I said to myself.

"Massa Barnes sho like to have his say," the harmonica player said as we carried the hammer and chisels back to the quarry to cut the new block.

He's going to tell off one man too many, I thought to myself, and end up with a hammer in his brain. All that morning while I was chipping at the new block, measuring and marking, sweating with the excitement of my anger as well as the work, I kept running through my mind plans for revenge. The thing I wanted most was to sink my hammer through his top hat into his skull. I saw the silk collapse and blood spurt as the bones crumbled. I chuckled with pleasure at the image.

And then I saw myself doing it all with my hands, fighting fair.

"A fist in the gut and a knee in the face when they double over," my cousin Nary liked to say. While chipping that extra block I must have kneed Barnes in the face a thousand times and seen the blood gush from his nose. I hammered until my eyes were filled with sweat and my breath was coming short. I hammered like it was Barnes's head I was cutting down to size.

Of course what some fellows would do was just walk away from a job where they talked to you that bad, then come back with their gun and shoot the rawhiding foreman. And I saw myself coming back with my shotgun and filling Barnes's belly with buckshot. It would take him days to die of peritonitis as he swelled up and screamed with the pain.

I worked so hard I was plumb exhausted by dinnertime when I had to walk back down to the bridge to get my dinner bucket. And as I walked I thought I was so mad because I didn't know how to talk back to Barnes. He had took me by surprise and the cat got my tongue. And it was only words. Sticks and stones, I kept saying, sticks and stones. His insistence on discipline and authority was what made Barnes such a good builder. I had learned a lot about masonry and also how to run a job, how you de-

mand that everybody meet the standards. By the time I got to the
bridge I was feeling better about the whole thing. I got my dinner
bucket from the spring and set down on the bank with Delosier
and the other masons. It was midsummer, and the jarflies was
loud in the trees all around.

"They do sound like rattlesnakes," somebody said.

"Except a rattlesnake's not up in an oak tree."

"You can't always tell where a sound's coming from in the
woods, especially if they's a big rock nearby."

Barnes come out of the little shed he used for an office. The
men lived in tents, but he boarded in the Lindsay house down
the river. He kept all his plans and instruments in the little office.

"Jones," he said. "We won't need that extra block after all.
We've already used the block you chipped on the inside." Then
he strolled away toward the spring. It was so hot he had taken his
jacket off, and his armpits was wet.

I was instantly mad all over again, that he had made me waste
a morning's work on that extra block. I imagined sinking an ax
into his spine as he walked away.

"I never knowed him to change his mind before," Furman said.

"He could have changed it before I wasted a morning's work,"
I said.

"Don't get riled up again," Delosier said. "That's the closest
I've ever seen Mr. Barnes come to an apology."

That evening I went back to dressing blocks before they was
hoisted into place, and was more careful than ever not to over-
chip a corner or side. But I didn't like Barnes anymore, and I
wished the job was already over.

When I woke up on the turnpike my head hurt like thunder.
My pockets was empty. I looked around for my dinner bucket.
They had throwed it down the bank, and my ten-dollar gold piece
was nowhere in sight. I set back down where I had crawled to
and held my head, which throbbed like it was in a vise. After a
whole spring and summer's work I had nothing to show. Clara

had put the corn in pretty much by herself, with a little help from the kids and from my brother Joe. She was now drying peaches and apples on the rooftop, and on sheets spread out on the bank behind the house. The stock would have less fodder for the winter, and there was no money for shoes or coffee. I'd have to find another job building a chimney or springhouse wall. I had wasted half a year and all I had to show for it was a bloody knot on my head.

"You seen the big ceremony," Clara would say. "And the rich folks going up to Flat Rock for their banquet. I guess that's your pay. You can tell everybody that."

I was just going to set awhile, to catch my breath and stop my head from swimming. They was tracks all around me in the dirt, but I knowed I could never identify them big rough brothers from their tracks, which could have been made by anybody's big brogans.

My head hurt so bad I thought it must be cracked. And I felt thirsty. There was a spring in the bend about a mile ahead. I'd have to stumble up there if I was to have a drink. I was about to gather my strength and try to stand when I heard somebody holler. The mountainside was steep there and it was hard to tell where the sound come from. But while I was looking and holding the back of my head, this cow come around the bend ahead, this big red cow, and then another, and two more, and three or four others, and still more behind them. Boys with switches run along beside them. They just kept coming down the turnpike like a flash flood of beef, hooking and slobbering.

"Stand aside," one of the boys called. "Hey, mister, stand aside."

I stumbled to my feet and backed over the edge of the road and stood in the leaves as they trotted past. There was men behind popping their whips and the boys with hickories run along side hollering "Aye, aye" when one of the animals slowed or started to turn aside.

You never seen so many cattle. They must have passed for twenty minutes, raising the dust and bawling, lifting their tails and spraying the ruts. Finally along come the end of it, a wagon loaded with cooking gear and blankets.

"Where you coming from?" I asked the driver.

"Why, friend, we've driv these cattle all the way from Tennessee," the man said.

"Where you going?" I said.

"Wherever they buy cattle," he said. "Augusta, maybe Atlanta."

Then they was gone and the dust was settling in the late summer light coming through the trees.

Son, I stepped back into the road and started up the mountain, but hadn't took more than ten steps when somebody hollered behind me, "Step aside, sir. Step aside."

I looked back and there was the prettiest carriage you ever seen with a black driver all in livery carrying his long stiff whip. They was lanterns of polished brass and glass on the corners and shiny black fenders. You never seen people dressed up like them inside, ladies with parasols and dresses so low you could nearly see the nipples on their bosoms, and men in top hats and silk cravats. And behind that carriage was other carriages, and buggies and a whole bunch of wagons carrying supplies and servants. It was some big party from the Low Country coming up for a picnic in the mountains. I've heard Fremont, the general and governor of California, was in that party. He was just a boy then. I stood back and let them pass, and they ignored me just like I was invisible.

Then when I did get started up the turnpike finally, stepping around cowpiles and horse apples, my strength coming back a little at a time, I met more drovers coming down the mountain. It was like they had opened a floodgate and flocks of sheep came along, baaing and pushing and jumping over each other, turning the road to dirty wool. And then a drove of hogs came, nosing and grunting, squealing when prodded by boys with sticks. I thought I had seen it all, but just then around the bend come a flock of turkeys, all gobbling and squawking. And behind them a bigger flock of geese come waddling, driven by more boys and followed by an old woman who carried a sack on her back.

"We's come all the way from Kentucky," she said.

Finally I thought I had the road to myself. I knowed I'd have to hurry if I got home by milking time. Clara was going to be mad, but there was no point in putting off the bad news.

"Watch out, watch out, sir," somebody called behind me.

It was a man in a buggy pulled by a shiny Morgan that just clipped along. He had a sack on the seat beside him. And I recognized Sam the peddler from Spartanburg. He used to come around with a pack on his back, and we almost always bought cloth and buttons and such from him and asked him to stay for dinner. And now he was driving a fine buggy with a carriage horse.

After he passed it seemed late in the evening. The road was already nearly in shadow. They was a buckeye laying in the tracks, but I couldn't tell if it was mine. It had been stepped on by a cow and I let it go. But I seen something shiny in the dirt ahead. It was my light mason's hammer. Them big rough boys had dropped it there as they run away. They didn't have no use for a mason's hammer, and thought it was too heavy to carry. I picked it up and wiped the grit off the handle and head before starting again for home.

Jill McCorkle

WAITING FOR HARD TIMES TO END

(from *The Southern Review*)

I haven't heard from my sister, Rhonda, in over a week now and I'm starting to get worried. My boss at Thriftway Grocery, which is where I work after school, tells me there's no reason for me to worry, that he bets Rhonda has better things to do than to sit and write out a card to me. "I know what kind Rhonda is," he said and laughed; I don't like the way he laughs or the way his bushy eyebrows go up when he talks about Rhonda. "You know what kind Rhonda is, now don't you, Bunny?" he asked, and I just shook my head and went back to counting up the cans of B&M Baked Beans.

I'm tired of being called Bunny but nobody in this town is going to change and call me by my right name, which is Saralyn. I've never minded that Rhonda called me Bunny because she made it up years ago because of the way my teeth look and because she said I always look scared and on the verge of bolting off. I do feel scared sometimes but I'm not always sure why. I'd be a whole lot less scared if I'd just hear from Rhonda. She left home two years ago when I was just fourteen and I have missed her ever since. We had some times, me and Rhonda. She used to make up my eyes and take me down to Ho Jo's where she was the hostess. "This is my baby sister," she would tell people, and

I'd sit up straight on my stool and nod at the person. "She's the sweetest," Rhonda would say about me and it made me feel so good. Sometimes Rhonda would buy me dinner and we'd sit at one of the tables and let somebody wait on us. The man who ran Ho Jo's would always want to sit with us and Rhonda would say, "Another time, Bill," then wink, so she didn't hurt his feelings. "This is mine and Bunny's night." Then when it started getting late, she'd put me in a taxi. "I don't want somebody trying to pick you up. Tell Mother I'll be home later after I'm through working," she would say and I would and my mother would get red in the face and shake her head, mad that I had on blue eyeshadow and was only thirteen. "Don't you be like her," Mama said.

I haven't seen Rhonda in two years, but almost every single day I have gotten a postcard. I'm the only person in my family that keeps up with Rhonda; nobody wants to hear what she has to say. Sometimes I get scared that they might not give me my card, so that's why I'm always there when the mailman comes and why I did not go to 4-H camp last year when everybody wanted me to. They wanted me to mainly because I had sewed the best dress and they thought I'd win our group a prize. I sew pretty dresses, all right, but they don't look good on me because of my shape; I don't have a shape. I have made Rhonda a pink silky party dress which I'm saving for when she comes home.

I love the cards that she sends; no two have ever been the same. I guess that's why I hate holidays so much—because the mail doesn't come. The only other times that Rhonda has not written to me for several days have been during what she calls "hard times." When I spread all my cards on the bedroom floor, I can see that there have been quite a few hard times but never one that lasted over a week. They'll start back real soon now. The first card to come after a hard time always says, "WHEW!" I'm expecting to get one of those any day now. Rhonda will say *Whew!* and tell me what happened.

The first card I ever got was two days after she left home. She had promised she would send one; she had hugged me so tight and told me that she would always keep in touch. "You are what makes it all bearable for me, Bunny," she had said. "You know that I love you the most?" I nodded and then she was gone and I did like she said. I didn't tell anybody that I had seen her; I didn't tell that she came by the Thriftway and had gotten herself a ride out of town with a man in a pickup. "There's a man in South Carolina that I need to see," she had told me. "He's in love with me and I need to decide what I'm going to do." She told me that I'd see one day that having a man in your life changes a lot of things. "But no man will ever change how I feel for you." I stood in front of Thriftway and waved until I couldn't see her blond hair flying out the window, couldn't see which way that truck had gone.

The first card has a picture of the Honeymoon Bed in the Honeymoon Suite of Pedro's Motel down in South of the Border, South Carolina. It is a beautiful bed with a rich-looking pink satin spread and little pillows, mirrors all around. I have never been to South of the Border, but I've heard of it, heard of fireworks and putt-putt ranges and gift shops and restaurants. I could've gone with the 4-H group last summer, but I passed because they were going to go on to Myrtle Beach and I would've missed the mail for three days. Rhonda isn't there anymore. When I first got this card I kept thinking about how wonderful it would be if I was there, how wonderful it would be if I was sitting on a stool right there near Rhonda while she introduced me to people.

Hey Bunny! I'm Mrs. Elwood Smith, now. We have been married one hour. I hate you aren't here with me. You know you're my maid of honor and if I had known I was getting married, I would have bought you a beautiful dress (and grown-up hose and high heels!) and had you here with me. But sometimes things just happen real fast. (You will know what I mean soon enough.) Just remember, you haven't lost a sister but gained a brother! (And you will like him better than Ned. HA!) I'm gonna live down here of course. I'll miss you but don't you worry! You'll be on a bus and visiting real soon. Elwood is in the shower. (Weddings make him sweat, he says. HA!) He is a card. You will love him like he will love you. Please tell Mama and Ho Jo's that I won't be back! Thanx 10,000 pesos! *R*

Nobody was happy for Rhonda and Elwood Smith like I was. Mama and my brothers, Ned and Billy, just frowned and shook their heads. Ned and Billy are both older than Rhonda and they're married. They married the Townsend sisters, who Rhonda always calls the "Gruesome Twosome." "She'll be back," I heard Mama tell Ned and Billy. "She don't have a pot to pee in."

"Well, well, well," that man at Ho Jo's said. "Wonder what it's costing little Rhonda Sue to live down there?"

The second card gave me all the answers, but nobody even wanted to hear about it. The Townsend sisters took me to buy some clothes, said I shouldn't be wearing Rhonda's hand-me-downs. I tried to tell them it was okay.

Bunny! Little Bunny! All of the clothes I left in my closet are for you! Elwood bought me a whole new wardrobe. See the dress Lady Di is wearing on the front of this card? Well, I have a black one *just* like it. Elwood doesn't look like Charles, though, thank God. HA! He has little ears, looks more like Al Pacino, you know? I hope one day you find someone like him and can move to a nice place like where we live. I go to the beach near about every day. I have a wonderful tan. I'll look into bus schedules to see when you can come. Elwood's paying so don't work too hard at the Thriftway and *don't* let any boys do to you what I told you they might try! Take it easy baby, *Rhonda*

Mama and the Townsends cleaned out Rhonda's closet and threw everything away. "She'll deserve that if she thinks she can show her face here again," Mama said, and I took Rhonda's blue-jean jacket with the diamond-looking things sewn in and hid it. I don't know why she hadn't taken that with her except maybe she wanted me to have it.

I can shuffle Rhonda's cards up and read 'em like little tiny stories or I can put them all in the right order and read them like a real long letter. That's what I do at night while Mama's watching TV. Right now I feel like shuffling and trying to remember where each one fits in the big piece.

Hard Times, Bunny. Forgive me for not writing. Enjoy being a little girl (you know what I mean) because being grown ain't all nylon hose and eyeshadow. The little girl on this card made me think of you. It made me cry. Look at her digging in the sand with her little pail. She is at Myrtle Beach and soon you will be, too. I want to wait until Elwood comes home, though. Stick your tongue out at the Gruesome Twosome for me and tell Mama, "Smile! Can't crack your face more than it's cracked!" Just kidding. HA! Love, *Rhonda*

Happy Birthday! Sweet Fifteen. I wish I could be there. I bought you a beautiful present but am going to save it for when you come. You keep asking *when* and all I know is that it depends on my job. I am moving right up in this world, work long hours. When you come, I can take off. I know what I was doing at fifteen and I hope you know what you're doing! Got a fella? I bet you do! I bet you look like the front of this card. I bet you don't even look like Bunny anymore! Buddy says, "Blow hard!" (He means the candles of course.) I'll call you this weekend when it's cheap. *Rhonda* P.S. Buddy is my neighbor, a real card! HA!

I turn that card over and stare at the picture of Marilyn Monroe, bent over, her hands keeping that dress from blowing all the way up. Boy, Rhonda couldn't really think I'd ever look like that, but Rhonda kind of looks like it, boobs and all. I had planned to tell her that but she didn't call that weekend. Buddy had been in a wreck, she wrote me later. He got twenty stitches in his head.

"Is she still with that man?" Mama asked me once and I just said, "No." I didn't tell her how Elwood had taken all of the money that she had saved and left. I didn't tell how Rhonda had herself a job as a restaurant manager and was making so much money she didn't know what to do with it except travel. She traveled all over the country, all the places you'd ever want to see. One of my favorite cards is of the Grand Canyon and it is beautiful. It says, "It'll take your breath away!"

Didn't take my breath! Still breathing, still smoking, too. HA! You're going to love this place, Bunny. I'm thinking I might settle here. I'll fly you out. OK? It's sweet what you said in your letter (before Elwood robbed me!) about how you've made me a gift. Just wait until you see all the gifts I have for you! They fill up one whole room of the condo I'm staying in. It'll be like Christmas when we get together. I'm glad you like that boy— what's his name?—in your 4-H group. Let him know you like him, you know? Take my advice. They will be lined up for you real soon like they are for me here. Whoops! There's Bronco (a nickname) right now. Love, *R*

I still don't like to think about the time I got that card. It's been over a year now, but I've never been able to look at Rudy Thompson since. I waited for him after the 4-H meeting. I remember it all like it's in a movie or a postcard. I was wearing Rhonda's blue-jean jacket and I had on some hoop earrings and some lipstick that I had put on in the bathroom right after our meeting. I had just been told that I had the best piece of sewing and Rudy had gotten a blue ribbon for his pet pig. "Hi there," I said when Rudy came out. I tried to say it the way Rhonda would; I let my eyes droop a little like Rhonda used to do to that man at Ho Jo's when she wanted the night off. "I need to talk to you," I whispered, because that's what Rhonda on the New Mexico postcard had suggested. "He'll have to step closer," she had written. "So wear some cologne so you don't smell like Thriftway."

"Yeah?" Rudy stepped closer and I felt my heart beating so fast when he did. "What is it?" He has green green eyes and kind of rusty-looking hair. He was wearing a belt buckle that had a big bull on it.

"I like your belt buckle," I whispered and closed my eyes, leaned back against a tree like Rhonda would do. "It's sexy." That was the part I had practiced the longest. Rhonda had said it always worked for her.

"What?" Rudy acted like he was frozen and it made me have to stand up straight, to smear that lipstick off a little with the back of my hand. "Bunny?" he asked, making the most horrible face like he'd been expecting Coca-Cola and got buttermilk. Then they were all there, everybody, listening in, Rudy's face so red I thought he might kill me. "Sexy?" a boy called out. "Wooo Wooo Rudy!" All the girls were just staring at me like I might have been green and I wished I was green. I wished I was dead, but more than anything, I wished I was with Rhonda in one of those fancy motels where she likes to go, places with big bathtubs for a bubble bath and champagne, though Rhonda says I have to wait a little longer, maybe a year, before champagne. I ran home as fast as I could; that word, *sexy*, sounded in my head over and over like the principal at school on the P.A. system or like what Rhonda had described when she was in that bar that got raided that time. Rhonda said the police had done that, called everybody out, took everybody to the police station, and made them spend the night. "And there I was just minding my own business," she had written. "What ignorant pigs! They made me take my clothes off! HA! I know why, too—a cheap thrill for the deprived slobs who work there."

I have never been able to look Rudy in the eye since. It has taken a whole year for people to stop teasing me. I'd be in the cafeteria line and I'd hear somebody say, "It's so sexy." Sometimes Rhonda doesn't stay in the same place long enough to get my cards, but she did get the one I sent that told what happened. She wrote me right back, too. She sent a card that she must have

saved from South of the Border way back, because it had a picture of that giant-sized Mexican Pedro which I still have not seen.
The 4-H people who can talk to me without laughing told me
that you can see that giant Pedro for miles. Anyway, now I don't
even have to see it for real because I've got the picture:

Bunny. I'm sorry that what's-his-name didn't bite the hook.
They don't always, you know? Why I had a man break up with
me just last week. (Of course, I had threatened to tell his wife. I
hear that's what Marilyn Monroe did to the Kennedy boys so I
figured what the hell?) DON'T mess with married ones. They
are *never* right in the head. That should just let you know that
what's-his-name is *dumb* like most of the men in that town. I
hate your boss. Did I ever tell you? He tried to get me to you-
know-what once and I was insulted. If he ever makes up bad
things about me, that's why. I'll be so glad when you can move
and be with me. Then you'll meet some nice people. Love, R

One of the funniest cards has Mona Lisa on the front and
Rhonda had written: "Well, I see Mama is *trying* to smile." And
then another has a cartoon of a two-headed Martian and the
Martian is disagreeing with himself. One head says, "I want to
go out," and the other head says, "I want to stay home." Below it
is printed, "Ever have trouble making up your mind? Two heads
are not better than one." Rhonda had written: "I see the Townsends haven't changed a bit! HA!" Of course, I would never show
any of those cards. I keep hoping that when I move and live with
Rhonda, Mama and Ned and Billy will start to be nice to her.

Another funny card has a picture of this dog peeing on a
tobacco plant and it says, "Have your cigarettes been tasting
funny?" Rhonda had written, "You better not be smoking. If you
do, you will love it and never ever stop. Jim and I go through
five packs a day." When I got that one I smoked one cigarette.
I hadn't liked it, but it had made me feel kind of grown up and
close to Rhonda. It was just last summer that I smoked it. I took
one out of my boss's pack and then I sat out back of Thriftway
on an orange crate and smoked it. It was kind of nice in a way be-

cause I could hear people talking inside and hear the big freezer humming, Willie Nelson singing on the radio, but I felt real safe. "You can always count on me, Bunny," Rhonda had just written on a beautiful silver valentine card.

But now I'm looking for those cards that came right after Hard Times, so maybe I can figure out what's keeping Rhonda so long from writing this time. There's the one after Elwood robbed her, the one after she had to take her clothes off and stay in the jail, and here's another one. It's from the Statute of Liberty in New York City. Rhonda had circled the blond head of a woman that's in the crowd looking, and from the back it really does look like her. "That's me!" she had written and then on the back:

Hey Bunny! Whew! I have finally seen the light. (Get it?) I've had hard times, have decided men aren't worth the trouble. You'll see. All they want is to get in your pants or steal your money. Don't fall for the tricks. I've been trashed too many times but now I'm starting over: good job/new friends. By the time you graduate (and you do need that diploma), I'll be ready for you to move in. Right now I'm staying with a friend who says I really should be an actress! Imagine!! This city has everything! I have a whole new life. I don't eat meat. Love and Liberty, *Rhonda*

I love the New York cards the best. They are so funny and happy. The pictures have all these bridges and lights and the Empire State building, places you only hear about. But there are still other hard-time cards. I had gone a week without hearing from her and then I got this one that has people at Niagara Falls. The water is so beautiful, falling there; there's a rainbow in the spray, and people are just standing there in yellow raincoats like the Safety Patrol people wear, standing so close to the little fence there before it drops off. I love the picture and I remember how glad I was to see it after having waited so long.

This is not a honeymoon so don't even think it! Randy (he's a good friend) came with me. I don't know what I would

have done that last week in New York without him! He saved
me. That's why I haven't written. Hard Times, but thanks to
Randy, I'm okay. He is such a card, looks real "sexy" in his
yellow raincoat. How are you? Knocking the boys dead? I bet
you are . . . more later. Love, *R*

After Randy ran off without a word, after she had taken care
of him, "practically supported him" for six months, there was
another lapse. That's why I was so worried at the sophomore
dance. I don't know if I would've had a good time anyway; I
went with Sandy Scott, who has teeth bigger than mine and a
neck like a giraffe. I wasn't going to go at all but Rhonda always
told me that I should go places "because you never know who
you'll meet. You can go on a date. It doesn't mean you have to
marry him! My God, I'd have been married a hundred times by
now!" Sandy Scott asked me to dance one time and the rest of
the night we just sat at our table and watched other people. He
folded his napkin in and out like an accordian and told me about
his daddy's heifer who had won a prize in the state fair. I guess he
had heard what everybody else had heard, that I had liked Rudy
that time. Everybody knew that Rudy's daddy *always* has prize
hogs and cows. Rudy was out on that floor slow-dancing and
it made me feel funny inside to watch him; I guess I felt funny
because of all that Rhonda told me about what men will try to
do, and because I hadn't heard from her. When I finally did hear,
she was back down in South Carolina and had gotten a job in a
Myrtle Beach bar. "It's a long way from Ho Jo's," she had said
and I was so relieved. When Sandy Scott called and asked me to
go see *Return of the Jedi*, I went, but I didn't meet anybody else
and I didn't have a very good time.
    I think that Rhonda has probably moved again and not had
time to write, or maybe she's been suntanning, or going to that
amusement park she's told me about. I close my eyes and try to
imagine all of the pictures in my mind before going to sleep. I
see Rhonda and a handsome man riding the Ferris wheel, while

I stand on the ground and look up at them, a huge teddy bear in my arms that a boy like Rudy has won for me over at the shooting range. Rhonda waves her hand, her yellow hair flying in the wind every time they hit the top, and me and that boy wave back, all of us so happy to be there together down in Myrtle Beach. I hear my door crack open and I know my mama's standing there like she does every night. She's checking to make sure I'm in my bed and have not run off like Rhonda. "She's like a prison guard," Rhonda told me years ago. "She will never get over the fact that she couldn't hold on to Daddy." I don't remember my daddy at all; I only know what Rhonda has told me, that he was good-looking and full of life and it would have killed him to stay there. "She's not going to keep me either," Rhonda had said. "And don't you worry, Bunny. I'll come rescue you one day." Now I hear Mama shuffling down the hall and it makes me wish that things were different for all of us. Sometimes I feel like I don't understand Mama at all.

"Did he touch you?" she'd asked when I got home from the dance. I shook my head and then she was crying and holding onto me. "I'm sorry," she kept saying, but I'm not sure for what. Maybe because Rhonda was gone.

It's been two weeks now since I've heard from Rhonda. I'm sitting out back on my orange crate and my boss doesn't even care. He's been asking about Rhonda lately, asking in a way where he doesn't laugh and his eyebrows don't go that funny way. "Where do you guess she is?" he asked just before I came out here. I told him I bet she has a new job in a new city, or maybe she's run off and gotten married. I hear the bell at the front of the store ring so I know I need to be getting back in so I can ring the person up. I'm just ready for the day to be over so I can get home and check the mail. I bet it'll be there, some funny message about the Townsend girls or Mama smiling.

"Hey," I hear, but I can't see through the wire mesh of the screen door to know who it is. Before I can ask, Rudy Thompson steps out here and leans against the building where somebody has spray-painted "Go to hell" in lopsided letters. "Haven't seen you at 4-H lately," he says. "Or school." That's true, because I haven't been in three days—been going down to Sikes Pond and sitting instead. "You been sick?"

"What's it to you?" I ask, remembering that that's what Rhonda had said to a man one time. Rhonda said, "That silenced the jerk!" I must have done it wrong because Rudy just shrugs and his face turns pink. Now I don't know what to say so I just wave a stick in the dirt and wait for him to leave. *They will always leave you. One minute he's there and the next minute he's gone.* How did he know I wasn't at school?

"I was just hoping you weren't sick." He steps forward and puts his shoe up on the orange crate; his foot is so close, I could retie his shoe if I wanted. *Oh yeah, they love you when they can get something. In your pants and in your wallet.* I shake my head and, for the first time in a year, I look Rudy Thompson in the face. *You got to learn to stare them down. Get the upper hand.* His eyes are just as green as before, as green as that Atlantic Ocean, Myrtle Beach, South Carolina, the Grand Strand. Where is she? "I been wanting to talk to you," he says and looks away. "You remember that time . . ." I know what he's going to say and I don't even want to hear it.

"No, I don't remember," I tell him before he can finish. *Sometimes I play dumb for Elwood because he thinks it's cute. HA!*

"Well, I wanted to tell you I was sorry that I didn't stick up for you," he says. "I just didn't know what to say. I mean, you looked so grown up that day and all, and I had never seen you look like that." *Wear my blue-jean jacket and make up your eyes like I taught you. That'll get him! I bet one of these days you look just like me, Little Bunny! (Hope you don't mind. HA!)*

I see the mailman's truck go by and I know his routine so well; he'll be at my house in fifteen minutes. "I gotta go," I say, and, standing, I take off my Thriftway apron.

"I wanted to ask you to go to the movies," he says, and I don't have time to think. I have fourteen minutes to check out with my boss and run home. "I've been wanting to ask you but . . ."

"I gotta go," I say. "Really, I have to go." I open the screen door, my mind on Rhonda and the card. If my mama gets it, it'll be gone.

"Will you think about it?" he asks, his forehead wrinkling, and I nod, once again looking at those clear green eyes. *Keep 'em guessing*. I have twelve minutes. "Can I call you?"

"Yes," I say and run through the store, the buzz of the freezer so loud, my steps so loud.

"Hey, what's the hurry?" my boss asks. He looks to the back of the store where Rudy is standing and still looking confused. Shaking his head, my boss laughs like he knows everything, but I don't take the time to hear what he's gotta say. I throw down my apron and I am gone, running so fast down the long street, the sun low and gold behind the big tree branches. Rudy Thompson's face keeps popping in my mind, but I don't have time to think about it all right now. *Sometimes people will ask you out just to use you.* I turn the corner just in time to see the mail truck stop in front of my house. I run faster and pretend that I don't see Mama out there on the front porch. She is walking down the sidewalk, but I get there first and reach my hand in.

"I need to talk to you, Saralyn," Mama says, and I wait for her to turn around so I can see if there's a card for me. "Why are you so eager for the mail?" she has asked before and I always come up with one reason or another. I haven't shown or told her about a card in months now, but I know she knows. I know because every time Rhonda's name comes up, which isn't real often, they all look at me like I know something. They have tricked me a few times by saying things like, "I bet Rhonda is in Canada," only to have me slip and give the real answer. I have quit talking.

"There's no card from her," Mama says and I turn slowly, so angry. "Rhonda has gotten herself killed."

* * *

I wait a long time before I go inside; I wait until it's dark and the light there in the living room comes on. When I get inside the doorway, I hear the policeman saying that they got no traces, that Rhonda was there in the Sleepy Pelican Motel somewhere near Georgia. I listen while he tells all about it: looked like there had been a struggle, looked like they had been drinking. Shot there in the heart. I don't want to even get a picture in my mind.

Nobody at school has said a thing about Rhonda to me. My boss just said he was sorry, real sorry. "Let it be a lesson, Sara-lyn," my mama said, and I wanted to be called Bunny so bad I thought I'd die. I went to the movies with Rudy Thompson and afterwards we went and sat down near the pond. He didn't ask me about Rhonda but I knew he wanted to know. Everybody wanted to know. *They will use you to get what they want. I can't wait for you to get out of that hole.* I kept hearing Rhonda talking to me the whole time that Rudy and I sat there. He held my hand and it made me feel so funny all over like maybe I was doing something wrong. He asked me why I never went on the school trips or club trips out of town, and I said because I didn't want to go anywhere, didn't need to go anywhere. "I know what it all looks like," I told him, and then I saw the real pictures, the motel room where they said she lived, the way they found her without any clothes at all. It made me feel cold all over and I told Rudy I had to go home. I told Rudy if he was after me to use me up that he better forget it. "I like you, Bunny," he said and I wanted so bad to believe him.

Rudy still calls me; he called just this morning to ask me if I wanted to ride down to South Carolina with him and his mama and daddy. "We're going to the beach for the weekend," he said. "You can tell your mama that my whole family's going." I imagined me and Rudy on that Ferris wheel, the stuffed bear, putt-putt ranges. But it was all too close.

"I've got to work," I told him. "But how about we go to the

show when you get back?" Rudy paused like he was disappointed, but then he said he thought he knew why I didn't want to go down there. He said he wanted to go with me, steady, just me, and I said all right.

Now I'm in my checkout and Henry (my boss) is sitting over on the counter. He's been real sweet to me lately, told me that he was sorry for things he had said about Rhonda, said he used to really like her and that she wouldn't have anything to do with him. "I would have done her right," he said, and part of me believed that.

"So, what's new with you, Bunny?" he asks, leaning back against the wall.

"Going steady with Rudy Thompson," I say. It's the first time I've said it outside the house. My sisters-in-law thought it was worth a Chinese dinner in Clemmonsville. My mama said she'd like for him to come by real soon.

"Well, well," Henry says and laughs. "I thought you looked different these days, all fixed up and smiling."

"Yeah," I say. *Having a man in your life will change a lot of things.* I look away from Henry to the street where the mail truck is passing right now. I feel myself ready to run from the store. Sometimes I keep thinking that I will get home and reach in that box and it will be there. "Whew!" it will say and there will be pictures of all the places she's been. I still feel that way and sometimes I wonder if I always will. Sometimes I think I'd just rather stay right here and get the pictures of all those places, the lights and the bridges. And then all of a sudden I will see the other picture, the real picture that never did and never will be on a postcard, that motel room, that night. *No man will ever change how I feel about you.* I wish I could tell her she was wrong. I wait for the mail truck to move out of my sight and then I tell Henry to call me Saralyn. "That's my real name," I say.

Thomas Phillips Brewer

BLACK CAT BONE

(from *The Antioch Review*)

I look at the picture of Herndon Avenue in Mobile taped to the wall beside my desk. Poor working-white street. There are two people in the picture, relaxed in a posture that comes only from years of practice in a tropical climate. She's sixty, wearing a sleeveless cotton-print housedress, bare legs spread comfortably apart, feet on the wooden porch boards; the man beside her has salt-and-pepper hair, and a short-sleeved checked shirt. They're sitting in two chairs of six lined up in front of the windows with blackened wire screens. The chairs are metal, painted aqua. Metal chairs are the only kind that hold up for any time here; it rains more in Mobile than in any other city in the country.

I look at the picture of Herndon Avenue and think about Roscoe's nephew. I look at the sinuous branches of the live oaks reaching across the lawns, dipping low, some low enough for children to clamber on, and wonder if it was one of these gently curving boughs, the grain twisted like steel rope inside, that Roscoe's nephew was hanging from the morning they found him. The picture in the paper three years ago showed the toes of his sneakers brushing the low St. Augustine grass. I didn't save that one. It looked like every other picture of the hanged—the apologetic nod, the closed eyes, the features cast in indifference with no mark of the final agony.

I look down the peaceful concrete street in the picture; pickup trucks are pulled up in the driveways and the men are home from work, eating supper inside where the lights are just coming on, or in the backyards drinking a cold beer. It's civil twilight and will be until eight-thirty or nine, when the light is gone from the sky; soon more people will come out on the porches to chat, to catch a little breeze at the end of the day, and look at the sky and say, "Wonder if it'll come a storm tonight." It must be an illusion—these neatly trimmed azaleas lining the walks to the front doors, these calm old pillars on the broad porches. One morning this street gave forth a corpse just by the sidewalk to greet the newsboy and the early morning workers leaving for the shipyard. And the dead boy was real; real as the black power poles, studded with fragile splinters from the climbers' iron crampons, as real as this old brown concrete street, roughened with its coarse aggregate of quartz and clamshells.

Swiveling my chair, I gaze at the other men in the drafting room: they grew up on streets like these. Neville is hunched down in his chair, meditatively patting the back of his new haircut. Although he's forty, it's the same haircut he had when he was a freshman at Auburn, and the same unlined face, quick to smile at a quip, or an overheard phone conversation, or a lopsided walk. On his lap is a green three-part folder with a structural steel bid; he's studying an *Organic Gardening* spread open over the handwritten columns of bent plate, and stud, and wide flange sizes. Beyond Neville is Ken, sitting straight up, jiggling his leg, phone in hand, talking rapidly (or what passes for speed in these parts), and writing on a pad. He's hard at it, although it's almost quitting time. The walrus mustache that almost completely covers his mouth moves nervously up and down. Mr. Energy, everybody calls him, or in saltier moments, Wonder Boy. ("That sapsucker don't solve no problems 'cept the ones he makes.") I look at these peaceful men for signs of the violent death that Herndon Avenue rendered up. And I see Neville's Hushpuppies run over at the heels; I see Ken, still talking on the phone, pick up a little steel bracket someone in the factory made for him—it's to hold down the boom on his sailboat when he trails it to the little lakes he likes to curve around on with his six-year-old daughter.

Of course, I don't exactly add up to them either. This picture I have on the wall of a second-rate street in the city where we live—what possible use could it be? It's gratuitous, absurd. But they don't have a problem with it, either. And since my speech has slowed down and smoothed out, they've forgotten I'm a Yankee—I didn't grow up in this city where I've lived for eight years; I'm still reinventing it in my imagination. I wear funny-looking hats, don't know who the characters are on "M*A*S*H," live in sin with my girlfriend, but it's okay with them. I also tell a lot of lies about my fishing, talk about what a horse's ass the boss is, come to work with a hangover. So everything's all right. They like to get along. It's not the same as the big city up north where I was raised; there, you're continually assigned to categories and defined by a thousand things—your clothes, your car, your last name, your first name, your school, your company, your wife, your necktie, the length of your collarpoints.

"Almost that time." It's the boss, slouched in the doorway at the other end of the room, making his last seat check of the day. I look at him with the usual dull disgust, my features blank. His tall skinny body fills the door frame, his polyester tie curving inward on his hollow chest. He's got a white hard hat on—he's been out in the factory. "I checked the modules," he tells us. He goes out there to chew and spit; he's embarrassed to hawk tobacco juice in his trash can.

At the sound of the boss's voice, Neville smoothly flips over the cardboard leaf in his folder, covering the magazine and revealing drawings of bolted steel-beam connections. "You found them?" Neville asks the boss, and chortles. He's telling the boss: you're so dim-witted you can't find the project we've been working on for the last two months. But Neville's smiling face is so guileless the boss doesn't get it, as always.

The boss drops into a seat in front of Mr. Energy's desk. "Oh, I found them all right. We're gonna make some changes. Gotta lot of work to do." He looks at Mr. Energy to include him in his comment. Mr. Energy continues his animated phone conversation and knee jiggling; he glances at the boss like an errant blip on his screen and looks back down at the pad he's scribbling on.

"Oh Lord, have mercy, sweet Jesus, have mercy." I hear Roscoe's mournful spiritual out in the hallway. The men in the drafting room look up and smile at each other. Roscoe appears in the doorway, pushing his janitor cart, humming the sad minor thirds and flatted sevenths. His six-foot frame is slightly stooped and his woolly hair is gray around the temples. He walks toward Mr. Energy's desk, a dust rag in his deep brown hand. The hand is very large and makes the rag look dainty. The hand is lumpy, and there are knots and gnarls on its back—badly aimed injections, and abscesses healed thirty years ago. But only Roscoe and I know that.

"Roscoe, is that your car out there?" The boss has been gazing out the second-floor window and sees Roscoe's old Electra 225 with the red tennis ball on the aerial and the gray splotches of spray paint.

"Where? Sure enough is. I told my wife to come down and bring me my medicine. I forgot my medicine. You ever meet my wife?"

"No. Is that her?" The boss stands up from his seat for a better look. Since the view is almost straight down from the second-floor window through the windshield, all that can be seen is two wide thighs in green pants, with big brown hands resting on them. Later, the boss will giggle about how fat Roscoe's wife is. I think about the boss's wife rationing out the pussy to him for good behavior—he always tells me in the morning when he's had his portion the night before. But Roscoe, I also know, gets what he wants, likes a "big-leg" woman with plenty of meat on her bones.

"Uh-huh. That my baby with her. He two." Through the windshield a fat hand can be seen shaking the tiny arm of a child. Roscoe's other son in Mobile is thirty-two years old. A city cop. Roscoe is proud of him also.

Roscoe turns to the boss, still making symbolic swipes with the dust rag on the table before the window. "He's big, ain't he? But that baby two years old. And I *know* that baby mine. Yessuh, I know that baby *mine!*"

Roscoe is tomming around now, and also referring to the fact that he is sixty-four years old. But, although Roscoe is tomming, the boss doesn't have anything to say; he's thirty-four, and had a vasectomy after the sensible two children.

Roscoe's Uncle Tom routine used to bother me, but now I know. It's a suit he puts on that makes him invisible. He goes everywhere, hears everything, does what he wants, and nobody notices him. The polite white folks call him Uncle Roscoe, in deference to his age. The medicine Johnnie Mae is bringing him is methadone, and Johnnie Mae is a razor-packing mama, although she gives up that leg when Roscoe wants it.

Johnnie Mae—Roscoe's new young wife. Last year, a man forced his way in Roscoe's door while she was home alone, demanded she give up Roscoe's stock from his little side business— his stash of junk. Johnnie Mae went to the kitchen to get it, came out of the drawer with a pistol. They both fired and the shotgun got her in the leg. She put two .38 specials in the man's chest, killed him. Roscoe said, "Willie, the doctors told me on account she got so much meat on her leg, that's what saved her." And Roscoe laughed. "You know, about two weeks after, we got a letter in the mail. Had five dollars in it. It say, 'You did a good job. Take this money and buy another box of bullets.'"

I sit in the office nights and talk to Roscoe. Twenty years at sea. Twenty years mess boy and cook in the freighters. He tells me about Algiers, Dakar, Maracaibo, Rotterdam, Lisbon, New Orleans. He buys ounces of heroin in North Africa that last the months at sea. Every time he gets a fresh supply in port, his cooking is inspired. He stays up all night, high, cooking special dinners for the crew, then tells them the next day, "That's it. I'm wore out, boys. No more rolled turkey breasts until we're back to Tripoli."

Back in the States, he tries living in Harlem. But, "All them niggers crazy," and he goes back home to Alabama. A man robs him, stomps him, breaks his ribs. The next time Roscoe sees the man on the street, Roscoe shoots him dead. "Willie, the judge told me: 'Roscoe, you should have let us handle it.' That's what he said!" Roscoe is shaking his head. In those days the sheriff usually wouldn't bother with arrests if it was just niggers robbing and cutting each other.

Five years at Atmore.

"What did you do there, Roscoe?"

"It was a farm. They had vegetables there. All kind of vegetables—peas, greens, corn. Cucumbers, I hated them things. I pick the vegetables. They make us get up early, 'fore day, and go out pickin'. We'd come back in when it got hot, middle of the day. But sometimes it'd rain the middle of the day, and them cucumbers, they'd swell up and grow back again. And they'd make us go back out. Twice in one day! Man, I hated them things. I still won't eat no cucumber!"

Now Roscoe turns from the window and picks the plastic bag out of Mr. Energy's trash can and moves toward Neville's desk. The boss straightens up, raps his knuckles on the table, and says, "I'll see y'all in the morning." I stall around cleaning my triangles and pointing leads while Mr. Energy finishes his phone call, and he and Neville leave. Roscoe's wiping off desktops now.

"Roscoe, you gettin' job-scared?" I ask. "You know they got another fifteen out in the factory today. And I hear the ax is going to start swinging up here soon."

"I know it. A boy down at the gate told me about it. The man's fixing to sell this place, you watch. But I ain't worried, no sir. They got to have somebody to clean up here, I don't care if they down to two people. And you know who they is."

"The president and the controller. They never had it so sweet, never had to do less and make more. They'll cut a guy's heart out and hand it to him before they'll get pushed out of this gravy boat."

"That's right. You right. And you think that man up in that corner office gonna empty his own trash can and wipe off his desk? You think Richard's gonna go out front by the secretaries and vacuum that carpet? Hell no, they ain't gonna do that. That the last thing gonna go—the janitorial. This whole place shuts down and the lights go off, they still gotta have somebody to sweep up and lock the door."

"I don't know, Roscoe. Old man Hogue told me he had a lock on the janitor job. He says he was here first. I asked him, are you worried and he said, 'I *got* me a good job.'"

"Don't tell me 'bout that old man. That's a nasty old man."

"He told me you better start washing out those fancy coffee cups they leave in the sink by the executive conference room. He said that's your job."

"My job! Ophelia's supposed to wash them cups and she ain't never do it. You know what that old man did? He called me around there one night, he was washin' them out. Say, 'Roscoe, come here. I want to show you what I think of these people.' He had all them cups where he had washed them and he was fixin' to put them away. He took out his dick and rubbed it around the inside of each one while he was puttin' them in the cupboard. That's right! Each cup! That's a nasty man."

"Roscoe, you gotta be shittin' me. That's great! Did he really do that?"

"Swear 'fore God. He take out his little skinny white dick and put it in them cups. Tell me, 'I hope they enjoy their coffee.' It like to made me sick."

"What a whacked-out old man! I bet Richard gets a tingle every time he takes a sip of coffee. Hey, you should work the roots on old man Hogue! What's that one you were telling me about? Saint John the Conqueroo'! Or the black cat bone. That's the one I like."

But Roscoe grows serious and turns his face down. "You don't know what you're sayin' there, Willie. That's somethin' you don't know nothin' about."

We're both silent a minute, Roscoe bending over his cart, getting out trash bags, me gazing at the green drawing board, one ear cocked toward the empty hallway door. Then I come out with it: "Anything happening, Roscoe?"

Roscoe walks slowly up to the front of the room with his bags, where he can see down the hall. "Willie, it's a bomb they got out there now. I got two from a boy in Birdville this afternoon and I like to fell out. It was fire! The thing is light brown with little speckles in it."

"That's that Mexican stuff. Mexican mud, they called it when I was in California."

"They did? That's the best thing they had out there in a long time. I pulled the spike out, I said what's goin' on here? My head was 'bout on my knees."

"The brown speckles were probably the dope. Heavy as they step on it here, that's probably all that's left is those speckles once you sort through the talcum powder and cornstarch and Bonita and beach sand and whatever else they dump in it. But I believe you. That brown I had in Berkeley was strong. It's not very refined, like the white stuff that comes from Turkey. You get those pins and needles from it. A strong flash. I think it's got a higher morphine content for some reason. Probably hasn't gone completely through the last stage of refining, still a lot of morphine base. They sold it in balloons. Dime balloons, twenties sometimes. I used to cop from a guy, he had his girlfriend carry them in her mouth. Give him the money and she'd give you a kiss— pass you a balloon. Remember that song: "Up Up and Away In My Beautiful Balloon?" We used to say the song was about junk. The guys who sang it were from California. Course, you get to thinking the whole world's as hung up on the thing as you are. You ever get it that way?"

This stuff pours out of me like a flood from a sink when

I'm around Roscoe. Master's degree, doctorate, postgraduate studies—twelve years; too much to know about the life and not tell anybody. My girlfriend's a square, I wanted it that way— thought it would help keep me out of trouble. The men in the office or the factory—might as well speak Swambolian as talk to them about junk.

And so I make a meet with Roscoe for when he gets off. I pull past the guard shack at the factory gate with all the station wagon's windows open; it's like a hot-air wind tunnel. By the time I get to Government Street and its canopy of live oaks, the sky is turning dark gray. It's time for the afternoon thunderstorm. The first big drops are hitting the pavement when I pull into the parking lot of the Château Rouge, and I run for the apartment.

I make it in the door—there's a little pile of mail on the kitchen table my girlfriend left before she went to school. A postcard is on top. I can see it from across the room. An event. I turn it over; it's from Sadie. Jesus. I told her not to put her name on anything my girlfriend could see. Postmark: Cuzco, Peru. *I'm here on a field trip. Decided to go back to school for a master's in archaeology. Peru is great. Viva coca!* I turn it back over. There's a picture of a mountain coming out of a tropical forest. I sit looking at the jungle on a shiny piece of cardboard while the rain pours down outside and thunder booms out over the bay, the kitchen light flickering, and my nuts tightening with viva coca and the junk I'm getting from Roscoe later, and Sadie, all mixed in together.

I concentrate on Sadie. It wasn't her real name, but she had taken to introducing herself that way when I met her. And it must have been for a while, because that's what the neighbors called her. She and her husband had been in the house for two years, since his transfer in the public health service; he was a doctor. Part of her name was probably the unsaid word: sexy. As though people might refer to her as sexy Sadie. She wasn't clumsy enough to be that overt, but it couldn't have been far from the front of her mind. And she was a sexy woman.

No makeup, no see-through blouses—she didn't have to play

peek-a-boo. What she had just vibrated out of her, a kind of energy everybody reacted to, whether they knew it or not. Her skinny frame said, I'm alive, I'm alive, it feels good. Suddenly, you noticed you were an animal too, felt your muscles relaxing, gathering, the phlegm in your throat, the sharp teeth behind your lips, and some part of you that slept most of the time said, Hey, come on, let's play.

She wasn't clumsy, or brazen either. The first time I was with her was on a sleeping bag in the side yard of her house. The side where there were woods. She had her husband's permission, but she didn't want him to be surprised, or have to make a mental adjustment, if he came home. The second time, he was there too. She lay between us, facing him, kissing and holding him, while I had her from behind. It was calm and warm. He came quickly, and I didn't come at all, having a methadone habit then. We all got what we wanted.

"My breasts are ruined," she would say as we stood under the shower together. They were somewhat sunken in around the nipples; she had had two children. She would smile as she said it cheerfully. I would hug her hips from behind. "I don't see anything wrong with you," I'd tell her.

A sudden quiet snaps me back; the rain has stopped almost as quickly as it started. Getting dark; almost time for Roscoe. I jam the postcard in my back pocket and go back out to the parking lot.

Easing the station wagon to a stop by a reedy marsh in Bulls Head, I hear baby frogs peeping from the water in the gulches by the dirt road. There's Roscoe's house across the gulleys and ruts—a sagging wooden box with flaking gray paint. A hundred yards down is his neighbor—the same kind of small wooden frame drooping on cinderblocks; there are three or four dead cars in front, and a clump of half-dead banana trees at the corner of the house. Hard to believe that this is inside the city of Mobile, and Mobile is in the United States—not some run-down nineteenth-century outpost in Martinique or Guadeloupe. But the French left here a hundred years before the war; the War between the States, that is.

Roscoe comes to the door in his carpet gliders and an old brocade bathrobe with frayed lapels. After poking his yellow eye out of the crack by the door, he says, "Huh. Stand up here for a minute." I can see no lights in the room behind the door.

He opens up again and with his large mahogany hand curled into a claw, moves it over my palm and opens slightly, dropping a folded tissue in. I squeeze it to make sure there are two caps inside. He pokes his head out the door frame a little and looks slowly up and down the dark road. There are no street lights, nothing to see except the tortured upraised hands of the scrub palmettos filling in his yard and straggling alongside the ditch by the road. "Be careful," Roscoe says.

Now I got the drive back with the junk sitting in my pocket like a piece of radium heavier than the dark side of the moon. I should know better, wasn't ten years of back wards and county lock-ups enough? An old, familiar tape. The old perverse wrestling match in my head. I think on Sadie instead, think about the part of her I like. I ease up to it gradually.

"But why did he do it? Did you ever find out, do you know?" I'm asking her. We're sitting up on the bed in her guest room, our backs propped against the wall.

"So we could be together in eternity. He left a note."

"You read it?"

"No. The police found it. I never went back to the house. Or my husband. When I left the hospital I moved into a place of my own."

"It was so bad, your life before?"

"It wasn't so bad, it was just so . . . empty. I kept going on, thinking I wanted new furniture, or maybe a new car. I had bleached hair. My husband worked in an office and worried about promotions. It wasn't only empty, it was so boring. That's why I started sleeping with the guy."

I look sidelong at her, to see what she looked like with a permanent. Impossible to tell; her thin chestnut hair hangs straight down, fanning out around her bare shoulder. Her eyes have circles under them. Those dark crescents draw me nearer—she's been too busy living to sleep. I put my hand flat on her belly, across the pale lines, move my palm a little to feel the ridges of the scars.

"You took acid with him?"

"No. I thought acid was sort of a kid thing—I was too mature for that! I was twenty-four. He was eighteen. It seemed like a big difference. I didn't find out until later he was taking it all the time."

"How did you find that out?"

"I read the legal papers. There were a lot, even though there wasn't any trial. Look at those sparrows." She covers my hand on her belly with hers and I turn to look with her out of the glass door beside the bed.

He threw himself under a bus. I want to know more. I want to hold it and turn it over and look at the little places. But I don't want to ask. I think again about her opening the door when she came home that night, and him pushing the knife in her liver. Trying to wrestle him off, her hand slipping on the blood on his wrist as he punches it in again. Her little girl dead on the couch when he runs away. He threw himself in front of a bus.

"Look at them now." The little birds are beating their wings up and down in a dusty hollow by the roots of a sycamore, taking a bath. "This is what I did the first month I was in the hospital," she says.

"What, lie in bed with a brown-eyed handsome man?"

"No, good-looking. Lie and watch the birds on the lawn outside the window. I couldn't do anything else. That's when I realized, that's when I understood. Your life is just too valuable, and too short."

"Too short for what?"

"To not live. To not do the things you dream about doing. To not enjoy." With her hand, she slides mine a little under the sheet.

"Please be careful," she asks me a few minutes later as we close our embrace.

I think of her eager, aching sighs all the long drive back into the center of the city. When I pull up to the Château Rouge, my apartment is dark. Sitting in the bathroom, with my girl-friend asleep in the bedroom across the hall, I make life the way I want it. I've got the way to do it here, the philosopher's stone. I start the familiar, forbidden ritual, slide the capsules apart, empty them in the spoon.

I sit at the Formica-topped table in the kitchen, dreaming of water dropping on the leaves of the sago palm outside the window. Dreaming about the power. Roscoe knows:

"How you make a black cat bone? You goes in a graveyard on a dark night when it's thunder and lightning and put a black cat in a pot of boiling water and boil all the meat and hair off until they go to the bottom. They's one bone that stays floatin' on the top. That the black cat bone. You make sure it the right one. Take it home and saw it back and forth across you teeth while you look in a mirror at midnight. It'll make a sound so shrill it'll break the glass. Then you got the power of the Devil and the Lord, both, and ain't nothin' can stop you. Can't be shot or burned up in a house neither. You can read a man's mind like it's you thinkin'. You can snap you fingers and pick money out of his pockets. Ain't nothin' can stop you."

Rick Bass

IN THE LOYAL MOUNTAINS

(from *Southwest Review*)

My girlfriend and I used to drive my uncle around the Texas hill country, in what was to be the last year of his life. We did not know they were his last days, then—though he did, I think—and we always had a good time. I'm married, now, and this girl we drove around with—Spanda—is not my wife, and I was never fooled into believing that one day she might be. Spanda and I were seventeen, that spring and summer. All this happened a long time ago—I have been saying ten years for so long that by now it is truthfully more like twenty.

My uncle, Jimy, was single, and had never been married, never had children. It's possible that he spoiled me. Jimy was a drilling pipe contractor and pipe-threader, and he always had money, unbelievable amounts of it. My father and mother used to laugh about it, because he never seemed to know how to spend it. My father was a professional golfer, of sorts—thirty-five years old, then, and still trying to make the big circuit—the tournament circuit—and he and my mother traveled a good bit. I was their only son, and I stayed with Jimy when they went on the road. My father and mother were very much in love, and loved to travel. They never seemed to have any grudge toward Jimy, the way I had read about other brothers and their wives having, because one of them had money, or success, and that was my favorite thing about Jimy: the fact that my parents liked him.

I had been born with one leg a few inches shorter than the other—a cruel joke, because it threw my golf swing way off—and understandably, my father had given up on my professional hopes by the time I was seven or eight. He had a grace, perhaps gotten from sport, of not pushing me, a compassion for persons weaker than himself.

What I am saying is that my father loved golf; and that he was a better person than he was a golfer—but he was still a very good golfer, just not the best, and he won or finished high often enough to raise me, if no others, and to support my mother.

My father had, and still does have, a bad back, and I remember that my mother was always rubbing it. She used a rolling pin. The way my father limped, after a match, when he got home; I was sometimes teased in school—this was in Texas, in the dusty, windblown sixties—and it was pretty widely believed that golf was a sissy game, with the manicured greens, and the caddies, the little humming electric golf carts, and the natty way of dressing. For a while, in younger grades, I had tried to get the other kids in school to believe that my father's nickname was "Mad Dog," but it never caught.

When he was home, and when he was not out practicing, my father walked around the house with a big plastic jug of aspirin in his jacket—and at night, in the pocket of his robe—and he was always opening the jug and shaking some out, swallowing them. I could tell by the way the jug sounded if he was almost out of them, or if he had just started on a new jug. I would never ask him how he was feeling—I felt it might remind him of his back pain, if he had somehow managed to put it out of his mind for a while—and so instead, I would sneak a look at the aspirin, whenever I could—when the jacket was laid out on the big table in the den (the one on which he got his back rubs, so that he could watch, on the television, on weekends, whatever tournaments were playing)—or sometimes, I would get up very early and go into the kitchen, and would check the jug then. He left it on the kitchen counter, and it was the first thing he went to, in the morning.

They were just aspirin. He wouldn't let himself take anything stronger.

I remember Uncle Jimy coming over to our house for dinner, whenever my parents got back from one of their road trips. That was always what they did for him, to show him their gratitude: fix him a huge, home-cooked dinner, on a weekend, and with all four of us, just a family, around the table. Mom would do all the cooking, but because Uncle Jimy was an outdoorsman—and because wild game was what he liked best—he would bring over the food that he wanted my mother to cook for us: pheasants and grouse from hunting trips he'd gone on in South Dakota, and venison roasts, and fresh fish he'd caught maybe that day, from one of the many lakes north of Houston—Livingston, Sam Rayburn, Conroe, even Toledo Bend. My uncle was a pilot, and would sometimes fly, by himself, to one of these lakes, landing at a little grass airstrip outside a tiny pine backwoods town, and he'd give one of the local men a hundred dollars or more, for the use of a boat—and he would go out to the lake by himself, in this other man's boat, and catch fish. Sometimes the local man would want to go with him, but my uncle always wanted to be alone. He was a good fisherman, and a good shot. His freezer was always full of fish and game.

At dinner, we would talk about my school, or my father's golf, or my uncle's recent fishing trips; or we would talk about other things, things that my mother might be interested in—politics, wars, morals—and about my mother's childhood, which she missed, I think. My mother came from a large family in Missouri—they had lived on a farm—and as I've said, she loved to travel, and loved my father, but she also loved to talk about growing up on that farm, and about the things her brothers and sisters used to do—nine of them, in all—and the trouble they used to get into.

She always had a story about them. Cooking the large (four of us), extravagant meal always reminded her, always brought out the best stories. We talked forever, worked past the hunting and fishing stories—going quickly and carefully over the golfing stories, the briefer the better, because golf was work, and this, the dinner, was play—and then, with a relish we'd been waiting for, we'd be on my mother's stories. They were what we most wanted to hear, and we'd be drinking wine, and the venison would have a thin sweet gravy over it, with sautéed mushrooms, the grouse would be stuffed with green apples and celery, and the fish were fried in mustard batter and black pepper, the way my father and uncle liked them, slender filets the size of a strip of bacon, so that we could squeeze lemon onto them and then dip them into the dill-and-chive sauce and eat them with our fingers, daintily, one after the other, and drink the wine, bottles of it, because they let me drink too, when I was sixteen, and seventeen—it was all right to get drunk, at the family dinner—and my mother talked about cold mornings, about doing the laundry by hand, and about new shoes; about what a thrill it was to get new shoes—she talked about all the old things.

My mother was living history, but beautiful, and young. We listened to her with an awe.

She used to be the one who would kill the chickens, on Sundays, for the big dinner after church. One of her older sisters would hold the chicken out on a stump, holding its neck between two nails driven into the stump, and my mother would hit the neck with the hatchet.

"One-Chop," my mother said proudly. "They called me One-Chop."

We ate so much at those dinners, whenever my parents returned from one of their travels. We would stay up late and eat and drink as far into the night as we could, as if trying to make up for, and gain ground on, some ache or loneliness that had happened, while they were gone—all of us. Jimy ate the most, drank the most. No matter how much food my mother fixed, or how many different bottles of wine were opened, we always finished it, everything—all of it—with Jimy leading the way, Jimy having four helpings, fifths, sixths—whatever it took—and my mother would be delighted, pushing more food on him, more freshly baked bread, handing him the honey to ladle over it, and pouring more wine—it would be midnight, sometimes one in the morning—and she would say, "My goodness, Jimy, Jackie must have been quite a lot of trouble, this time!"

My uncle slept in the guest room, the nights of these huge welcome-back dinners. We scraped the fish bones, the grouse keels and lemon rinds, into the garbage; piled all the dishes in soapy water in the sink, and left all the empty wine bottles on the table, and fled, leaving everything for later, for when we would be better able to face it.

"Jimy, you were *insatiable*," my father would always say, as he and my mother went down the hall, leaning against each other, to their bedroom. My father would look back over his shoulder. "You were just an *animal*!" he'd tease. It was a joke they had had between them for many years, a joke that had begun with their father. Even then, I had heard, Jimy had had an enormous appetite, and a great, almost brute strength, and that had been their father's, my grandfather's, nickname for him: "Animal."

"Good-night," my uncle would tell us, pausing at his doorway. "Good-night, all."

I remember, in my room, reeling drunk, pretending I was a gut-shot actor in a Western, spinning in the dark, pretending I had caught a bullet in the stomach; and clutching it with both hands, I would do a slow, triple-spin, all for Hollywood, for no one, pirouetting, before toppling to the bed, landing on my back, asleep almost as soon as I hit.

I am a plain man. What I do for a living has little to do with the way I sometimes feel about things. I'm an accountant, and a junior one at that. I'd like to be something with power— sweeping power, the power to change things, to right wrongs— a judge, or a lawyer, a surgeon—but because I do not do these things, does not mean they are not in me.

My uncle was a crook. His death was a suicide, as he felt the evidence closing in—questions arising from (where else?) the oil companies' accounting departments; and letters, meetings, queries from lawyers for explanations, polite at first—all of these things are in his dusty files, his long-ago files, which I felt the need to get, after his death, and which I keep in my attic—and it must have been a very tough time for him, getting near the end, with no way out—and I wish that he could never have been caught, that he could have held out forever. There were no lakes in prison, is what he must have been thinking, no woods in which to hunt, no grass airstrips to float down onto, in the middle of a week, on a hot June Wednesday afternoon.

What *could* he have been thinking? It is not right for me to try to guess. But it is fair for me to remember.

I think that he was bored—but that is not the real answer.

I think that he felt some sort of hunger, something sharper than most of us ever know; and that he felt he had nothing, but that he wanted everything, and that he would take what he could get. I would like to believe that his actions amazed him, but that he was also glad that they amazed him, glad for the danger, and for doing a thing that he could not understand.

My mother might have thought it was a burden, a trouble to my uncle, for him to keep me while they were gone—or again, she might just have been teasing him, she might have realized how much he truly enjoyed the company, my company—but whatever her opinion, I do not think that she ever realized what an absolutely great time we had. I am sure she never knew what fun we had—my uncle and I, and then, once I hooked up with her, Spanda.

Spanda came from what would be called in another city the wrong side of the tracks—though in Houston, at that time, there were no tracks, either literally or figuratively—and she did not go to my school, and sometimes did not go to her school.

What I am trying to say is that Spanda was not a nice girl. I thought she was lovely—and she *was* lovely—but she was a little rough, a little mean, and she did not have many odds in her favor, except to be rough and mean.

My leg excited her: the shorter one. It's not proper or relevant to go into how much it excited her; it was her business, and mine. But it did—she loved the leg—and though she did not love me, it was the first time I had ever felt such a thing, someone *attracted* to my leg, and to me, and it gave me a confidence I needed badly. It did not hurt either that Uncle Jimy was almost always around, his pockets bulging with dollars, like a caricature of the old-style Texans, the kind everyone used to love, until they learned to make fun of them—generous, big-minded, and loose dollars trailing, fluttering in the wind, whenever he reached his hands into his pockets and pulled them out—and Uncle Jimy liked Spanda, too, and he saw to it that she always got what she wanted, when she was with me, saw to it that she was always happy.

I was seventeen. This was clover for me. I believed in things, rather than understanding them. What we are talking about here is innocence, no different from anyone else's.

Would it be safe to say that Spanda did not have her innocence anymore? But now it sounds as if I am beginning to feel sorry for her. There would be no reason for that. Perhaps I do feel a guilt, for having been so happy then, and for being so content now— but it is a mild, loose guilt, and certainly a much better feeling than pity. My family did not ever teach me pity, and for that I am glad, and it may in fact be the reason for my contentedness.

Uncle Jimy was wild, like a big kid, when he was away from my parents, and away from his office. He was a loner, and when I got in from school, those times I stayed over at his house—and there were many, that year, because my father was getting older, and was making his last hard run at the circuit, at going over the top, and it seemed he was traveling all the time, that year, traveling not as if running from something, but rather, chasing it—and even then, I knew there was a difference—and then my uncle and I—after he had changed out of his suit, and into his old coveralls—would drive out to the practice range, to hit golf balls.

It would be around three-thirty in the afternoon, a weekday, and Houston was simply a working town in those days, growing, and because there was neither any unemployment nor any affluence—neither of these things, yet—the driving range would be empty, and my uncle and I could practice our swings, with no one around to watch. Sometimes there might be a housewife or two—matronly, yellow-haired, overweight, dressed up in their ridiculous tight bermudas, and a bulging yellow knit shirt, and meat-eating spikes, for gripping the earth on long drives, long drives that gave them much pleasure, I could tell—but they never embarrassed me by looking at me because I was used to their looks, had seen them before—looks of pity and what they thought was knowledge—and as such, it was easy to ignore them.

Jimy had a couple of golf pros who would meet us out there sometimes, Will and Dougal—athletic young men who were patient, courteous, and who did not know pity, either—but they were unable to correct my swing, or rather, unable to help me develop one with which I could play, either competitively or recreationally—and so, I think, my uncle must have fired them, because after a while they stopped showing up, and it was just my uncle and me again.

"This'll be a great surprise," he would say, sitting next to me on a soap crate in his coveralls, looking like a mechanic, as I swung, and swung, and swung—"This'll be a big surprise," he would say, and for a long time, I believed him. It was an easy thing to do, and I believed that I could—with my uncle's wild, insatiable view, I could picture it, could picture coming in the house one day, after my father got back from one of his road trips—golf clubs slung over my shoulder—and tossing the keys to his car onto his table, where he would be lying, resting, stretching his back—and saying, "How 'bout it, Pop, want to go play a few rounds?"

I could see pictures better than that, too; we both could, my uncle and I, that hot, humid Houston spring, with no one else out at the driving range. I shudder to think, now, of what kind of pictures my uncle must have been able to see, to imagine.

Even hitting one-legged, as it were, even hitting off balance, I had my uncle's great, strange strength, and after several weeks, I was hitting the balls farther than we could have hoped for—but I could not hit them straight, I would always send them, with my twisting swing, into a wild, sail-away slice, or almost as bad, into a horrid, rocketing, never-to-be-seen-again hook—and I think our pictures finally began to dim.

My uncle would sit on the soap crate, sweating, toweling his face off with a handkerchief, just sitting in the sun, watching me and sweating, and drinking beers, which he kept in a little icebox by his side—and I would swing harder and harder, but along with my uncle's and father's strength, I had my father's back—and sometimes it hurt so badly that I would almost want to tell my uncle that I did not want to play golf anymore—or at least, not anymore that day—but there would be this almost wild, glassy look—an eager look, a look of childlike expectation on his face as he sat there, motionless on the wooden crate, and studied my swing. And so I would shut my eyes, and take my best cut, and away the ball would soar, disappearing to the left or the right, never traveling straight, and sometimes I would be so frustrated that I would roar, would shout as loudly as I could— shouting at the frustration, and also at the cramps in my back— and the lady golfers would move away from us, would sometimes even pack up their clubs and leave, but my uncle liked the shouts, liked them very much, and he would nod, and take a sip from his beer, and then lean forward and hand me another bucket of golf balls, another handful of the brightly colored wooden tees.

My father was having a very good year, that spring. He won one fairly large local tournament, and for the first time in several years was selected to play in a prestigious tournament overseas. He was getting offers again, finally, to do endorsements, but he wisely rejected them, and concentrated on his golf, and did even better.

He was often written about in the sports pages, and I was extremely proud of him, the pride coming like a flood, along with—again—perhaps a little guilt, from all the days in school at a younger age, when I had tried to change his name, and when I had wished he did a sport more violent, more bloodthirsty, than golf. . . . The newspapers were always saying what a gentleman he was, what a good sport, and how he brought class to the game, class to the city.

He was almost a hero.

I began to eat aspirin, the way he did. My uncle never saw me eating them, but it was not long after my father won his tournament, his first first-place finish in several years, that my uncle and I stopped golfing, anyway. And I felt a flood of relief, again, and though I know that I may be attributing too much wizardry to Jimy, I am wondering now if he knew exactly what he had been doing, all along.

I was delighted to never pick up a golf club again, delighted not to ever even watch the game being played again.

Uncle Jimy brought Spanda home from work with him one day, later that spring, saying simply that her father worked in his plant, and that she, Spanda, was new in town, and didn't know anyone—and that she wanted to meet someone her own age, and so my uncle had volunteered me for the job. He hoped I didn't mind.

Lies! Lies! Many children are wise at the age of seventeen, but I was not one of them—and I believed in luck then, as I still do, only even more so, then—and I believed my uncle, as did so many other people, it seems. Spanda was beautiful, Cherokee-looking with old blue jeans, a purple tie-dye shirt, a tan face (and body) and long black hair, and a headband, no makeup. We got along famously. It doesn't matter what I think, now—wondering whether we would have, had it not been for my leg, and more importantly, for my uncle, and his money. It is in the past, and unlike some things in the past, it does not matter. We got along famously, on all levels.

We played cards, we listened to the radio; we went for drives together, along with my uncle—driving his truck. At night,

Spanda came into my room downstairs, and got in bed with me. My uncle slept upstairs, and slept heavily, not even arising until after I had left for school.

Spanda was angry at a lot of things, at most things, and she had a wonderful vocabulary of curse words, which she used against establishments of all kinds—traffic lights, policemen, rainy weather, everything—but she was not angry at me, or at my uncle. I felt like a hero. And I think that upstairs, in his bed, drifting into sleep, eyes shut, perhaps imagining things—I think that my uncle, too, probably felt like a hero—as well he should have.

Into the hill country we'd drive, once summer came, staying in hotels in the little German tourist towns—Fredericksburg, Boerne, New Braunfels—getting separate rooms, a room for Spanda and me, and a room for my uncle—and driving through the wild, rocky country that was in no way like the rest of the state, and certainly not like the gentle, windy Gulf Coast where we lived. We stopped at beer gardens in the little towns and sat outside on the patios in the shade, drinking cold beer and eating huge amounts of food—my uncle sometimes ordering one of everything on the menu, unable to make up his mind—and then we would walk up and down the streets of the little wide-streeted towns, window-shopping in the dazzling heat, with hardly anyone else out, the heat far too great, and we would buy whatever Spanda desired, whatever she or my uncle saw, and wanted, on a whim—an old sewing machine in the window of an antique store, or a rocking chair, in the same—fresh-baked loaves of bread, a gingham dress for Spanda, a cane for me, with which to walk—and then we would put more beer in the ice chest in the back of the truck, and we would leave the little towns, sated, and would head up into the wild country, up the twisting, climbing back roads, into the mountains of cedar and rock, cactus and heat—heat rising in shimmers and mirages from the dusty white caliche roads, always a drought in the summer—and then sailing down into the little valleys between the hills, rattling across creek bottoms, and highwater caution dips, through the water-seeking shady live oaks, barreling along, my uncle with a beer in his hand, and one foot mashed on the accelerator, and the other propped up and hanging out the window—and Spanda and I would drink beers too, Spanda sitting in my lap, with her arms around me, her hair swirling, her eyes fuzzy and distant, looking out at the countryside as she drank her beer. . . .

Roadrunners scurried across in front of our mad flight, and grazing herds of little deer leapt away from us in mild alarm, vaulting gently over barbed-wire fences and disappearing, with flagging white tails, into the tangled cedar. Sometimes we would see flocks of wild turkeys, shining bronze in the sun, taking dust baths along the side of the road. Hawks circled overhead, and buzzards too. We were heading for an obscure mountain range that we knew about, a small chain of mountains in the center part of the state that were not even on any map—the Loyal Mountains.

The Loyal Mountains were the most beautiful place I had ever been. There was a stream, Willow Creek, that flowed through the little mountains' heart, and along which there were many great boulders, and sandbars, and the huge shady live oaks. We would take out driving across someone's pasture in the truck, bouncing over rocks and logs, my uncle still driving with his foot hanging out the window, driving and singing "Red River Valley," and we'd drive 'til we couldn't go any farther, and then get out and hike up the canyon, following the creek upstream to a large shady spot we knew about, where we could picnic, and nap in sweet ferns, and go swimming in a pool beneath a small waterfall.

We'd stay there until dark, drinking Jim Beam, and shooting pistols—my uncle had a whole tool chest full of them, which he would sometimes carry with him up to the picnic spot, lugging them like a chest of stolen gold, while Spanda and I carried the ice chest—and Jimy would lean back against a tree, all three of us unbelievably drunk—Spanda floating on her back out in the little pool, once we got there, naked, with her long hair floating all around her, sun-dappled, the sun trying to make it down through the heavy canopy of the live oaks—and Jimy would sing, and shoot his pistol at the boulders, causing the bullets to ricochet all around with mean, zinging whines, but we were too drunk to care.

"Yeah I've played the Red River Valley," he would bray, half-shouting, half-singing, "and sat in the kitchen, and cried . . ."

The water in the pool beneath the waterfall was deep and cool. Spanda and I would climb up onto the boulders above the pool, both of us still naked, and would practice our best dying-actor, shot-from-the-stagecoach falls, while the bullets ricocheted all around us. It was impossible to imagine what my father and mother would have thought, had they been able to see us. My uncle wasn't drunk, so much as just crazy.

Spanda and I would clutch our hearts, spin slowly, and topple, falling slowly into the deep water below us. Sometimes we died holding hands, hitting the water together. It's a miracle my uncle didn't get carried away with the game, and begin shooting directly at us, forgetting that the bullets were real; and it's a lesser miracle that we were never hurt in any of the falls, and that none of the ricochets ever hit us. I believe so strongly in luck.

My uncle could have been my father! What if I had been raised by him, instead of by my father—raised full-time? We all had the same beginning, the same genes—their father I knew little about, only that he too had been very strong, physically, and that he had called my uncle "animal."

Driving back, too tired to drink any more, and too tired to attempt the long drive back to Houston, we would check back into our hotel. Very often Uncle Jimy would not feel like eating—and he would appear to have sobered, once we left the woods, which was always a slight disappointment to me, because I was beginning to think I liked him better wild than tame—and he would give us some money for supper, and the keys to his truck, and he would go to his room, where he would not sleep, but would sit up with all the lights on, watching television.

But on the drive back in, leaving the waterfall—Jimy driving, and me in the front, as usual, with Spanda in my lap, achingly in my lap—the windows down, and cool washing smells of the hill country at night sweeping in over us, cactus blossoms, cedars cooling in the night, creek water, the nectar of late-season blue-bonnets—and with fireflies blinking slow and green, out in all the meadows—we would race across the roads, up over the hills, plunging down into the little valleys and meadowlands, swerving to dodge the red-eyed deer, bucks with their antlers in summer velvet, and does with spotted fawns that hurried across the road, just ahead of the play of our headlights—in the truck like that, Spanda would be kissing my neck, kissing my face, my eyes, licking my ear, everything—it would be dark, and we'd both still be drunk, and I wouldn't care that we were sitting right next to my uncle.

Spanda would be like a wild animal, feasting on me. Jimy would be driving straight and true—suddenly—responsibly—and he would be humming.

Spanda and I were always ravenous, after the long afternoon of play, and the drinking, with the alcohol finally beginning to lose its edge, slightly; and we'd eat barbecue, ordering it the way my uncle had taught us, one of everything, and then we'd go back to our room as if we were adults, as if we were married—as if we had all of life figured out—and we would make love on and off all through the night, falling into it like a trap, like a slow, tumbling dive—all we wanted, and more—though now that I am older, and have seen more, I realize—sadly—that it was with more of a dutifulness that Spanda moved, there in the dark, than the passion she had, or appeared to have, driving back in the truck, with my uncle present.

But sometimes after I fell asleep, I would awaken later in the night, and she would have the lamp on, and she would have the covers pulled back from me, and would be sitting up in the bed, looking at my leg. She did this several times, and at first I was flattered, and felt special; but as it happened more and more, it began to trouble me a little.

I was not a nincompoop, was not an utter dolt; thoughts would come into my head, about Spanda, and where she had come from, but they went away, or I put them away.

"Jackie's father is a golfer," my uncle would tell her, sometimes—always telling it as if forgetting he had mentioned it, or more, saying it not so much with the intent of informing her, but rather, telling her so he could get her reaction, which was never anything, which seemed to please him, and he would drop the subject.

Sometimes, in the hotel rooms, right after I had made love to Spanda, or had had love made to me by her, and was about to fall asleep, with my head against the pillow, and the room quiet, Spanda's hand on my chest, her face next to mine, I could hear the TV in the next room, in my uncle's room. There would be the sound of the TV—the news, usually—and then of my uncle's voice, talking not to himself, and not to anyone else, but to the person on the television. He would argue, usually—arguing with the weatherman about the forecast, or with the sportscaster, about the replay of a close play at the plate.

Once, as I lay there listening, I heard the sportscaster talking about a golf tournament, the one my father was in, and I heard my father's name mentioned. Spanda was already asleep, and I sat up to hear better, but my uncle must have gotten up and turned the set off, because the sound suddenly went silent.

I could hear the crickets outside our room, and could hear an occasional car passing. We were in the hill country, on the edge of the Loyal Mountains, and I felt bad, not knowing if my father was winning or losing.

We never had Spanda over for any of the dinners. I wish now that we had—I wish it very much, because it is past, and can never be claimed again, cannot be done, now—but I knew better, then, than to even mention her to my parents, much less show them her picture, or have her over for dinner.

"Pass the fucking meat loaf, please," I could picture her saying, after a glass or two of wine. I could see her getting up from her chair and coming over and sitting in my lap, and putting her tongue in my ear. These were the thoughts I had then, though of course I realize now that she would have behaved like a professional, as she always did, and that she would have been charming—and so I wish we had invited her, even just once, for that reason, and also so that she could have heard my mother's stories.

Listening to my mother's tales of childhood—and sitting there in the midst of us, with his brother, and his nephew, his sister-in-law, and her stories—my uncle was not my uncle, then, but was a tame, admirable man—he was my father's brother, and we always had a wonderful time—always.

"My sisters and I had a pet Brahma bull," my mother said, "named Skippy. We got to ride him to school, each year, on the last day of school. He was so tame, so gentle."

My uncle listening, with a gentleman's interest, and also, I could feel, some kind of hunger, some kind of loss.

"In the winter, we used to hook him up to a harness, and use him to pull people's cars out of the snow, after they slid off into the ditches," my mother said.

My father laughed. "We used to use Jimy," he said. "Jimy would lift up the back ends of cars and trucks that were stuck."

My uncle smiled, modestly. "Those days are over now, I guess," he said, looking down at the table.

"They certainly are," my father agreed, and he held his hands out in front of him and flexed them, looking at his big hands, muscular hands. Arthritis was already beginning to set in, and he had to have been able to see that he could have only three or four more years left, at best, for doing what he did.

My mother poured us each another glass of wine. It sparkled, golden, in the light of the chandelier. We made toasts, often.

* * *

My mother and father were not home much, that summer. I feel now almost as if I aggravated my uncle's condition, though I know it is what he desired. When he could not travel to the hill country—when he had to stay close to Houston, for business meetings, and to finish deals—he would instead take us to the fanciest restaurants in the city. We would all dress up—he would buy Spanda a new dress, and would give me money to rent a tuxedo (it would have been a waste to buy one for me, for I was growing, and would quickly have outgrown any one we purchased)—and I'd have the shop pin the cuff up on my left leg, and we would go out to dinner, and would go to a baseball game afterwards, still wearing our tuxedos, Spanda still in her evening dress.

We drove in my uncle's truck, and as always, the radio would be on, and he would sing along with almost all of the songs, even the ones he did not know the words to, had never heard before. His favorite was "Inna Gadda Da Vida," and it was a scary thing to hear.

Some nights we would drive out to the little country airport where Jimy kept his plane—Lakeside Airport, out west of town, in the flat prairie rice-field country—no clouds, a clear night, but no stars either, the dome of light from the city even then, in the sixties, obscuring them, washing them all out—and we'd park and get out and walk over to Jimy's plane, a little red-and-white Cessna, which he did not keep in a hangar, but merely tied down to little eye-bolts set in the ground, so that the plane was more like an animal, tethered—and he would run his hands all over the plane, feeling its smoothness, the coolness of the metal, and sometimes, though not that often, he would ask if we wanted a ride—I always did—and so we'd get in, and he would start the engine—shouting out the window as he did so, "Clear!" out of reflex, to warn anyone standing nearby to get out of the way of the prop, though it was silly, of course, there was no one else out, no one around at that time of night—and the engine would catch, cough, and then roar, and the little lights in the instrument panel would come on, illuminating my uncle's face with an eerie green light, and the gyroscopes would all suddenly be spinning wildly—and my uncle would be transfixed, as serious as a heart attack, examining all the gauges and meters, to make sure everything was all right.

Spanda would be crouched in the back, terrified, but trying not to show it—one hand gripping the back of my uncle's seat, and the other one clutching the back of my seat, for it was only a two-seat plane, and I was the co-pilot—I think she felt very strongly that this was not part of her duty, and it's possible that this, unlike anything else, any of the other, was the part she did for love, if indeed there was any—which I believe there was— and then we would be spinning, turning toward the runway, and lumbering across the grass—my uncle paid no attention to the paved taxiway that was there for that purpose—and then, always, out on the runway, the best part, the moon shining down on it, making the runway look wet and shiny, like the end of life, and the beginning of a newer, finer, more glorious thing— something inviting—then, the best part, putting the throttle in, all the way.

My uncle was a good pilot, and it was very hard to tell when we had left the ground, at first—at what point we were completely, totally flying—though I think Spanda could sense it, beneath us—a certain feeling of lightness, of being lost, for a minute, or even longer—and we would rise above the little trees, and above the airport, and we would be able to see all of the lights of the city out to our left, but always, we would bank and make a turn back into the darkness, away from the disorientation of the city— all those streams of light, and the silhouettes of tall buildings, rising as if through a mist—and we'd fly out in circles above the prairie, flying circles in the dark, out over the rice fields, flying straight and true, my uncle all the while watching the gauges, and looking out for other things. It might seem that he would be a wild pilot, prone to doing loops and barrel rolls and crazy-eights, whether he had been drinking or not, but up in the air like that, with everything at stake, he was the picture of calm, he was the picture of my father, even: responsible, cool, and caring.

The little plane's roar was loud, and we had to shout to each other whenever we wanted to say something; but mostly, we just flew, and looked back at the city, and at the darkness below us. Sometimes, feeling chivalrous, I would hold Spanda's hand, would squeeze it, and she would smile weakly, in the greenish light.

It was impossible to believe that this was the uncle who had ricocheted bullets all around us, up in the hill country. He looked like somebody's grandfather, up there in the air like that, cautious and reasonable, calculating.

He looked tense, but also calm at the same time, somehow—reassured, perhaps.

We'd land, then, when the gas gauges began showing less than half-full, and would tie the plane back down to its grommets—the hood of the engine warm and ticking in the night, and the sound, again, of crickets, and farther away—much farther—the sound of one of the interstates. Spanda would go straight to the truck and wait for us in it—and then, driving home, with the radio playing, my uncle would be as calm as a mare, would not sing along with any of the songs, would not backtalk any of the commercials that came on, and he was thinking about something else, and he was so tame that again he could have been my father.

His pipeyard was on the way to his house, and we would often stop there and drive through the chain-link gate—putting a card in a slot, to open the gate automatically—and then my uncle would get out on the huge crushed-shell parking lot, and look at all the stacked pipe on the racks, pipe lying silent in the night, with big floodlights all around the yard, to prevent vandalism. It was the most boring-looking thing in the world, all that motionless pipe, and I did not understand how anyone could do that for a living, did not even understand how such a boring-looking thing could make money, or be worth anything.

In August, during the worst of the heat, my uncle developed gout, and had to take medication for it, and had to stay off his feet. He got an electric wheelchair, for his dealings at work, and that was when Spanda and I began to drive him around, rather than having him drive us. We would head up into the Loyal Mountains at every chance we got.

My uncle was not a good sport, and he had not changed his diet. He would ride up in the passenger's seat—Spanda sitting between us, with her legs on either side of the stick shift, though she had to be careful not to bump his foot with hers, because it would cause him intense pain—and he was in pain anyway, and was trying to suffer it silently, but he was not as good at it as was my father; he bellowed, whenever we hit a bump, and would immediately take a swallow of whiskey, or shake down a handful of the pills he was taking, of which the first doctor had told him to take only four a day, but which my uncle had been able to obtain in bulk. . . .

He rode with a shotgun in his lap, and would shoot at the coveys of quail that we would often see huddled along the road, bathing in the dust; he would fire into them as we drove past, always hitting them, and sometimes he would kill or injure the entire flock, and he would have me circle around and go back and pick them up.

He'd clean them in the truck, then, as I drove, turning around and heading back for the Loyals, and Spanda would be grim-lipped, not even looking at him, but looking away, looking straight ahead, or to the side, out my window. Feathers would swirl around in the truck as he plucked the birds, putting the entrails and feathers in a brown paper grocery bag that he had brought for that purpose. The insides of quail, unlike those of dove and other birds, smell rotten, for some reason, even when freshly killed, and we had to drive with the windows down, in order to breathe. I know now that Spanda was being paid to be with me, but I do not care. It's in the past.

Jimy would cook the quail in his hotel room, that evening, over a little can of Sterno he'd bought at a convenience store, skewering them on a coat hanger and cooking them for an after-dinner snack, basted with butter and pepper, as he watched the news, and as Spanda and I thumped around next door.

Mornings in the hill country were, and still are, beautiful; a heavy dew, even in the summer, and the sounds of roosters, and of cattle lowing. My uncle could not make it to the picnic spot anymore, so often Spanda and I would go by ourselves. My uncle insisted upon this; and he would stay in the hotel room, with a pitcher of beer, and he would have stacks and stacks of paper spread out all over the desk, all over the bed, when we got back—papers everywhere, frantic-looking, and an adding machine plugged in, and the bottles of pills, for the gout, and the Jim Beam, half-gone. . . . I could tell that the numbers with the adding machine, and all the loose papers, were troubling my uncle, and I wished that there was something I could do to help him, I wished I knew about numbers, knew how to line them up so that they all made sense, and so that they would not be troublesome. I wanted to walk down the Main Street and window-shop with him, window-shopping with him and Spanda, and eat, and drink, and drive the back roads.

When the news came that my uncle had shot himself, it was raining, and we were all three at home, my mother and father and I, and I wanted the news—a phone call—to be taken back, to go away somehow; and my father wilted, and sat down on the couch, and it was as if he was not my father anymore, it was as if he was not anyone, anymore—as if he had his identity taken away—and I felt as if I had betrayed him, somehow.

"One-Chop," said my father, with his head in his hands—he called my mother that often—"I need to be alone."

"No, you don't," my mother said, and came over and sat down

by his side—and I did not know what to do, or where to go. I stood there and watched them sitting on the couch together.

"We should have been able to see it coming," my father said, "should have been able to see it coming like a freight train." He was shaking his head, and my mother's arms were around him.

"No," she said. "No."

After a long while my father's color started to come back. He stood up and said to us, "I have to go identify the body now." I thought what a bad task that would be, that it would be like looking at himself, and worse, that there would be guilt.

"Do you want me to come?" my mother asked. She looked over at me. "Do you want us to come?"

"No," my father said. "I will be all right."

My family history—I am frightened of it, but I am proud of it. My father is as normal as pie: a retired golfer, is all now, a middle-aged grandfather, and a gentleman. His back still hurts him, but he is silent about it, as ever. My mother still tells us stories about her family, and her childhood, but there's a loneliness, and the stories are not devoured with as much of an eagerness—can never be devoured with as much of an eagerness as they once were, by my uncle. A picture of my father, from one of his golf tournaments, wearing the winner's jacket—the victor—is in a frame on my wife's and my dresser, an old photograph, from twenty or more years ago.

What lies ahead? Sam, my son, is strong, and prone to tempers. Sometimes, knowing the past—and not knowing parts of it, too—I am frightened, worried, almost to the point of paralysis. He may be some kind of athlete—Sam. He is often sweet to his sister, but he can throw horrible tantrums, too—or can turn distant and moody, on the drop of a dime, only three years old but reminding me of something, and I overreact, I panic, and it is my wife, Marilee, who has to calm me.

"He is so strong," I say, "already, he's so strong."

Or when he's crying, and throws his fits, and turns his back on us—so cold, as if he doesn't need us!—I react poorly; I panic, and it feels as if there is nothing I can do.

"Hold him," Marilee says, when Sam grows distant, sometimes for no reason. She's large with our third, coming soon, but she shows no fear, no worry, only a willingness to dive ahead, to move on into the future.

She picks Sam up and hugs him tightly, holds him close to her, strokes the side of his face, and smiles at me.

"Hold him like this," she says, rocking him, and smiling at me. "Like this."

Nanci Kincaid

THIS IS NOT THE PICTURE SHOW

(from *Story*)

Me and Pat Lee go to town every Saturday. It is a social responsibility. Only the country kids don't go because they have to feed chickens and stuff, which we think is the saddest of circumstances.

When we get to town we buy five-cent bags of boiled peanuts first thing from crazy old men who sit on the sidewalk, some with their legs cut off and their pants all folded and pinned in strange arrangements, some blind who take all day making change, feeling each coin, counting out loud, and some who are okay on the outside, but crazy in the head the way they sing songs without words, or make a bunch of kissing noises when they see me and Pat Lee walking up.

"Shut up, you stupid old men," Pat Lee mumbles.

Mother says these crazy old men are left over from the war or else let out of Chattahoochee Mental Hospital. She drops us off at the park right where they sit and says, "It's pitiful. You two be nice to those pitiful men." And every Saturday of our lives we pay one of them our nickel and get ourselves little warm, wet bags of juicy boiled peanuts.

Then we roam through all the stores in downtown Tallahassee looking at merchandise. Actually we are looking for other junior-high people who are also roaming. When there are seven or eight of us, maybe more, we go from place to place, trying out 45 records in the listening booths at the Sammy Seminole Music Store. Sometimes we connect the dots on the acoustical tiles to see what they come out to be. (Once we fit thirteen people in one listening booth, just for the heck of it, and played Chubby Checker records on 78 speed, which is the funniest thing you ever heard.) Then we eat French fries at the Rexall and write messages on the tabletops without getting caught. Me and Pat Lee make up initials, like T.B. + V.D., and paint them on in fingernail polish, knowing other people will come along and try to figure out who it is. The waitress has never mentioned a thing about it.

After that everybody rides the elevator at Mendelson's Department Store. We hold the buttons down and just keep going up and down—not stopping to let any other people on. We do that ten or fifteen times and then we go to the cosmetics counter and spray each other with sample cologne. Until, finally, it is time for the picture show and we all walk down the street to the State Theater.

Now the State Theater does a good business. They could show black-and-white slides of "How to Care for Houseplants" and we would line up to see it. It is fifty-five cents to get in and for another nickel you can get an all-day Sugar Daddy on a stick, which we always do. If you are ever going to have any experience with boys this is the place to get started with it, which makes me nervous, although I manage to be as suave as the next girl about it. I have to be. Because of Pat Lee and all.

It comes natural to her, driving boys crazy. She does it by acting rotten to them. She does it by being mad at them all the time, or bored to death or aggravated with them for some reason they never can figure out. I've seen boys get in a fistfight outside the State Theater over who was going to sit by Pat Lee, only to have her get mad and refuse to sit by either one of them. I've seen her sit by Bobby Castle all the way through an Elvis Presley movie with her arms crossed, pouting, not saying a word to him. But he still bought her buttered popcorn, an Orange Crush, and a box of Milk Duds. And when the movie was over he asked her if he could sit by her again the next Saturday, tried to make her promise, and she walked right out of the theater without even looking at him. That night he called and asked her to go steady. It's like that all the time.

Pat Lee says the reason the boys don't like me as much is because I'm too nice to them. She says I make her sick going around smiling and being thoughtful. She says no boy will ever take me seriously until I stop it. I try to tell her that I don't mean to smile this much, it's just that my face seems to automatically go into a smile, even when it's in a resting state. Pat Lee says it's disgusting and is trying to get me to start saying "shit," and "tits," and "screw" and a bunch of other words that will wipe this smile off my face. She gives up on me all the time. She says deep down boys cannot stand a nice girl. "You're prettier than me," she says, "but I'm a whole lot more popular than you. So I guess it balances out." I can only hope she's right.

Pat Lee's popularity got started in the sixth grade when she was the fastest runner in the school—and nobody could beat her and almost every boy in the class tried. She did not throw like a girl either, which made boys go crazy over her. They would line up at P.E. just to watch Pat Lee pitch a baseball. And she could hit home runs and shoot baskets from midcourt and do a backward flip off the high dive in her red bathing suit. Everything boys respect. Then all that admiration just mushroomed into this other thing. And Pat Lee is the most popular girl at Augusta Raa Junior High School. She gets elected to everything she tries out for. And I kind of like it because I get the spillover from her popularity. If a boy can't sit by Pat Lee, then he wants to sit by me, since I'm her best friend. I don't have to go to much trouble over it. I even let Proctor James sit by me, despite the fact he never washes his hair. He sat by Pat Lee first, but she got up and moved, making all the rest of the boys laugh at him. The next thing I know I felt so sorry for Proctor I was smiling at him.

"You're hopeless," Pat Lee said to me. "I swear to God, you're hopeless."

"He's sort of nice," I lied.

The only boy Pat Lee thinks is nice is Tony Kelly, and that's only because Tony is almost as mean as she is. And he is a country boy too—not like the rest of the boys at the picture show on Saturday in their penny loafers. His brother lets him out in front of the State Theater in a souped-up green truck—which anybody else would be embarrassed over—and Tony neither speaks nor looks at a single person in the picture show line. And he wears boots, which are not in style at all. And sometimes lights up a cigarette like he has a perfect right to do it. He does not fit in in any way, and doesn't even try to, and so people can't help but stare at him and wonder just what he thinks he's doing. I stare at him myself.

The first Saturday he showed up at the State Theater all the regular junior-high people got quiet and looked at him. He didn't care. And before you know it Pat Lee walked over to Tony—the whole civilized junior-high population gawking—and said, "Hey, Tony. You here by yourself?"

"You see anybody with me?" he answered.

"Do you want to sit with me and Connie Jean?" (I was hoping he'd say no. Pat Lee had already promised to sit with Bobby Castle.)

"It depends," Tony said.

"On what?" Pat Lee said, not smiling exactly, but sort of playing with her hair.

"I don't like a bunch of talking when I go to the picture show," Tony said. "I'm not paying my money to listen to girls talk."

Pat Lee didn't get mad, and she sat beside him that Saturday and every Saturday since. Nobody can understand it. She has let Tony kiss her three times. Once at *Beach Blanket Bingo*, once at *Pillow Talk*, and once at *Fort Apache*. I was sitting right next to her every time. When they start that, it makes my hands sweat. And worse than that, it gives the town boys the same idea. They think Pat Lee is practically a goddess now that they know she will kiss in front of everybody.

And Tony, even though his hair is too long, he doesn't peg his blue jeans, and just wears white T-shirts all the time, nobody makes fun of him. If he walks into the State Theater late and Pat Lee is sitting with Bobby Castle because she thinks Tony is not coming, all Tony does is walk down the aisle with his hands in his pockets, not even looking for Pat Lee, just maybe chewing a toothpick, and he goes and sits by himself and waits. And when Pat Lee sees him she hurries over there, saying, "I'm sorry. I didn't know you were coming." And Tony says, "Shhhhh, I'm trying to watch the show."

At school Tony will not speak to Pat Lee. He's in the dumb classes for one thing, the vocational boys, woodshop and all, and so he just minds his business at school. If you ask me he's failed a grade or two. It wouldn't surprise me if he'd been to reform school. Pat Lee laughs and says I'm crazy when I tell her that. "You're jealous," she says.

"I don't have anything against boys from reform school," I say.

"You don't have anything against anybody," she says. "That's what's wrong with you."

Pat Lee tried to save Tony a seat at lunch once, but he said, "No," and took his tray and sat at a table all by himself.

She got so mad she stormed over there saying, "I don't see what gives you the right to go around acting like you're better than everybody."

"Go sit with your friends," he said.

I thought for a minute Pat Lee was going to cry. But she said, "Are you coming to the show Saturday?"

"Maybe," he said.

Me and Pat Lee usually get to the State Theater early but we are probably the only two people in junior high who don't always get to see the show. Our mothers worry about appropriateness.

On this occasion, when *Gypsy* was the Saturday show, our mothers said, "I can't think of a reason in this world why two young girls need to see a movie about a stripper!" So we had to just stand outside the State Theater and watch everybody else go in. We could just see all the junior-high people sitting in the first rows, and it made us miserable to think we wouldn't be sitting there too. It made Pat Lee even more miserable than me, for fear Tony would come and she would miss seeing him, or worse, that some other girl might try to sit next to him and he might let her do it.

We stood on the sidewalk sucking soft-boiled peanut hulls, then spitting them on the ground. We stood there until every single person had filed inside and there was no one left but the two of us.

"I guess he's not coming," Pat Lee said.

"Who?"

"Who do you think?" Pat Lee said, shoving me down the street. "Let's go to Woolworth's."

Woolworth's is two doors down from the State Theater and they have this banana-split special. They have a bunch of balloons taped to the wall above the counter. The customer picks out one and the waitress pops it and gets a piece of paper out of it with the price of the banana split on it. Sometimes a person gets a banana split for a penny, but most of them are thirty-nine cents.

We sat in the booth up by the window, chose our balloons and sat waiting for our thirty-nine-cent banana splits. We have never paid less for a banana split and don't know anybody else who has, but we believe in the game and remain hopeful.

Pat Lee is one of the few people I can talk to in a serious way. We've been best friends since third grade, and over the years we developed a radar. For example, I knew, without Pat Lee saying so, that she was watching every vehicle that went down Monroe Street, hoping to see that souped-up green truck.

"You still looking for Tony?" I said.

"Nope."

"You know why he makes you so miserable?" I said. "It's because he's as mean as you are."

"At least I don't hold hands with Proctor James."

"I DID NOT HOLD HANDS."

"You sat by him."

"ONCE."

"You are so nice you make me sick," Pat Lee said. "I bet you grow up and marry one of those boiled-peanut men."

"Shut up," I said.

"This is the real world out here," she said. "This is not the picture shows."

The waitress brought our banana splits just then, two beauties with beehives of whipped cream on top and red cherries sliding, leaving pink trails. She set them down carefully, trickles of chocolate dripping down the sides of the glass boats. As soon as the waitress left, Pat Lee said, "Yours is bigger than mine."

"Good," I said.

"But your banana has a rotten spot on it," she said, scooping a mound of vanilla ice cream into her mouth, "so it balances out."

Pat Lee is my best friend. But she can make me hate myself sometimes. It's because she's honest, I think, which Mother says never has been in style and never will be. Mother says that honest is another word for rude. Like if somebody is fat Pat Lee'd say, "Lord, that girl wears her groceries, don't she?" When Beth was too flat-chested to undress in P.E., Pat Lee said, "Listen, Beth, get you a bra and stick some toilet paper in it. That's what Caroline does." Caroline was mad at Pat Lee for a long time, but Pat Lee didn't care. You'd think her mother had never mentioned the first word about good manners.

I don't hold this against Pat Lee, though, because she is Catholic and I feel like that has something to do with it. My mother says that Catholics just do what the Pope says and they don't have to think for themselves, so I always keep that in mind.

We paid the waitress and began wandering up and down the

dime-store aisles. We know the store by heart, same as we know every store in Tallahassee.

Neither one of us really felt like hanging around uptown by ourselves, knowing the rest of the world was in the dark theater watching some grown woman undress to music.

"Today's been a bomb," Pat Lee said. I was surprised at Pat Lee sounding ready to go home. She usually loves to stay in town more than anybody. "Let's walk over to Penney's," she said. "I'll call Mother to come get us."

JCPenney's is between Woolworth's and the State Theater. It is the official place where people call their mothers. I gave Pat Lee a dime to call with, since it was her mother coming to get us. Things are always confused at her house. They have eight kids. It usually takes a lot of time just to get the right person to the phone and then her mother has to remember where everybody is or should be. It is mass confusion, which is why Pat Lee doesn't like to be home much and doesn't like people to come over to her house and see what a mess it always is. One of her brothers has drawn a Sears truck on the living room wall with an orange crayon. Now they have to paint the whole room. There is a lot of crying going on over there and screen doors slamming. That's why Pat Lee prefers to come to my house. It's quiet. My mother spends her life cleaning everything up. After saying "okay" about ten times, Pat Lee hangs up.

"Mother said she has to take Missy to tumbling class at the armory and then she'll come get us. She said to meet her in front of Penney's because her hair is rolled up and no way is she going to trek through the Penney's store looking for us with her hair rolled up."

"Okay," I said. "Let's go upstairs and look at the clothes a few minutes."

They had a whole rack of new bathing suits set up. We both headed straight for it. "Are you getting a two-piece this year?" I asked Pat Lee.

"Probably. If you don't, boys think there is something the matter with your body." She held up a little butterfly bikini. "Shoot, I bet seeing me in this could straighten Tony Kelly out. Bet this could turn the boy nice."

Pat Lee was greatly exaggerating her powers—believe me—and besides, her mother would never in a million years let her buy a bathing suit like that.

"Good gosh," she said, pulling out a second bathing suit and waving it around in my face, "they must have chased a nigger down for this one."

"Shhhhh," I said on instinct. I looked around us, afraid some colored person would hear her. Afraid some colored person would get mad and give us that quiet look I hate more than anything. There were a couple of salesladies at the counter deep in whispered conversation, and some girl older than us carrying a dress into the fitting room. "Be quiet," I said.

"This bathing suit is even too tacky for a nigger," Pat Lee said.

And then I saw her—an old lady, who came walking from between some racks of raincoats. Pat Lee was analyzing bathing suits a mile a minute by this time.

"Hey," she said, "get a load of this."

But I was watching the old lady. She moved slow, like she was dragging something, watching her feet every step she took. On her head was a black straw hat—the kind old ladies wear—and she carried a big tourist pocketbook with gaudy flowers all over it and the word FLORIDA stitched in red straw across it. She stood at a counter of madras shorts and as slow as Christmas picked up one thing, put it down, picked up another thing, put it down.

She had on a pair of old Hush Puppies—somebody probably gave them to her—and dark stockings with a run in both legs, showing streaks of skin. And her dress, it probably used to fit somebody just right, some other woman a long time ago. There was a hole in the elbow of her sweater, which it was too hot to be wearing anyway. But it wasn't her clothes that got my attention, it was her face and the fact that I couldn't see it. She was stooped over and her eyes stayed down. Just that black hat on her head shining out like a blank face with the eyes, nose, and mouth erased off of it.

I guess she'd picked up and put down every item on that table. Her back was to me now. And with unnatural stillness she moved her arms at such a slant, like she was reaching for something, and that pocketbook of hers came open. Then quick—so quick I wasn't sure I saw it—she stuffed a handful of shorts into her pocketbook, and it was closed again.

I got hot all over. There I was watching her and the old lady stole something. My heart was beating away, like it was me doing it, stealing. I couldn't move my eyes away from her.

"What's with you?" Pat Lee was hollering. "Hey, what are you staring at?"

"Shhhhhh," I said.

Pat Lee turned to see what I was looking at. When she did, the old lady was sticking some more clothes in her pocketbook and Pat Lee saw her too.

By this time I knew it was the real thing. But Pat Lee felt that same shock like I had. "Good gosh," she whispered. "Look at that. She's stealing. Would you look?"

I couldn't quit looking.

The old lady should have felt us staring at her. Our eyes should have seemed like little bullets going into her back.

"We've got to tell somebody," Pat Lee said. "Come on. Let's tell somebody. She can't come in here and clean the place out. Shoot, a granny like that."

"Wait a minute," I said, grabbing Pat Lee's arm so she couldn't go. "She's old."

"Have you gone crazy?"

"Look at that pitiful dress," I said. "It's so pitiful." It crossed my mind that this old woman might be a sister to some of those old men that sat in the park selling peanuts. She might be crazy like some of them and have spent her whole life at the Chatta-hoochee Mental Hospital and just got released into Tallahassee without having any idea how to act in the regular world.

"What's right is right," Pat Lee said. "You know that."

But I didn't. There is nothing in this world that I am sure of. "What do you think they'll do to her if we tell?" I said.

The old lady didn't look anything like my two grandmothers. Both of them are fat. I knew for a fact it had never crossed either of their minds to steal anything.

"It's our duty to turn in people when they start robbing the place blind," Pat Lee said, her eyes contracting into slits. "You wait here if you're chicken. Just keep your eye on her. Don't let her get away."

I tried to act regular watching the old lady shuffling around the counters. Maybe it was a terrible thing—shoplifting. It probably was, since they send people to jail over it. What if everybody did like me and watched old ladies steal shorts from the junior-teen department? JCPenney's would have to close down in no time.

If she could be a colored woman stealing, I thought, well, then it would make sense and I wouldn't be so worried about it, because everybody knows colored people have certain reasons for what they do. But everybody also knows there is no good reason for any decent white woman to be stealing. My mother has explained it to me, that any wrong thing a colored person does, it is because we make them do it. Us. White people. But I don't know where she gets that. Because I can honestly say that I, myself, have never made a colored person do anything.

I stared at the old woman like she was stark naked scooting around in nothing but those Hush Puppies. It was not my fault she was poor, was it? It was not my fault she had that wrinkled face and wore that pitiful dress and had got caught stealing like any other thief in the world. Why did it seem like my fault?

I thought about running up and telling her to empty that tacky pocketbook before the police came. I thought about screaming for her to run like heck. I could have warned her. But then I bet Pat Lee would say it was her duty to turn ME in as an accomplice. I would have to go to court, which would break my daddy's heart and make him divorce Mother for the crazy ideas she put in my head. I would be sent off to reform school, where I would turn into one of those vocational girls who takes cosmetology classes, dyes her hair, and wears bras as pointy as two sharp arrows. They would probably kill me at reform school because I am so nice. They would tie me up in ropes and leave me on a cold cement floor, or else beat me with slats of lumber until I go unconscious. And they would scream, "You are too nice. This is what you get for being so nice!"

The old woman floated like a small gray ghost around the store. I am afraid of any person who will not let you see her face. It seemed forever before Pat Lee came back. Some man wearing a name tag came with her. And it was done.

"Let's get out of here," Pat Lee said. "We've done our part. Besides, Mother's probably waiting out front."

The man with the name tag walked over to the old lady, taking hold of her arm. "You'll have to come with me," he said.

A great puff of air seemed to go out of the woman, shriveling her the last bit, but she was obedient and allowed herself to be led away, shuffling along beside the stern, closed-faced JCPenney's man, clutching her Florida bag with its cheerful straw flowers. "I need to call my grandson," she said.

"Yes, ma'am," the man said with strange politeness. Maybe, like me, he believes this is all somehow his fault.

"Hurry," Pat Lee said. "Mother will kill us if she has to get out of the car with her hair rolled up."

The man slowly escorted the little bent-over robber downstairs to call the police. They passed in front of Pat Lee and me, the old lady watching her step, staring at those hand-me-down Hush Puppies.

We passed a full-length mirror in the men's department before we reached the front door. Pat Lee stopped a minute and looked at herself, pushing her hair up with her fingers, puffing it.

"Do you think I ought to start ratting my hair more?" she said. "I bet it would make me look older. I bet Tony would like it."

"You're too nice to Tony," I said. "Every other boy you treat hateful and they all like you because of it, but Tony you're nice to and he hardly pays you any attention at all. You make a fool of yourself acting so nice."

"You don't understand," Pat Lee said, fluffing her hair again, twirling around, holding her arms out at her side. "It's love," she said, grinning. "It balances things out."

Pat Lee's mother was late. We stood on the sidewalk for twenty minutes, waiting, before Pat Lee finally went back into Penney's and called her mother again. "She forgot us," Pat Lee said, coming back out of the store, "but Missy says she's on her way now."

Just as Pat Lee finished speaking, like the timing in a movie, that green pickup truck Pat Lee had hoped to see all day came lurching to a halt in front of JCPenney's. Tony sprang out of the front seat, leaving the door hanging open, and hurried toward us. His brother sat in the driver's seat and kept the motor running. He was smoking a cigarette and had a tattoo on his arm. He looked like one of those men my mother sees and says, "The army would be the best thing in the world for him." He did not look like Tony, who has not got so sour yet, and who walked past us full of intent, his boots clicking across the sidewalk.

"Hey, Tony," Pat Lee said, but he seemed unable to hear her or see her, either one. He seemed only able to see what was directly in front of him and he walked straight ahead toward it, whatever it was, right past us, and through JCPenney's swinging doors.

"He didn't even speak," Pat Lee said.

"He didn't see you," I told her.

Just then Pat Lee's mother pulled up in her station wagon and began blowing the horn, as if we were likely to miss seeing her otherwise. She had brush rollers with pink spikes stabbed through them all over her head and a scarf tied uselessly over them. She was happy because she and Pat Lee's daddy had been invited to dinner at Tallahassee Country Club that very night.

They were not members but socialized with lots of people who were. Her fingernails were painted red and she had the radio going, playing Glenn Miller's "Little Brown Jug." Three of Pat Lee's younger sisters were huddled in the very back of the station wagon with a scattered set of paper dolls to keep them busy. One of her brothers sat in the front seat with his arm hanging out the window. "Hurry up," he said. Me and Pat Lee got in the backseat after scooting over some bags of groceries that were piled in our way.

"You won't believe what we saw," Pat Lee said to her mother. "There was this really old woman in Penney's teen department . . ."

As Pat Lee was speaking, the old woman appeared, walking out of Penney's, shuffling slowly, looking down. She was holding on to her grandson, who walked patiently beside her, extending his crooked arm so that she could brace herself walking.

"Isn't she pitiful," Pat Lee's mother said, noticing the old woman and craning her neck to look harder. "So pitiful."

The pair moved across the sidewalk to the waiting green truck and its open door, she in her Hush Puppies and he in his pointed cowboy boots and white T-shirt.

Tony gently helped his grandmother into the truck. It didn't seem to matter to him whether she was crazy, or a criminal, or wearing raggedy mismatched clothes. It didn't seem to matter to him that she had just got caught stealing, and it would probably say so in the *Tallahassee Democrat* the next day. It wouldn't matter to him if she was just released from Chattahoochee yesterday or due to check in tomorrow. He spoke softly to her and when she was seated in the truck cab he slid in beside her and slammed the door closed.

The green truck jerked out into traffic right in front of us, and when it did Tony caught sight of Pat Lee, her face watching him from the backseat of the station wagon. His elbow was jutted out the window, and keeping his arm still he lifted his hand in recognition as he passed, raising a couple of stiff fingers and nodding slightly.

Pat Lee fell back against the seat, silently. And I understood it. Why Tony makes her smile like that. Why she loves him more than any other boy in Tallahassee. For a minute there, I loved him myself.

Reynolds Price

HIS FINAL MOTHER

(from *The New Yorker*)

Crawford Langley was twelve years old and still a child; but the first traits of manhood were on him—tall for his age, no baby fat, no pointless smiles, a broad forehead and steady gray eyes that gave his head a claim on the dignified notice of adults. So it was early in that crucial year when he took what he saw as his first grown step. He managed to stamp out his old nickname. It was nothing more obnoxious than Ford, but he calmly told his friends not to use it.

A few children laughed and tried to taunt him with Fordie or even Model T. He smiled but then refused to know them; and since he was anyhow the main child to know in his town and school—the funniest surely, the most openhanded—they all came round in a matter of days, his teachers included and the baseball coach; even his mother, who privately called him Strut and Dub. All but his father. Crawford's father stuck with Ford since that had been his own father's name. Crawford liked and trusted his father enough to humor him, and causes for that came thick and fast once his mother was gone.

She left in an instant—no warning or pain, so far as they knew. She was in the backyard, hanging an ancient quilt on a clothesline, and then she knelt. Crawford and his father had left for the day, but the cook had watched it clearly from the porch. She said, "Miss Adele went to her knees like somebody needing to pray, *hard*. Then it look like she needed to rest her head—she went right on down slow to her side and smoothed the grass and stroked her hair. She was cool as a window by the time I touched her."

The cook phoned school and Crawford was home on his bike in ten minutes (his father was an hour away, taking an Irish-setter pup to his lonely aunt). By then the ambulance men were there; her body was covered in the dim front hall. Young as he was, Crawford walked straight to her, lifted the sheet, and leaned in a slow curve to kiss the forehead. *Cold as glass*—he thought it before the cook could warn him. And though he loved his mother deeply, they'd understood that her racing heart would take her soon.

He expected tears, and when none came he told himself his natural feelings were in shock now. But before he took his hand off her arm, a tall new thing stood up in his mind. It was not a thought or even a feeling. It was more like watching his hands grow stronger in a slow instant. He hoped it was one more sign of manhood. It calmed him at least and dried his eyes.

He told the ambulance men where to go, Bond's funeral home. Then he tested the newborn strength again—it poured right through him like iron in his blood. So he thanked the cook and asked her to wait till his father was back. She nodded and went to fix normal supper. Then Crawford thought he had to go pray. The word surprised him—*Pray for what?* But when the cook had shut the kitchen door, he obeyed himself and climbed to his room.

There he stood in the midst of the rug and waited to see if any word came, any message from him for God or man. But again his mind was still and firm. He thought he'd taken another step on-ward, no need to lean on others or the sky. He could handle this trial with his own strong body and his new brave mind—brav-ery was still his main ambition. He went to his shelf and found the old copy of *Robinson Crusoe*, his pick among books in recent months. Then he stretched on his bed and turned to page one.

Crusoe was sunk in waste and shame, and hellbound for ship-wreck, before Crawford thought of himself again or the world below his silent room. What brought him back was his father's car door, slamming in the drive. Crawford said one sentence aloud to his ceiling, "This'll kill Dad, too, and I'll be gone." He knew it was hardly courageous thinking, but he didn't wait to understand the solemn further questions he raised—*Gone where and why?* He sped downstairs to tell the sizable news before his father could step indoors and call "Adele?" and find her vanished. One of the main things Crawford knew was fresh in his mind as he faced the father he'd long since tried to shield from harm—*This boy is a whole lot shakier than me.*

Later that night, when their friends were gone, Crawford's father said they better take a walk before bedtime if they meant to sleep. They hadn't gone walking at night for years—since the time they had to admit in silence that they had nothing better to talk about than baseball or school—and tonight anyhow Craw-ford wanted to keep on reading *Crusoe.* But his father stood; so the boy said, "Yes sir." And they went right out, through a kitchen that now was broad and empty as the plains of Gobi.

After a speechless fifteen minutes, they left strong moonlight and entered the woods. His father was leading, and though they were taking their same old path, the whole idea of a walk was strange. So Crawford asked himself, *What will we be when all this settles?* He was still not asking, *Where are we going, here tonight?* In any case, no answer showed. He guessed he was safe though and tried to keep step, but his father stumbled a time or two, and then Crawford brushed his enormous back, which seemed too hot for the time and place.

The woods stopped sooner than either one expected, and their feet were on the verge of the river before their eyes had opened enough to see the sudden end of the path. Crawford laughed a little at the near escape.

But his father said, "It might have been better."

"Sir?"

"Drowning tonight, no waiting around—I mean me, Ford. Not you, not yet."

Crawford knew his father was an excellent swimmer; so he thought the words were no cause for worry, just some kind of smoke from the hot pain in him. The boy moved on into reaching distance; but his father stayed still—no touch, no look. Then fear, like a tickling feather in sleep, flicked Crawford's mind. This man could do his will on a boy—*Has he lost his mind? Does he blame me?* So the boy chose his latest version of a grown man's voice and told his father, "Sir, she's fine now. You just need to wait."

"For what?" His father's voice was changing, darker and deep.

Crawford said, "You mostly tell me time's the big doctor."

"I've told you some lies."

The fear struck now in Crawford's throat and begged him to run, but the boy knew he had to keep talking. "What I really meant—she's waiting for you. In Heaven, all well."

The man's throat rasped at itself, to spit; and his new voice said, "You don't believe that."

Crawford was suddenly shivering cold, though the night was warm. He told himself the man was wrong. With his mother's encouragement, for years the boy had thought of her long-dead pitiful father as safe in Heaven, literally hunting and a far better shot than ever on earth. And since Crawford's own father prayed every night, and often commended the habit to him, the boy now felt a huge trapdoor fall open in the ground nearby—if he took three steps in any direction, he'd surely drop through an endless hole. In an almost final hope of rescue, the boy said, "Sir, I don't feel right about any of this."

The man said, "Then you must be growing."

"Sir?"

"Nothing's right and won't ever be again. Get that through your head."

It was already there; Crawford felt it as a hot ball stuck far back in the quick of his mind. So he said, "I need you to calm down now."

The man's big hand shot out and seized Crawford's neck.

The fingers were colder even than the boy, though he thought he recognized the scrape of his father's thick palm. Crawford said, "I'm still not strong as you." The man's grip eased. Then suddenly he seemed to be gone, that strange and quick. Crawford waited for a clue and finally spoke, as strong as he could, "Am I out here alone?"

From what seemed a far distance, the man said, "You always were."

The boy had roamed these woods his whole life and was all but sure he knew the way home, even in dark this heavy and close. But he thought that if he moved, any way, he might crash into his father's body or whatever changed man waited out here. So he tried again to say a prayer, *Our Father . . . Lord, please.* Crawford knew the words—they gleamed in his head, as hard as signs—but some new way, the world around him, the actual air, refused to let words out of his lips. He'd read of men abandoned by God—young Crusoe himself, for his worldly wrongs. Still what had *he* done, Crawford Langley, to pay like this? Had he somehow caused his mother pain, in broad daylight, alone in the yard? At the thought, an arm of the night rushed the boy's cold face and choked his words.

What felt like half his lifetime passed, though a real forty minutes; and then Crawford broke through the maze of dark woods. There, set in a space that looked familiar, was a house he guessed was his own old house, dark in every window and door. In all his years he'd never seen it completely dark. Hadn't he and his father left it well lit? The boy was past a child's automatic fears—of falls and darkness—but it came to him now that, in this house, the man who left him alone by the river was hid and ready.

Crawford also knew there was nowhere else. He had school friends, and their parents liked him; but he couldn't turn back and run to them with such a wild story, not this late. All he could think was to set his face and volunteer for the rest of what was stored up for him, life or death.

He recognized the dent in the doorknob as he entered the kitchen; but from there on through, the dark was so thick he might have been walking on the far side of Venus. After four steps Crawford saw in his mind, as clear as fact, that his father was hid right now in his path. He saw a butcher knife in the hand that had never once punished him, so much as a slap. He saw the gray eyes wide as a panther's, fixed on a boy and perfectly aimed.

Still the boy put out both arms before him, to grope his way toward the foot of the stairs. If he got that far, and his heart still worked, he knew he must try to find his own room and wait on his bed for a key to the meaning of this fresh news. Like all sane children with baffling, even murderous, parents, he understood that something he himself had done—some unintended but last-straw fault—had brought this fate down on him, and rightly.

Each individual stair creaked out; but once Crawford stood intact at the top, he paused to test the air for warnings. Never in all his life in this house had it been so absolutely silent. He held in place till he heard his mind want one of two sounds—either the final slash of his father's vengeful knife or Crawford's own voice promising, *Dad, I'm sorry for my whole life. I swear I'll be anything you say.*

But still the boy was in one piece. So he crept on past his father's door (no crack of light), found his own empty bed, and stretched on his back. This time he never tried to pray. What he tried was a thorough backward search of his recent life. His mind was clear and a thousand details marched past his eyes. But no fault showed, nothing worth much more than a "God damn it, Ford" from his tired, patient father.

So the boy kept coming round to the fact that, as lately as two or three Sundays ago, he and his father had walked an hour out into the fields. There'd been a hard rain the night before; and that was always a lucky time for the hobby they shared—arrowheads, shot or lost by the Tuscarora ages past (no Tuscarora left in the state for two hundred years).

And when Crawford dug out a clear quartz knife, white as

glass—a priestly knife they'd only dreamed of—he trotted to his father, held out his shut hands as in a child's game, and said, "Pick one." At once his father tapped the left hand. Crawford grinned, cried out "It's Father's Day!" and opened his palm on the stupendous find. Father's Day was months ahead, but his father took it with a look that deeply underlined what he mostly showed and had said more than once—he prized this boy. Surely this moment the sacred point was on his father's desk downstairs with the only other treasures he kept—a bullet dug from an ancestor's leg and, locked in a tiny glass box, one curl of his father's sister's hair (she'd died at two weeks).

For a moment Crawford wanted to find the crystal knife. What else now under this strange new roof might bring him luck or help defend him? But then he thought, in some terrible way it might be used in the night against his heart. He remembered how Aztec priests had cut the beating hearts from men with just such points to feed their gods. At the chance—almost the certainty—of that, Crawford spread his arms wide and shut his eyes. Still facing up, he only waited—balked as any mind can be but likewise ready, he told himself, though soon he slid into scrappy dreams, then exhausted sleep.

Crawford knew it was day, well before he woke. His last dream told him he'd lasted the night and that now he was fully a man but alone. His eyes came open—no, still night. Then, as he lay in the ongoing quiet, he knew that, yes, a light was growing but not at the window. In another minute he saw a glow was actually blooming, a great slow flower of morning light, till his ceiling was patterned with numerous leaves in shades of cream and gold like nothing he'd ever seen or heard of. He wondered if he'd already died and this was his next home, high or low. But the same old lighting fixture hung there and, on a short string, the one plane model he'd ever finished. Whatever then, the mild colors and gradual speed of the bloom were saying that he was past the threat in the heart of the night.

He rose on his elbows and looked to the door. He'd left it half-open, and now he saw where the light came from. It streamed from the hall in a narrow shaft, then spread in these strange shapes through his room. In a long stretch from the bed, he could reach and carefully test the beam with his hand. It was not only fine to see but the same temperature as his skin. So he had to be safe. He'd get up and make his way to what caused it.

The time it took to walk up the hall through the streaming glow seemed longer even than the moment when he touched his mother this afternoon and knew he was somehow as changed as she. For the first full time, in his mind Crawford saw her welcome face and heard her voice, which had been the better part of what he loved for his first six years. He thought the day was bound to come when he'd miss her bitterly—not yet tonight. This hunt he was on, through what still seemed his father's house, was all he could manage here and now.

By now he stood at his parents' door. Never before had he seen it closed (his father's only dread was of traps). But the stream of light was coming from there, around the edges of the door and beneath it. The boy bent slowly and laid his ear on the wood to listen. At first he thought he could hear a whole crowd of friendly voices, but he couldn't hear words. He waited there till his ears adjusted. It was just two voices, a man and a woman—more likely a girl, that young and bright (he'd only begun to lean toward girls). Soon he knew the man was his father but younger too; the girl stayed strange. The boy never understood a word, though he knew from their tone and slowness they were peaceful.

A thing he'd always respected was privacy, even more now as his own body grew its secrets. But here this late on this big day, his heart had got so huge in his chest that he knew he had no other hope than to turn this knob and take what came at his eyes or mind.

After maybe two minutes his pupils narrowed enough to see, in the core of the glare, his father seated at the foot of his bed. His father wore his regular pajamas, cool sky blue and neatly pressed. That much was normal. He sat like that, each night of his life, for five or ten minutes with both eyes shut, saying his prayers in a deep silence (his painful kneecaps kept him from kneeling). Now though, his head was tilted up; and his eyes were halfway open in the blaze. His lips were moving as if he went on saying whatever he'd said while Crawford listened outside at the door, but if words came they were swept away. Crawford thought his own body might also drown or burn past hope; but in his new bravery, he knew not to leave.

In another minute the boy's reward began to rush him. Either she somehow came from above or had been there right along, too bright to see. Whatever, suddenly a girl stood clear and tall by his father: the single sight both boy and man could watch from then on. It took Crawford another slow wait to see her face and know it was someway kin to the face that hung in a frame by his father's bed—Crawford's mother before her wedding, lovely and strong as he still could see her, in occasional dreams from his cradle days. The picture showed no more than her head, a graceful neck, and the top of a yellow dress. The girl here now wore the same dress, which seemed to fall right down to the floor, though it drowned in light; and her dark eyes were surely the same.

The boy thought he was brave enough to say her name; at least he felt the powerful need. Let her hear his voice and then just laugh and call him Dub or Strut a last time. But before he stoked his courage for that, her face turned gradually in his direction and all but smiled before she faced his father again, closed his eyes with two long hands; and (like the mother she once had been) she helped him lie in place on the pillow before she was somehow gone again; and his father was covered with the old quilt, plainly asleep and harmless as any new pine in the woods.

The light continued long enough to see Crawford back to his own bed, then faded quickly. He sat at the foot and knew his father had surely prayed her back to life to tame him down and save her son. Then the boy slowly asked himself if he wanted to beg for a similar visit—*now*, he knew, was the only chance. But didn't that girl's face belong to his father, the girl he picked when he was not much older than Crawford tonight? The boy's oldest memories rose—himself in his mother's arms in a chair by the sunny window, each consulting the other's eyes for secrets, then laughing together at what they found. It was still the face the boy loved most; it would be that all his life on earth. And though it was gone from his daily world, it was maybe changeless and better in dreams.

Next he thought he could steal downstairs, find the quartz knife, and bury it deep in a moonless corner. That would keep it safe, and him and his father, and leave it ready as food again for the hungry gods, if they were there still watching man. But no, he was tired and knew he was rescued. He gave one thought to how his mother had looked this morning, cheerful and firm but calling him back from the edge of the yard, giving him one last kiss on the brow, thumping his skull with a healthy finger and saying, "Strut, *fly!* or you'll be late," when she was the one who'd flown in time.

So the tired boy stood, shucked his clothes (the room was still warm), and then, for the first time, entered his sheets as naked as he left her lovely body long ago, in pain and blood. As his head lay back, he felt—again and for the last time—the hardness of that long black first trip to reach daylight. But the pain subsided and, through the rest of that short night, he slept like some boy thoroughly safe, whose days hereafter will each be brave, whose nights will bring him—whenever he calls—the face and voice he understands are utterly gone: his only mother, lost forever, young and free for good and all.

BIOGRAPHICAL NOTES

Rick Bass was born in Fort Worth and grew up in Houston. He has worked as a biologist in Arkansas and a geologist in Mississippi, and now lives in Montana. He has received writing fellowships from the Mississippi Institute of Arts & Letters and the National Endowment for the Arts. He is the author of *The Watch*, a short-story collection, and, most recently, *Winter*, essays.

Thomas Phillips Brewer, formerly of Fairhope, Alabama, now lives in New York City. He grew up in Chevy Chase, Maryland, where he was introduced to writing by his grandfather, a columnist for the *St. Louis Post-Dispatch*. He is at work on a second novel.

Larry Brown is the author of two collections of short stories, *Facing the Music* and *Big Bad Love*, and a novel, *Dirty Work*. He is a retired firefighter and lives with his family at Yocona, Mississippi. His new novel, *Joe*, is forthcoming.

Robert Olen Butler lives in Lake Charles, Louisiana, where he teaches creative writing at McNeese State University. He has published six novels since 1981, the most recent of which is *The Deuce*. His short stories have appeared in many literary magazines, including *The Virginia Quarterly Review*, where he won the Emily Clark Balch Award. His first collection, entitled *A Good Scent from a Strange Mountain*, will be published early next year.

Barbara Hudson was born and raised in El Paso, Texas. She did her undergraduate work in Nashville, Tennessee, where she lived for twelve years, and received an M.F.A. in writing from the University of Pitts-

245

burgh. She currently lives and writes in Norfolk, Virginia, with her husband and daughter.

Elizabeth Hunnewell was born and raised in Richmond, Virginia, and graduated from Hollins College. Her fiction has been published in *The Virginia Quarterly Review*, and she contributes regularly to the *Boston Globe*. She lives in Wellesley, Massachusetts, with her husband and their three children.

Hilding Johnson has had work selected for *Story* magazine, *Story Quarterly*, and for *Best American Short Stories* and other anthologies. She is a television commentator on PBS.

Nanci Kincaid was born in Tallahassee, Florida, and lives now in Tuscaloosa, Alabama, where she is working toward an M.F.A. from the University of Alabama. Her stories have been anthologized in *New Stories from the South* and *Homecoming: The Family in Southern Fiction*. Her first short-story collection is forthcoming from Putnam this fall.

Bobbie Ann Mason is a native of Mayfield, Kentucky, where she grew up on a dairy farm. Her first book of fiction, *Shiloh and Other Stories*, won the Ernest Hemingway Foundation Award for first fiction in 1982. She is also the author of *In Country, Spence + Lila*, and *Love Life*.

Jill McCorkle is the author of four novels, most recently *Ferris Beach*. She teaches creative writing at the University of North Carolina at Chapel Hill and is working on a short-story collection to be published in 1992. Her hometown is Lumberton, North Carolina.

Robert Morgan was born in Hendersonville, North Carolina, and teaches at Cornell University. His most recent books include *The Blue Valleys*, stories, and *Sigodlin*, poems. He received a Guggenheim fellowship in 1988. His next book of stories, *Watershed*, will be published later this year.

Reynolds Price has published twenty-two books. He lives in Orange County, North Carolina.

Mark Richard was born in Lake Charles, Louisiana, and grew up in Texas, Virginia, and North Carolina. His first collection of short stories, *The Ice at the Bottom of the World*, received the 1990 PEN/Ernest

Hemingway Foundation Award. His stories have appeared in *Esquire*, *Shenandoah*, *Harper's*, *The New Yorker*, *Grand Street*, *Antaeus*, and *The Quarterly*.

Susan Starr Richards was born and raised in Winter Park, Florida, and graduated from the University of Florida. For the past thirty years she has lived in Kentucky, where she breeds racehorses and writes. She has been a NEA Fellow in Fiction and has published stories in *The Kenyon Review* and *The Sewanee Review*, as well as essays in *Ms.* magazine and *Essence*. Her book, *Horse Fables*, is in its second edition.

Lee Smith, a native of Grundy, Virginia, is a current fellow at the Center for Documentary Studies at Duke University. A longtime resident of Chapel Hill, North Carolina, she teaches at North Carolina State University. Her most recent books are *Fair and Tender Ladies*, a novel, and *Me and My Baby View the Eclipse*, short stories.

Peter Taylor was born in Trenton, Tennessee, in 1917. He and his wife, Eleanor Ross Taylor, now live in Charlottesville, Virginia. He has published six volumes of short stories and two novels. For his novel, *A Summons to Memphis*, he received a Pulitzer Prize in 1986.

Shannon Ravenel, the editor, was born and raised in the Carolinas—Charlotte, Camden, and Charleston. She served as series editor of the *Best American Short Stories* annual anthology from 1977 to 1990 and edited *The Best American Short Stories of the Eighties*. She is editorial director of Algonquin Books of Chapel Hill and lives in Chapel Hill, North Carolina, with her husband, Dale Purves, and their two daughters.

allegorical—
you can read it on
one level, but you
can take it to a
second level &
read it symbolically